The Supernatural Tales
of Fitz-James O'Brien

The Supernatural
Tales of
Fitz-James O'Brien

Volume One: Macabre Tales

Edited, with Notes and an Introduction, by
Jessica Amanda Salmonson

Doubleday

NEW YORK

1988

Acknowledgments

Thanks to the University of Washington's Suzallo Library, the London Museum, and the Seattle Public Library. Thanks to Darroll Pardoe and Richard Dalby for help in obtaining scarce material. Thanks to Jules Faye for miscellaneous labors and comforts. Thanks to Pat LoBrutto for his enthusiasm for this project at Doubleday and to David Hartwell for moral support. Thanks to Susan Lee Cohen for helping with loans when monies were scarce and to Eileen Gunn for the same financial assists.

U.S. CIP data applied for 87-36525

ISBN 0-385-24562-9
Copyright © 1988 by Jessica Amanda Salmonson
All Rights Reserved
Printed in the United States of America
First Edition

To Richard Dalby,
like me, a bibliomaniac,
with the emphasis
on maniac.

And to the late Francis Wolle,
who made this book possible.

Contents

Fitz-James O'Brien,
America's Splendid Bohemian:
An Introduction by
Jessica Amanda Salmonson

I like a dirty slum; not because I am naturally unclean, but because I generally find a certain sediment of philosophy precipitated in its gutters. A clean street is terribly prosaic.

—"The Wondersmith"

I

Fitz-James O'Brien is the most important figure after Poe and before Lovecraft in modern horror literature. The nineteenth-century Irish-American's classics "What Was It? A Mystery" and the hauntingly beautiful "The Diamond Lens" have been anthologized scores of times, praised by every commentator on weird literature and the short story generally, and imitated by such authors as Ambrose Bierce, Guy de Maupassant, and F. Marion Crawford.

William Winter reported that Fitz's tales "revived the fashion of the weird short story, and provided a model for subsequent compositions of that order," while America's greatest short-story anthologist Edward J. O'Brien pointed out that in the decade after Poe's death, the short story was in a moribund state, revived by Fitz, widely recognized as the true inheritor of Poe's mantle. Without Fitz-James O'Brien, the flourishing of supernatural literature in the last half of the nineteenth century would never have occurred. The weird tale would have peaked and died with the trinity of Irving, Hawthorne, and Poe.

In spite of his highest status in the field of supernatural fiction, many of his stories, excluded from William Winter's 1881 *Life, Poems and Stories of Fitz-James O'Brien*—which has served as the closest thing to a standard edition—have never been reprinted from various magazines and newspapers of the 1850s. They often appeared anonymously and have remained practically unknown. More surprising still, because Winter edited Fitz's work posthumously, the texts even for his most widely known classics have never been reprinted in their unaltered entirety.

Edward J. O'Brien, long the editor of the *Best Short Stories of the Year*, which he founded in 1915 and which is still issued annually, was but one champion of Fitz's genius. In 1923 he wrote, "A young man who came to New York in the early fifties of the last century to make his literary fortune would have had one great immediate ambition, especially if he were a writer of short stories. He would have blushed with pleasure if he had been introduced to Fitz-James O'Brien, just as a young man who came to New York fifty years later would have written home with pride that Richard Harding Davis had shaken hands with him or O. Henry had bought him a drink. Davis and O. Henry are not yet forgotten, but how many people today could tell you what stories Fitz-James O'Brien has written? And yet O'Brien seems to me rather the more significant in our literary history than either Davis or O. Henry, and to his contemporaries he was little short of a god."

We must wonder that to this day Fitz's work is best known to the connoisseur while lesser writers are force-fed to unwilling readers from an early age. It was nearly twenty years after his death before a significant amount of his work was gathered into one volume, despite long efforts on the part of William Winter, who wished to do a second volume as well, of some five hundred pages of additional material, but was never able to convince a publisher.

Given that Fitz was one of the giants of his day, known to one and all for "The Diamond Lens" and still a topic of conversation in magazines of the 1890s, decades after his death, we must wonder all the more that publishers shied away from his collected works. Having died a hero's death in the Civil War, it seems likely that even a minor writer, if only out of sentiment, could easily have been given a posthumous collection of a scant thousand copies.

There was a prejudice afoot that slowly impressed itself upon my awareness as I read all that I could find of Fitz's New York years and of the dandyism his type epitomized in a city that even Baudelaire likened, in however testy a tone, to Paris. Louis Stephens, Fitz's contemporary, wrote defensively of Fitz's "strain of manliness underlying his erratic habits" and of "something that may well be left unsaid." Winter himself intimates that Fitz's lifestyle was part of the reason it took nearly two decades to get even a limited edition to the public.

Puzzled by so many yet vague allusions, I was left to surmise their meaning. Could they be referring to Fitz's hot temper? But this was the *first* thing they liked to talk about, his pugilistic encounters being the stuff of high adventure. His fabrications or enlargements upon his history? This too was subject to constant speculation, making him illusive and the more intriguing. His habit of begging loans never to repay them? Again, his chums were resigned to this and found moments of humor in such habits, as when Thomas Bailey Aldrich gave him money for what was supposed to be a crisis, which Fitz used to throw a fancy dinner. Tom's chief complaint was that he had bankrolled the affair and not been invited!

No, Fitz's mystery was something other. But I'll address this mystery in some depth later.

II

He was born in County Cork very likely in 1826 rather than in Limerick two years later as often cited. With gentry origins, he grew up in Limerick with good schooling. For his class this included equestrianism, swordsmanship, and marksmanship with a variety of private tutors. He was an only child, doubtlessly spoiled even beyond gentry norms, and forever after just a little startled that life didn't give him his own way. With an inheritance he went to London and very likely Paris, where he succumbed to the dandyism then current, as espoused by Henri Murger and Jules Barby d'Aurevilly.

This was almost exactly mid-century. Within two years he had squandered his fortune in high living. Little is known of his companionships or doings at this time, but that he published poems and prose anonymously and was at least glancingly acquainted with Dickens, for he arrived in New York with letters and sufficient credentials that gained him instant access to editorial offices. A few of his pre-American works have been identified; the rest never will be.

The matter of his birth presents unique problems, as he was a dandy and as such worshipped youth and physicality, much in the manner of the samurai, the Dorians, or the ancient Greeks. He was not apt to admit to the passing of years. Ferris Greenslet in his 1908 book on Thomas Bailey Aldrich and Richard Coom Beatty in his 1936 book on Bayard Taylor reported Fitz's birth unequivocally as 1826. Most other places give it as two years later, failing to note that Fitz would certainly have availed himself of the opportunity of shaving a couple years from his life at mid-Atlantic. Lewis Pattee and Edward J. O'Brien were unwilling to hazard his real age. With some friends, as with his teenage chum Frank Wood, editor at *Vanity Fair*, Fitz claimed 1830 for his birthdate, doubtless in an effort to seem less the cradle robber. He took the added opportunity to officialize this date near the end of his life for his Union Army records.

William Winter categorically refutes the 1830 date and remembered that among Fitz's compatriots, it was widely understood that he was older than he wished to admit. A satirist in *Vanity Fair* teasingly described Fitz as about fifty-one though seemingly much older, wickedly letting on that everyone knew he lied about his age. In Fitz's favor, it seems to have been unimportant to him whether or not he was believed in this regard, but out of physical vanity always thought of himself as younger. His friend George Arnold remembered him as "a disciple of the church of St. Biceps," and Fitz himself suggested that he would not like to live so long as to see his body decay.

On his Irish pilgrimage, O'Brien scholar Francis Wolle was confident that he had established that Fitz was born in Cork, although this information has not made it into general reference works. In the 1850s tens of thousands of immigrants, many of them Irish, flooded into New York. Generally they were Corkmen and lower-class. Fitz did not wish to be thought in any manner connected with these rude fellows, who bore the brunt of shocking prejudices. It was easy enough to claim Limerick, where he was raised, as his birthplace.

Wolle, however, even in Cork, was unable to uncover Fitz's birth record, possibly because he was searching two years off, possibly because a specific effort had been made at some point to expunge the black sheep O'Brien from family chronicles. Records do undoubtedly survive, however; until an obsessive enough scholar uncovers the definitive proofs and publishes this information, many problems of Fitz's birth and ancestry will remain.

Fitz's disdain for the uneducated Cork immigrants has often been interpreted as a disdain for the very nation of his birth. William North, once a close friend but soon Fitz's outspoken enemy, portrayed Fitz in a bizarre novel called *The Slave of the Lamp* (published posthumously in 1855) as hateful to his parent Ireland. But there was not an iota of truth to the matter. In his early poems, in a handful of his stories, in his most successful play produced in New York, as well as by his pieces signed "The Irishman" in *The American Whig Review,* it is perfectly clear that he loved Ireland and was, in fact, ever ready to brawl in her behalf.

This often-repeated bit of mythology of his despising his own heritage is typical of the way Fitz has been remembered. I recall a heated exchange with another researcher, when we encountered one another in the hallway of a convention hotel, as I yelled Fitz was honest in his own way, and my friend hollered as vehemently that he was the devil's own liar. But I remain inclined toward the Edward III theorem—that the finest are often the most maligned.

It is too often assumed he lied regarding his education, his travels, his military record, his work for Dickens's magazine . . . The greatest mistruths he perpetrated—that of his age and county of birth, and a bit of subterfuge to excuse his confirmed bachelorhood—have been the least questioned. Fitz was a consummate boaster and exaggerated everything. His hints of being in the British Army are entirely likely, although it was probably brief and undistinguished service or he would have been less vague about it. As he was visited by British Army veterans in New York, he could certainly not have faked military experience with them, even though his proven skills with sword and revolver were typical of the gentry and not necessarily gained in much action.

Fitz undoubtedly stayed in Paris, perhaps for many months, where he gained his dandy's philosophy of Bohemia, his perfect mastery of French, a lifelong interest in French literature and theater, and counted Frenchmen among his friends. Georges Clemenceau, for two years an impoverished physician in New York, was one of Fitz's Bohemian chums, and it would have been impossible to pretend knowledge of Paris to France's future Prime Minister. Fitz's compatriots Ada Clare and Henry Clapp, Jr., who were also inspired to Bohemianism by their Parisian stays, would have seen through any ruse on Fitz's part.

Francis Wolle tentatively identified works by Fitz published anonymously in Dickens's *Household Words*. One of these, "An Arabian Nightmare," is certainly structured along the order of Fitz's later stories "The Crystal Bell," "How I Overcame My Gravity," and "A Dead Secret." Fitz may have exaggerated the importance of his work for Dickens, who he admired greatly and imitated in "Three of a Trade; Or, Red Little Kriss Kringle" and "The Child That Loved a Grave," but was not fabricating his association from nothing.

Lastly, Fitz claimed an education at Dublin University Trinity College, which has been roundly denied by later researchers because his name does not occur among graduate records. But Fitz cleverly never claimed to have graduated. His loafer's attitude wouldn't have given him much chance of doing so. As he was chums with comedian and *Lantern* editor John Brougham, a graduate of Trinity, it would once more have been impossible to perpetrate a fraud, though exaggeration was easy.

Those contemporaries who doubted Fitz's veracity were those who knew him least, or emotionally unstable enemies, notably William North. That researchers have been eager to believe the worse may be partly that some of them were colorless people desiring to tear down the Byronic image of so remarkable a man, deflating him out of disapproval or envy or simply because he was incomprehensible to their more limited understanding of how lives are lived. Also, not realizing that his age was the one thing he would lie about—any proper dandy would—researchers have quite rationally seen that there wasn't time before his arrival in New York for him to have done all that he claimed in Dublin, London, Paris, and the British army. However, given that he was in all likelihood two years older than commonly accepted, he could well have done all he claimed.

III

Many things conspired to bring Fitz to New York. First among them would seem to be that he owed too many people money. His definition of Bohemians was that they were "writers who cultivate literature and debts, and, heedless of the necessities of life, fondly pursue the luxuries."

In said pursuit, he squandered seven thousand pounds of inheritance in London.

He was also adventurous at heart and might not have required much impetus to seek new territories of urban decadence. He may well have felt it would be easier to make a lasting mark upon the world from upstart New York when compared to London or Paris. Very likely the deciding factor was his fascination for Poe, which had all but displaced his worship of Dickens. New York was Poe's city.

New York of the 1850s was at once a hideous and a gorgeous monster. The streets were crowded with English, Irish, and German immigrants. Housing shortages led to horrible tenement environments. Opium dens and bawdy houses were barely disguised as cellar restaurants. There were an estimated five thousand prostitutes of every variety, vicious gangs of children on the docks, and a corrupt or incompetent police force.

There was also a vital and international theater, pleasant excursions to the beaches of Coney Island, the beautiful window displays at Christmas, and the comings and goings of carriages. There was the eating of ices, the drinking of beer and coffee. There were boat parties floating down The Narrows. There was stepping rudely into the paths of wealthy old aristocrats of the Hudson. There was a publishing industry less staid than Boston's, hence potentially more exciting, though less lucrative, for the writers.

Fitz arrived in 1852 with very little money in his pockets. He introduced himself to the city by checking into the most expensive hotel, running up an exorbitant wine bill, then slipped out before anyone caught on that he was all but penniless.

Armed with letters of introduction, he was instantly taken into positions as editor, author, and poet for various papers and magazines.

The Harper brothers recognized his value at once; they became the chief publishers of his columns, essays, poems, and fiction in *Harper's New Monthly Magazine* and the tabloid *Harper's Weekly.* The Harpers provided the only well-paying magazine until the founding of *The Atlantic Monthly,* so having Fletcher Harper as his supporter was a fine piece of good fortune. Fitz became the intimate of young Joseph W. Harper, Jr., and years later, marching off to the Civil War, he was in the company of John Fletcher Harper, son of Wesley. Many a time, when Fitz found himself literally homeless but never friendless, the Harpers came through with a particularly good payment for a poem or story to put Fitz on his feet until next time.

Although the term had not yet become widely used, Bohemian circles were already forming as Fitz stepped off the boat. John Brougham the comedian, along with his staff and the authors of the *Lantern,* met at Windust's for weekly dinners. Francis Henry Temple Bellew, a well-known illustrator in his day, formed the Ornithorhyncus Club that met at a restaurant of the same name run by a widow, for whom Bellew provided the signboard: a platypus smoking a pipe.

Fitz's first circle of friends included Dickens's favorite illustrator Sol Eytinge (who produced a famous portrait of Dickens and of Fitz-James as well); the poets Bayard Taylor and Richard Stoddard (with whom Fitz wrote burlesque poetry); Fitz-Hugh "the Hashish Eater" Ludlow; and the doomed William North, author of a number of morbid tales and, within two years, the first Bohemian suicide, whose act "cast an aura of tragic romance" upon these young artists.

Fitz seems to have done well enough in the first two or three years. In 1852 he was uncommonly attractive: wavy brown hair, fair complexion, athletic, a sweetly resonant voice, and beautiful eyes. Later, hardship was to reduce him to a rough visage, short-cropped thinning hair, a nose flattened by a pugilist, though still handsome due to his good laughter, musical voice, expressive gray-blue eyes, and cheerfulness with companions.

He likely arrived in New York with some trunks of possessions from his London and Paris days, and certainly his association with the Harpers allowed him, for a time, to obtain easy credit to add to earnings. The poet George Arnold remembered Fitz with "elegant rooms, a large and valuable library, pictures, a wardrobe of much splendor, and all sorts of knick-knackery." But his possessions were soon scattered along a trail of evictions. There were to be many times when he could not afford the pen nibs and paper with which to draw himself back up. "What Was It? A Mystery" was written in Thomas Bailey Aldrich's room during one homeless stint, and the poem "The Sewing Bird" was written in William Winter's quarters after another eviction.

Winter said Fitz was "the most industrious idler I ever knew," and in truth the legend of his abject laziness looks exaggerated considering the vast body of work produced in only ten years. It was true he breakfasted in the afternoon and when not in need, which was seldom, was apt to fall into idle ways. But he was usually working on something. The real source of his financial distress was a combination of low pay from most magazines, extravagant tastes, generosity to others when he had money in his pockets, and creditors' eventual realization that he was reliable in one thing only: never paying them back.

Many a tale is told of Fitz and his New York nights, one of which will suffice to capture the intensity of his public persona. At a dinner party in a fine restaurant, the topic of William Tell was bandied about, with several diners doubtful that such marksmanship was possible. Fitz suddenly drew a pistol from his coat and, to prove such skill *was* feasible, fired thrice in rapid succession, utterly destroying three ornaments of a chandelier. A waiter, somewhat aghast, suddenly appeared with a platter of birds. Fitz shouted, "Ha! Now we can have some real shooting. Let fly the birds, waiter!" To which the fellow replied, "But, sir, the birds are fried." "Fried!" Fitz protested. "Then let us shoot the cook! A cook who would fry birds deserves death. Tell him to come up and be killed instantly!"

IV

Every memoir of the 1850s, by a variety of that decade's survivors, draws Fitz as unforgettable and larger than life. William Winter remembered him as "the most striking figure" among the Bohemians, "at once the most potential genius and the most original character." Even in his old age Winter was obsessed with this remarkable companion of his youth, so much so that Caroline Ticknor of the publishing family, in her recollections of the elderly writer, was struck mainly by his stories of Fitz-James O'Brien. Winter's son as well remembered his father's tales of night-long sorties through low neighborhoods with other young men in the company of the older Fitz, who served as guide and protector.

Biographies about other authors of the Bohemia summer may mention Fitz only in passing, but what a bright passing each biographer imagines. Beatty, in his book on Bayard Taylor, captures Fitz in these few words, calling him "the Richard Steele of nineteenth-century American literature. Like Captain Dick, he was dashing, brilliant, often in debt, a delightful person to know."

Yet it would be more than misleading to leave the reader with a picture of a devil-may-care heartwinning rake. Fitz could not have written the stories he did, in the manner he wrote them, if there weren't a dark, brooding, melancholy side to him that ran deep. His exhibitionistic tendencies hid a quieter aspect.

He often describes himself in stories and once, under the amusing subterfuge of anonymously reviewing the poems of Heremon (who was none other than a pseudonymous Fitz) in the December 1852 *American Whig Review*, Fitz manages to discuss the gloomy underpinnings of his creative urges:

"A strain laden with ghostliness and death rises from the harp of the weird contributor. Well may he have chosen the darkened face for his crest. A veil seems to shroud his nature, and his soul revels in mystery. Terror is the monotone which his heart utters when the wind of inspiration sweeps across its chords. His dwelling should be in some dark, German castle, with long corridors, deserted chambers, and pictures that occasionally come down from the wall of their own accord. A clanking spectre should stand every night at his bedside, and he should wear a 'deathwatch' in his fob. With such adjuncts as these, he and the darkened face might be qualified to fill the niche left vacant by Mrs. Radcliffe, or edit some ghastly magazine, which might perhaps be entitled 'The Pyramid of Horrors.' "

(Fitz's idea of a horror magazine in 1852 is interesting in itself.)

So we can see that while many a portrait gives Fitz as always charming and aggressive, full of vitality, cheerful even in a fight, there were indeed a few who knew him as a melancholy man resigned to a pauper's plight but scarcely glad of it.

The 1850s could be viewed akin to the 1950s' "Lost Generation," a time of joys, excesses, and untimely deaths. Many of the Bohemians died of suicide, alcoholism, drug addiction, pneumonia in a damp and freezing garret, or, in Fitz's case, of war. Ada Clare, the Queen of Bohemia, wrote a treatise on suicide. The Bohemian "King," Henry Clapp, Jr., a liberal and acidic wit, was notoriously morose in the manner of Poe.

William North's feud with Fitz may have been one-sided. They had been fast friends, but it was Fitz's nature to quarrel with chums at least once. It was even said that no one was truly his friend until they'd had a battle or two. But he was incapable of grudges and there is no evidence he reciprocated North's unebbing anger. When North committed suicide by drinking prussic acid late in 1854, with only twelve cents to his name, Fitz soon after published the poem "Willy and I" that runs, in part:

> Together we hid in the scented hay,
> Or plucked the blooms of our English may,
>   Willy and I.
> I called him husband, he called me wife,
> We builded the dream of a perfect life . . .

and so on to a grave parting. The poem provoked comment in its day as too vague, being about some tragedy Fitz is not very specific about, though his closest friends would have known the story. North may have idealized Fitz unduly so that disillusion turned his love to hatred. His portrait of FitzGammon O'Bouncer in his only novel, *The Slave of the Lamp,* is really dispicable and adds to North's tragedy—that he should be remembered today primarily because he tried to insult Fitz.

An unknown advocate of North's, after his death, charged that Fitz plagiarized "The Diamond Lens" from North's lost story "Microcosmos." The press presented several commentaries which outraged Fitz. The final word on the matter came from Dr. Guernsey, one of *Harper's* editors, who had read North's story and rejected it, but years later accepted "The Diamond Lens," although Fitz withdrew it when he found himself in the way of publication of the newly founded *The Atlantic Monthly.* Dr. Guernsey found no resemblance between the two stories.

North published a handful of weird tales interesting for their morbidness and there is rather more of O'Brien's influence on North than vice versa. His choosing death rings inevitable from these stories, although the whole of New York's Bohemia romanticized suicide. The most spectacular case was that of Henry Herbert, who wrote as Frank Forester and is still read by hunters and fishermen today. Abandoned by his younger wife, he invited several friends to his house for dinner on May 16, 1858. He concluded the evening's entertainment by standing before a large mirror and shooting himself in the head.

Stephen Fisk was one of those who remembered Fitz as melancholic. "The idea of suicide was often in O'Brien's mind." His temperament was not actually morbid, but the theory of suicide was fashionable and a perfect verbal expression of a haunted, sorrowful streak so evident in his stories.

Henry Clapp, Jr., who drank himself to death many years later in conscious if belated emulation of Poe, once said to Fitz, "Death is a consuming, intolerable curiosity." Fitz replied, "That is my feeling exactly, and I intend to satisfy my curiosity without waiting for the slow decay of nature.

With such a fascinating problem as death before us, I cannot imagine how anybody can be satisfied with the monotonous stupidity of living."

Fortunately, his barely hidden dark side came forth not in self-immolation, but in the penning of strange stories. Yet, feeling as he did about the agony of existence and the attraction of death, we might find it less tragic that he was fated to an early death.

V

Fitz was gregarious. He involved himself in many cliques, such as "The Bees." These were Bohemian actors, dramatists, and critics who so cleverly ridiculed the theater that they came to be feared. He was a regular at Richard Stoddard and Elizabeth Barrow Stoddard's saloons, though these were rather low-key by Fitz's standards. He attended motley gatherings in various bars and restaurants, in one bar being waylaid by someone he had criticized in print, and got himself beaten by a gang of hired thugs.

The group that became a thing of near legend was the at first nameless gathering of artists in Pfaff's Cellar. Charles Pfaff's establishment served excellent coffee and German beer, a variety of burgundies, and passable meals served by buxom wenches. Whitman and George Arnold wrote poems to Charlie and his cellar. The impoverished artists and street philosophers and radicals who met there were soon called *The* Bohemians by the press, a label eagerly accepted.

Pfaff's Cellar was on Broadway. Under the sidewalk in the far recesses of the café as veritable tourists and would-be Bohemians, wishing to share the life of New York's "Left Bank" of Bleecker, Bond, and Spring, where there were plenty of boardinghouses.

The press condemned them as "a threat," going so far as to recommend Bohemians be arrested on sight. Others satirized and belittled them. The group responded with admirable manifestos scribbled collectively at Pfaff's. They also planned many magazines around that table, most stillborn or failures, with only *Vanity Fair* becoming a notable success.

A list of illuminaries would be exhausting, but three representative members deserve focus. First is journalist and poet Ada Clare, who said, "Above all, the Bohemian must not be narrow-minded; if he be, he is degraded back to the position of mere worldling."

Ada was nationally known in her day, yet little of substance has been passed down to ours. The type of woman she epitomized and who took part in the Bohemian heyday are poorly represented in the memoirs and monographs. To read William Winter, who knew Ada well, one would think she never existed. Only a few other women's names have come down to us, so a glimpse of Ada must suffice to help us understand one aspect of women in the arts of this decade.

She smoked and exchanged witticisms with the best and was proud of her son Aubrey, born out of wedlock, who called her Ada. She gleefully offered self-introductions of "*Miss* Ada Clare, and son." Castigated by the press, she insisted her fellow Bohemians rush to her rescue. When they were too slow with their pens, she adopted pseudonyms to praise the ravishing Miss Clare in her own words. She fancied herself a new kind of purity, pictured herself with great white wings, and saw her destiny to bring uplifting beauty into the lives of all Bohemians. She was worshipped by her fellows, who put the word out that Aubrey was the product of Immaculate Conception.

Her story is told more completely in Albert Parry's *Garrets and Pretenders* (1933), reissued by Dover. You are recommended to this volume, but consider Ada's sexual adventures with a grain of salt. Parry in some instances appears misled by his own or others' romanticism. He makes too much of her friendship with Charles Warren Stoddard, the California poet, during a Pacific voyage. It was not likely to be a romantic affair at all, since the author of *A South Sea Idyl* (1869) is one of the key figures in the history of homosexual rights and writings. Ada didn't fit his preferences, despite the fact that she cut her blond hair scandalously short and parted it as a boy's.

Contrasted to the "Queen of Bohemia" and her erotic legend is the Bohemian "King," Henry Clapp, Jr., who strove to appear as sexless as possible, and whose furtive liaisons were subject of speculation even among those close to him. He founded *The Saturday Press*, a Bohemian newspaper, and proceeded to tweek "brownstone respectability" and to champion liberal causes. No cows were too sacred to slaughter and Henry's wit still carries much of its bite. An advocate of women's rights, he suggested that *The Nation*, lacking women on its staff, be renamed *Stag-nation*. He dubbed Cuba "home of the slave, land of the flea." Asked about a famous evangelist, he said the man was only waiting for an opening in the holy trinity. It was Clapp who said of Horace Greeley, "He's a self-made man and worships his creator." Clapp was a brilliant man about whom many humorous tales are told, but whose later life was tragic and embittered.

The third mainstay of Pfaff's was Walt Whitman. He was in attendance nightly, eager to be admired. Emerson, who found the Bohemians rude and noisy, was disappointed in Whitman's desire to remain a dominant figure among them. He had already published *Leaves of Grass* and his presence gave the Bohemians more credibility than Emerson, and many others, thought they deserved. The Civil War changed Whitman, but in the 1850s he liked nothing better than to sit in the cellar with doting comrades, baring his muscular chest.

There were many, many others, famed and not, the best of them destined to die young, their obsession with Edgar Allan Poe perhaps symptomatic. This admiration for Poe lent the Bohemians to the perpetration of melancholy posturing as a matter of fashion. In reality they were having a grand time, as though there were no future, as for many there was little enough. Poe was decidedly out of favor to the world at large, hence the Bohemian admiration was one of the key factors that set them apart, and this was as true of Bohemianism in Paris and Moscow.

Fitz was always considered the most exact representative of Bohemianism, by historians and by the Bohemians themselves. One of the tales of his role in this legended society merits repeating, as it reflects Fitz's marvelous nature and the comic-morbid tone of his community.

Prone to fisticuffs, Fitz was often hauled off to the Jefferson Market jail for fighting strangers. One evening he arrived at Pfaff's cave with a blackened eye. He answered the queries nonchalantly. "I argued about right-of-way on the sidewalk." He then removed from a pocket a vial with a leech in it. He attached the leech to his injured orb and from the other pocket removed a piece of paper on which he'd composed something that very afternoon at Hone House, where he was residing. He commenced a dramatic reading, in his sonorous voice, of the ghostly poem "The Lost Steamship," the leech dangling the whole while.

In a more troublesome encounter on June 14,1858, Fitz engaged an expert pugilist too readily, and got his nose flattened. It was not his first scar, but it was by far the worst, yet he jestingly asked the surgeon to retaylor his nose to be more Roman than Semitic.

VI

In 1890, on the death of Charles Pfaff, the *Herald* waxed nostalgic: "Clapp, Wilkins, O'Brien and the rest have a lot of beer and pipes ready to welcome Pfaff over there." In many references in magazines late in the century is every evidence that the Bohemians retained a touch of tragedy and glamour in the public imagination for at least forty years, despite the fact that the key members were long in their graves.

Which leads us again to the puzzle of Fitz's collected works being such a hard thing to place with publishers. It wasn't that his name had fallen into obscurity. "The Diamond Lens" remained one of the most popular stories of the century, with nothing quite as popular until Edward Everett

Hale published "The Man Without a Country" and Frank Stockton "The Lady, or the Tiger?" Though William Winter finally obtained a partial collected works, the stories from which were reprinted on more than one occasion *sans* poems and sketches of Fitz's life, it had been an uphill struggle. And a second volume, readied for press, never was sold, though William never gave up and chatted with publishers about it whenever he had a chance.

"The Diamond Lens" can be read as an impossible quest for the ideal of beauty and of perfect, unachievable love. In Fitz's poem "A Fallen Star," a melancholy, musical and somewhat debatable theme captivates the reader. It is filled with homoerotic allusions, of which this verse is not even the most overt:

> The air was rich with fumes of wine
> When next we met. 'Twas a feast,
> And he, the boy I thought devine,
> Was the unhallowed priest.

Fitz expended a bit of energy encouraging the belief that his bachelor nature was due to a sorrowful romance with some nameless lady love of Britain. He otherwise made no excuses for surrounding himself with young men when the chance arose. Scholar Albert Parry refers to Fitz's "reckless but obscure love affairs," though it hardly seems they were that reckless if so obscure. Certainly he was never emotionally tied to women of the Bohemian circle, which is not to say he necessarily forswore the easy opportunities of urban life. In his "Man About Town" column, he admitted to a flirtation with a tall cultured Negress met in a café. His romantic poem "Amazon" suggests a masochistic fascination for cruel women. An inclination toward men does not mean he mightn't have liked women too.

Fitz's worship of the male body was obvious to all, just as Walt Whitman was fond of his own brawny body and wanted it admired. Since Walt is the member about whom the most is definitely known, we might safely look to him as an exemplar of Bohemia and Eros. "In the history of homosexual emancipation," writes Jonathon Katz in *Gay American History* (1976), "Whitman emerges as a founding father." Walt would never have spent night after night at Pfaff's if the men were generally not available. The fact that libertine mores are always part of Bohemianism is confessed by all, yet far too many researchers have conducted their studies with lead-lined blinders to ignore the obvious.

In the prewar decade such mores battled staid, even Calvinist norms. To a limited degree—as among impoverished artists, authors, poets, and

actors—radical liberalism won out. But the Civil War brought retrench-
ment, much as McCarthyism rose in the wake of World War II and
Nixon/Reagan conservatism after Vietnam. In the 1850s, Fitz's fine combination of machismo and dandyism was colorful and exciting—in its
place—but dangerous and unacceptable after the war.

Thomas Bailey Aldrich wrote his poem "At the Café," addressed to
"the man I loved," with the merry line: "You will kill me with laughter,
some day, my dear owl!" And it continues as a jealous diatribe against
some vixen trying for the dear owl's attention, failing because the owl is
asleep. The mature Tom Aldirch never allowed this poem to be collected
into any of his books.

Tom was a beautiful youth of nineteen when he first met the older Irish
dandy. They remained close friends for the rest of the decade. Fitz on
drunken sprees would show up at Tom's place of employment, a book-
shop, looking to be nursed. It was during one long stay in Tom's rooms
that "the dear owl" made the suggestion, "Let's live in the Venetian
manner!" "What's that?" "Why, sleep all day and live all night!" Which
they did, for a while.

Years later, as a Boston conservative at the center of literary matters,
Tom remembered his Bohemian days with a touch of bitterness, except
where Fitz was concerned. He claimed to have met more generous souls in
a month in Boston than in all his years in New York. This was likely
because his youthful poems were dismissed by Whitman as "tinkles" and
he was generally treated as Fitz's emotional if not physical catamite rather
than as a serious artist in his own right.

On his deathbed Fitz called for another teenage companion, Frank
Wood, who would have rushed to Fitz but that word came too suddenly of
the soldier's death. Frank, an editor for *Vanity Fair*, and who called his
staff and authors "the vanity fairies," was Fitz's choice of two literary
executors, but Frank died very young and was unable to see his friend's
wishes met.

It is evident that Fitz loved to surround himself with handsome young
men and had therefore to seek mental stimulation elsewhere, such as in
the company of Whitman and Clapp and Ada Clare, or with the poets
Bayard Taylor and Richard Stoddard. The young William Winter and
others with whom he passed many an all-night foray simply were not
Fitz's intellectual equal.

Winter told a tale of Fitz at the Manhattan Club in which Fitz seems
to be satirizing himself, though at another's expense. The overwhelming
Count Gurowski was pontificating his knowledge of court etiquette, a
typical dandy topic, but with many interruptions and corrections from

Fitz. The count, in a pique, demanded to know how such a rude Irishman would know a thing about it. Fitz silenced the borish count by replying gravely, "I was for several months a resident of the Court of St. James, as maid of honor to the Queen."

But only Thomas Davis, an attorney with whom Fitz lived on Staten Island just before the war, writes uncryptically and with a degree of pride regarding Fitz's "delicate, womanly sensibility which formed a large part of his hidden character," going so far as to boast of Fitz's promise to settle down with him after the war and begin to write in earnest.

Even more whimsically revealing is Tom's telling of Fitz's relationship with the Scottish author Donald McLeod. They were in bed together when they fell to discussing Irish versus Scottish excellence. Fitz, forever apt to press a friend to anger, finally raised Donald's blood. "I'll not allow this!" cried the Scotsman; "I demand satisfaction!" "Very well!" exclaimed Fitz, reddening with anger and pulling the blanket over himself; "Very well, sir! You know where to find me in the morning!"

In our modern era of gay rights and the recapturing of gay American history, it is perhaps possible to view Fitz more honestly and without sensationalism. As Edward J. O'Brien said, "Good work is always sure of resurrection," so that today, prejudices brushed aside, a complete edition of his supernatural fiction can be presented.

VII

It remains only to tell of our samurai poet's bold demise.

A novel by Harriet Beecher Stowe had successfully riled a divided nation. More Americans would die than in all our other wars combined. In patriotic fervor, Fitz felt that he had found a noble use for his athleticism, his skill with sword and gun, his leadership capacity. He began to raise a regiment to be called the McClellan Rifles, hoping to achieve the rank of colonel.

In New York he rounded up recruits by force, "dragging hoodlums to his recruiting station." Many of the recruits were Bohemians and pampered dandies who, it turned out, did not take well to camp life. Others were such scoundrels, Fitz could not control them.

In one encounter with a "mutinous, abusive, dangerous soldier," Fitz shot the man and risked the firing squad himself for wounding a fellow Union soldier. He lived with Thomas E. Davis on Staten Island during the inquiries. Although little came of it in the long run, his dreams of his own regiment were lost.

Tom Aldrich received a commission by telegram but was not in the city to receive it. Fitz took the opportunity of taking the commission as his own. As aide-de-camp to General Lander, Fitz needn't have risked his life unduly. But he was not all bluster and boast. If there was to be fighting, he must be in it, and could not be restrained from bold action.

His impressive military record is detailed by Francis Wolle in a book-length study of Fitz, but I will skip to "the beginning of the end," drawn chiefly from a contemporary account left by the artist Albert F. Waud.

Waud was a companion of Fitz's at the front. They were on their way to rejoin General Lander at Harper's Ferry when Fitz had a premonition he would be shot. He sang the tune "Don Caesar de Bazau," which runs: "Then let me as a soldier die." He would not be talked out of his belief that doom was certain, but parted from Waud cheerfully.

That day, in a pistol duel on horseback with the rebel Colonel Ashley, "twenty paces asunder," three shots were exchanged. Fitz took a shot in the shoulder, reducing the bone to two hundred fragments. The bullet exited at the elbow. Fitz held his saddle and dispatched his adversary.

"In a state of weakness and agony," he rode twenty miles to a doctor, an inept man for this age of injury, or Fitz might have been saved. By the time a creditable surgeon saw him, it was weeks too late. Our heroic dandy lingered long and suffered greatly from gangrene. He wrote a few final poems and letters, including a letter to Tom Davis, sadly predicting, "After I am dead I may turn out a bigger man than living."

In New York, Henry Clapp recollected that Fitz had taken Aldrich's commission and quipped, "Fitz has been shot in Tom's shoulder." But it is clear from the notices in all the magazines for which Fitz wrote that all Bohemia mourned his passing on April 6, 1862.

In a poignant, tearful mood, William Winter was to write the obituary for an entire era: "The music is hushed. The fires are put out. The gypsies are all gone. There is no Bohemia anymore, nor ever will be, except in imagination's dream."

Fitz's body was returned to New York. Eventually a marble stone was set over him, engraved with praise for "a brilliant poet who, whatever his faults, had the saving graces of genius and high principle."

Time and weather have erased the marble clean.

—Jessica Amanda Salmonson
Seattle, 1987

Proem

The Ghosts

Pale shapes advancing from the midnight air,
Beckoning with misty fingers round my bed,
Bending your faded faces o'er my head,
I have no fear of ye! I seem to share
Your dim vitality—mine's well-nigh fled.
I feel the human outlines melt away;
These thin, gray hands that lie on the damp sheet
Are almost vapory enough to meet
Yours in the grasp of fellowship. My hair
Seems turning into cloud. The quickening clay
That walls me in is cracking, and I strive
Towards ye through the breach. Am I alive?
Or are ye dead? All's vague—a wide, gray sea.
Hark! the cock crows! Now, spirits, welcome me!

—F.-J.O'B.
The Knickerbocker, January 1859

The Supernatural Tales
of Fitz-James O'Brien

The Lost Room

It was oppressively warm. The sun had long disappeared, but seemed to have left its vital spirit of heat behind it. The air rested; the leaves of the acacia-trees that have shrouded my windows, hung plumb-like on their delicate stalks. The smoke of my cigar scarce rose above my head, but hung about me in a pale blue cloud, which I had to dissipate with languid waves of my hand. My shirt was open at the throat, and my chest heaved laboriously in the effort to catch some breaths of fresher air. The very noises of the city seemed to be wrapped in slumber, and the shrilling of the mosquitoes were the only sounds that broke the stillness.

As I lay with my feet elevated on the back of a chair, wrapped in that peculiar frame of mind in which thought assumes a species of lifeless motion, the strange fancy seized me of making a languid inventory of the principal articles of furniture in my room. It was a task well suited to the mood in which I found myself. Their forms were duskily defined in the dim twilight that floated shadowily through the chamber; it was no labor to note and particularize each, and from the place where I sat I could command a view of all my possessions without even turning my head.

There was, *imprimus*, that ghostly lithograph by Calame. It was a mere black spot on the white wall, but my inner vision scrutinized every detail of the picture. A wild, desolate, midnight heath, with a spectral oak-tree in the centre of the foreground. The wind blows fiercely, and the jagged branches, clothed scantily with ill-grown leaves, are swept to the left continually by its giant force. A formless wrack of clouds streams across the awful sky, and the rain sweeps almost parallel with the horizon. Beyond, the heath stretches off into endless blackness, in the extreme of which either fancy or art has conjured up some undefinable shapes that seem riding into space. At the base of the huge oak stands a shrouded figure. His mantle is wound by the blast in tight folds around his form, and the long cock's feather in his hat is blown upright, till it seems as if it stood on end with fear. His features are not visible, for he has grasped his cloak with both hands, and drawn it from either side across his face. The picture is seemingly objectless. It tells no tale, but there is a weird power about it that haunts one, and it was for that I bought it.

Next to the picture comes the round blot that hangs below it, which I know to be a smoking-cap. It has my coat of arms embroidered on the front, and for that reason I never wear it; though, when properly arranged on my head with its long blue silken tassel hanging down by my cheek, I believe it becomes me well. I remember the time when it was in the course of manufacture. I remember the tiny little hands that pushed the colored silks so nimbly through the cloth that was stretched on the embroidery-frame—the vast trouble I was put to to get a colored copy of my armorial bearings for the heraldic work which was to decorate the front of the band—the pursings up of the little mouth, and the contractions of the young forehead, as their possessor plunged into a profound sea of cogitation touching the way in which the cloud should be represented from which the armed hand, that is my crest, issues—the heavenly moment when the tiny hands placed it on my head, in a position that I could not bear for more than a few seconds, and I, king-like, immediately assumed my royal prerogative after the coronation, and instantly levied a tax on my only subject, which was, however, not paid unwillingly. Ah! the cap is there, but the embroiderer has fled; for Atropos was severing the web of life above her head while she was weaving that silken shelter for mine!

How uncouthly the huge piano that occupies the corner at the left of the door looms out in the uncertain twilight! I neither play nor sing, yet I own a piano. It is a comfort to me to look at it, and to feel that the music *is* there, although I am not able to break the spell that binds it. It is pleasant to know that Bellini and Mozart, Cimarosa, Porpora, Glück, and all such—or at least their souls—sleep in that unwieldy case. There lie embalmed, as it were, all operas, sonatas, oratorios, notturnos, marches, songs, and dances, that ever climbed into existence through the four bars that wall in melody. Once I was entirely repaid for the investment of my funds in that instrument which I never use. Blokeeta, the composer, came to see me. Of course his instincts urged him as irresistibly to my piano as if some magnetic power lay within it compelling him to approach. He tuned it, he played on it. All night long, until the gray and spectral dawn rose out of the depths of the midnight, he sat and played, and I lay smoking by the window listening. Wild, unearthly, and sometimes insufferably painful, were the improvisations of Blokeeta. The chords of the instrument seemed breaking with anguish. Lost souls shrieked in his dismal preludes; the half-heard utterances of spirits in pain, that groped at inconceivable distances from any thing lovely or harmonious, seemed to rise dimly up out of the waves of sound that gathered under his hands. Melancholy human love wandered out on distant heaths, or beneath dank and gloomy cypresses, murmuring its unanswered sorrow, or hateful gnomes sported and sang in the stagnant swamps, triumphing in unearthly tones over the knight whom they had lured to his death. Such was Blokeeta's night's entertainment; and when he at length closed the piano, and hurried away through the cold morning, he left a memory about the instrument from which I could never escape.

Those snow-shoes, that hang in the space between the mirror and the door, recall Canadian wanderings. A long race through the dense forests over the frozen snow, through whose brittle crust the slender hoofs of the cariboo that we were pursuing sank at every step, until the poor creature despairingly turned at bay in a small juniper coppice, and we heartlessly shot him down. And I remember how Gabriel, the *habitant*, and François, the half-breed, cut his throat, and how the hot blood rushed out in a torrent over the snowy soil; and I recall the snow *cabane* that Gabriel built, where we all three slept so warmly, and the great fire that glowed at our feet painting all kinds of demoniac shapes on the black screen of forest that lay without, and the deer-steaks that we roasted for our breakfast, and the savage drunkenness of Gabriel in the morning, he having been privately drinking out of my brandy-flask all the night long.

That long haftless dagger that dangles over the mantle-piece makes my heart swell. I found it when a boy, in a hoary old castle in which one of my maternal ancestors once lived. That same ancestor—who, by-the-way, yet lives in history—was a strange old sea-king, who dwelt on the extremest point of the southwestern coast of Ireland. He owned the whole of that fertile island called Inniskeiran, which directly faces Cape Clear, where between them the Atlantic rolls furiously, forming what the fishermen of the place call "the Sound." An awful place in winter is that same Sound. On certain days no boat can live there for a moment, and Cape Clear is frequently cut off for days from any communication with the main land.

This old sea-king—Sir Florence O'Driscoll by name—passed a stormy life. From the summit of his castle he watched the ocean, and when any richly laden vessels, bound from the south to the industrious Galway merchants, hove in sight, Sir Florence hoisted the sails of his galley, and it went hard with him if he did not tow into harbor ship and crew. In this way he lived; not a very honest mode of livelihood certainly, according to our modern ideas, but quite reconcilable with the morals of the time. As may be supposed, Sir Florence got into trouble. Complaints were laid against him at the English Court by the plundered merchants, and the Irish viking set out for London to plead his own cause before good Queen Bess, as she was called. He had one powerful recommendation; he was a marvelously handsome man. Not Celtic by descent, but half Spanish, half Danish in blood, he had the great northern stature with the regular features, flashing eyes, and dark hair of the Iberian race. This may account for the fact that his stay at the English Court was much longer than was necessary, as also for the tradition, which a local historian mentions, that the English Queen evinced a preference for the Irish chieftain of other nature than that usually shown from monarch to subject.

Previous to his departure Sir Florence had intrusted the care of his property to an Englishman named Hull. During the long absence of the knight this person managed to ingratiate himself with the local authorities, and gain their favor so far that they were willing to support him in almost any scheme. After a protracted stay Sir Florence, pardoned of all his misdeeds, returned to his home. Home no longer. Hull was in possession, and refused to yield an acre of the lands he had so nefariously acquired. It was no use appealing to the law, for its officers were in the opposite interest. It was no use appealing to the Queen, for she had another lover, and had forgotten the poor Irish knight by this time; and so the viking passed the best portion of his life in unsuccessful attempts to reclaim his vast estates, and was eventually, in his old age, obliged to content himself with his castle by the sea, and the island of Inniskeiran, the only spot of which the usurper was unable to deprive him. So this old story of my kinsman's fate looms up out of the darkness that enshrouds that haftless dagger hanging on the wall.

It was somewhat after the foregoing fashion that I dreamily made the inventory of my personal property. As I turned my eyes on each object, one after the other, or the places where they lay—for the room was now so dark that it was almost impossible to see with any distinctness—a crowd of memories connected with each rose up before me, and, perforce, I had to indulge them. So I proceeded but slowly, and at last my cigar shortened to a hot and bitter morsel that I could barely hold between my lips, while it seemed to me that the night grew each moment more insufferably oppressive. While I was revolving some impossible means of cooling my wretched body, the cigar stump began to burn my lips. I flung it angrily through the open window, and stooped out to watch it falling. It first lighted on the leaves of the acacia, sending out a spray of red sparkles, then rolling off, it fell plump on the dark walk in the garden, faintly illuminating for a moment the dusky trees and breathless flowers. Whether it was the contrast between the red flash of the cigar stump and the silent darkness of the garden, or whether it was that I detected by the sudden light a faint waving of the leaves, I know not, but something suggested to me that the garden was cool. I will take a turn there, thought

I, just as I am; it can not be warmer than this room, and however still the atmosphere, there is always a feeling of liberty and spaciousness in the open air that partially supplies one's wants. With this idea running through my head I arose, lit another cigar, and passed out into the long, intricate corridors that led to the main stair-case. As I crossed the threshold of my room, with what a different feeling I should have passed it had I known that I was never to set foot in it again!

I lived in a very large house, in which I occupied two rooms on the second floor. The house was old-fashioned, and all the floors communicated by a huge circular stair-case that wound up through the centre of the building, while at every landing long rambling corridors stretched off into mysterious nooks and corners. This palace of mine was very high, and its resources, in the way of crannies and windings, seemed to be interminable. Nothing seemed to stop any where. Cul de sacs were unknown on the premises. The corridors and passages, like mathematical lines, seemed capable of indefinite extension, and the object of the architect must have been to erect an edifice in which people might go ahead forever. The whole place was gloomy, not so much because it was large, but because an unearthly nakedness seemed to pervade the structure. The stair-cases, corridors, halls, and vestibules all partook of a desert-like desolation. There was nothing on the walls to break the sombre monotony of those long vistas of shade. No carvings on the wainscoting, no moulded masks peering down from the simply severe cornices, no marble vases on the landings. There was an eminent dreariness and want of life—so rare in an American establishment—all over the abode. It was Hood's haunted house put in order, and newly painted. The servants, too, were shadowy and chary of their visits. Bells rang three times before the gloomy chambermaid could be induced to present herself, and the negro waiter, a ghoul-like looking creature from Congo, obeyed the summons only when one's patience was exhausted, or one's want satisfied in some other way. When he did come, one felt sorry that he had not staid away altogether, so sullen and savage did he appear. He moved along the echoless floors with a slow, noiseless shamble, until his dusky figure, advancing from the gloom, seemed like some reluctant afreet, compelled, by the superior power of his master, to disclose himself. When the doors of all the chambers were closed, and no light illuminated the long corridor, save the red, unwholesome glare of a small oil lamp on a table at the end, where late lodgers lit their candles, one could not by any possibility conjure up a sadder or more desolate prospect.

Yet the house suited me. Of meditative and sedentary habits, I rather enjoyed the extreme quiet. There were but few lodgers, from which I infer that the landlord did not drive a very thriving trade; and these, probably oppressed by the sombre spirit of the place, were quiet and ghost-like in their movements. The proprietor I scarcely ever saw. My bills were deposited by unseen hands every month on my table while I was out walking or riding, and my pecuniary response was intrusted to the attendant afreet. On the whole, when the bustling, wide-awake spirit of New York is taken into consideration, the sombre, half-vivified character of the house in which I lived was an anomaly that no one appreciated better than I who lived there.

I felt my way down the wide, dark stair-case in my pursuit of zephyrs. The garden, as I entered it, did feel somewhat cooler than my own room, and I puffed my cigar along the dim, cypress-shrouded walks with a sensation of comparative relief. It was very dark. The tall-growing flowers that bordered the path were so wrapped in gloom as to present the aspect of solid pyramidal masses, all the details of leaves and blossoms being buried in an embracing darkness, while the trees had lost all form, and seemed like masses of overhanging cloud. It was a place and time to excite the imagination; for in the impenetrable cavities of endless gloom there was room for the most riotous fancies to play at will. I walked and walked, and the echoes of my footsteps on the ungraveled and mossy path suggested a double feeling. I felt alone and yet in company at the same time. The solitariness of the place made itself distinct enough in the stillness, broken alone by the hollow reverberations of my step, while those very reverberations seemed to imbue me with an undefined feeling that I was not alone. I was not, therefore, much startled when I was suddenly accosted from beneath the solid darkness of an immense cypress by a voice saying,

"Will you give me a light, Sir?"

"Certainly," I replied, trying in vain to distinguish the speaker amidst the impenetrable dark.

Somebody advanced, and I held out my cigar. All I could gather definitively about the individual that thus accosted me was, that he must have been of extremely small stature; for I, who am by no means an overgrown man, had to stoop considerably in handing him my cigar. The vigorous puff that he gave his own lighted up my Havana for a moment, and I fancied that I caught a glimpse of a pale, weird countenance, immersed in a background of long, wild hair. The flash was, however, so momentary that I could not even say certainly whether this was an actual impression or the mere effort of imagination to embody that which the senses had failed to distinguish.

"Sir, you are out late," said this unknown to me, as he, with a half-uttered thanks, handed me back my cigar, for which I had to grope in the gloom.

"Not later than usual," I replied, dryly.

"Hum! you are fond of late wanderings, then?"

"That is just as the fancy seizes me."

"Do you live here?"

"Yes."

"Queer house, isn't it?"

"I have only found it quiet."

"Hum! But you *will* find it queer, take my word for it." This was earnestly uttered; and I felt, at the same time, a bony finger laid on my arm that cut it sharply, like a blunted knife.

"I can not take your word for any such assertion," I replied, rudely, shaking off the bony finger with an irrepressible motion of disgust.

"No offense, no offense," muttered my unseen companion rapidly, in a strange, subdued voice, that would have been shrill had it been louder; "your being angry does not alter the matter. You will find it a queer house. Every body finds it a queer house. Do you know who live there?"

"I never busy myself, Sir, about other people's affairs," I answered, sharply, for the individual's manner, combined with my utter uncertainty as to his appearance, oppressed me with an irksome longing to be rid of him.

"Oh! you don't? Well, I do. I know what they are—well, well, well;" and as he pronounced the three last words his voice rose with each, until, with the last, it reached a shrill shriek that echoed horribly among the lonely walks. "Do you know what they eat?" he continued.

"No, Sir—nor care."

"Oh! but you will care. You must care. You shall care. I'll tell you what they are. They are enchanters. They are ghouls. They are cannibals. Did you never remark their eyes, and how they gloated on you when you passed? Did you never remark the food that they served up at your table? Did you never, in the dead of night, hear muffled and unearthly footsteps gliding along the corridors, and stealthy hands turning the handle of your door? Does not some magnetic influence fold itself continually around you when they pass, and send a thrill through spirit and body, and a cold shiver that no sunshine will chase away? Oh, you have! You have felt all these things! I know it!"

The earnest rapidity, the subdued tones, the eagerness of accent with which all this was uttered, impressed me most uncomfortably. I really seemed as if I could recall all those weird occurrences and influences of which he spoke; and I shuddered in spite of myself in the midst of that impenetrable darkness that surrounded me.

"Hum!" said I, assuming, without knowing it, a confidential tone, "may I ask how you know of these things?"

"How I know them? Because I am their enemy. Because they tremble at my whisper. Because I hang upon their track with the perseverance of a blood-hound and the stealthiness of a tiger—because—because—I was *of* them once!"

"Wretch!" I cried, excitedly, for involuntarily his eager tones had wrought me up to a high pitch of spasmodic nervousness, "then you mean to say that you—"

As I uttered this word, obeying an uncontrollable impulse, I stretched forth my hand in the direction of the speaker and made a blind clutch. The tips of my fingers seemed to touch a surface as smooth as glass, that glided suddenly from under them. A sharp, angry hiss sounded through the gloom, followed by a whirring noise, as if some projectile passed rapidly by, and the next moment I felt instinctively that I was alone.

A most disagreeable sensation instantly assailed me. A prophetic instinct that some terrible misfortune menaced me; an eager and overpowering anxiety to get back to my own room without loss of time. I turned and ran blindly along the dark cypress alley, every dusky clump of flowers that rose blackly in the borders making my heart each moment cease to beat. The echoes of my own footsteps seemed to redouble and assume the sounds of unknown pursuers following fast upon my track. The boughs of lilac-bushes and syringas that here and there stretched partly across the walk, seemed to have been furnished suddenly with hooked hands that sought to grasp me as I flew by, and each moment I expected to behold some awful and impassable barrier fall right across my track, and wall me up forever.

At length I reached the wide entrance. With a single leap I sprang up the four or five steps that formed the stoop, and dashing along the hall, up the wide, echoing stairs, and again along the dim funereal corridors until I paused, breathless and panting, at the door of my room. Once so far, I stopped for an instant and leaned heavily against one of the panels, panting lustily after my late run. I had, however, scarcely rested my whole weight against the door, when it suddenly gave way, and I staggered in head-foremost. To my utter astonishment the room that I had left in profound darkness was now a blaze of light. So intense was the illumination that, for a few seconds while the pupils of my eyes were contracting under the sudden change, I saw absolutely nothing save the dazzling glare. This fact in itself coming on me with such utter suddenness, was sufficient to prolong my confusion, and it was not until after several moments had elapsed that I perceived the room was not alone illuminated but occupied. And such occupants! Amazement at the scene took such possession of me that I was incapable of either moving or uttering a word. All that I could do was to lean against the wall, and stare blankly at the whole business.

It might have been a scene out of Faublas, or Grammont's Memoirs, or happened in some palace of Minister Fouque.

Round a large table in the centre of the room, where I had left a student-like litter of books and papers, were seated half a dozen persons. Three were men, and three were women. The table was heaped with a prodigality of luxuries. Luscious Eastern fruits were piled up in silver fila-gree vases, through whose meshes their glowing rinds shone in the con-trasts of a thousand hues. Small silver dishes that Benvenuto might have designed, filled with succulent and aromatic meats, were distributed upon a cloth of snowy damask. Bottles of every shape, slender ones from the Rhine, stout fellows from Holland, sturdy ones from Spain, and quaint basket-woven flasks from Italy, absolutely littered the board. Drinking glasses of every size and hue filled up the interstices, and the thirsty German flagon stood side by side with the aerial bubbles of Venetian glass that rested so lightly on their thread-like stems. An odor of luxury and sensuality floated through the apartment. The lamps that burned in every vacant spot where room for one could be found, seemed to diffuse a subtle incense on the air, and in a large vase that stood on the floor I saw a mass of magnolias, tuberoses, and jasmines grouped together, stifling each other with their honeyed and heavy fragrance.

The inhabitants of my room seemed beings well suited to so sensual an atmosphere. The women were strangely beautiful, and all were attired in dresses of the most fantastic devices and brilliant hues. Their figures were round, supple, and elastic; their eyes dark and languishing; their lips full, ripe, and of the richest bloom. The three men wore half-masks, so that all I could distinguish were heavy jaws, pointed beards, and brawny throats that rose like massive pillars out of their doublets. All six lay reclining on Roman couches about the table, drinking down the purple wines in large draughts, and tossing back their heads and laughing wildly.

I stood, I suppose, for some three minutes, with my back against the wall staring vacantly at the bacchanal vision, before any of the revelers appeared to notice my presence. At length, without any expression to indicate whether I had been observed from the beginning or not, two of the women arose from their couches, and, approaching, took each a hand and led me to the table. I obeyed their motions mechanically. I sat on a couch between them as they indicated. I unresistingly permitted them to wind their arms about my neck.

"You must drink," said one, pouring out a large glass of red wine, "here is Clos Vougeot of a rare vintage; and here," pushing a flask of amber-hued wine before me, "is Lachrima Christi."

"You must eat," said the other, drawing the silver dishes toward her. "Here are cutlets stewed with olives, and here are slices of a *filet* stuffed with bruised sweet chestnuts;" and as she spoke, she, without waiting for a reply, proceeded to help me.

The sight of the food recalled to me the warnings I had received in the garden. This sudden effort of memory restored to me my other faculties at the same instant. I sprang to my feet, thrusting the women from me with each hand.

"Demons!" I almost shouted, "I will have none of your accursed food. I know you. You are cannibals, you are ghouls, you are enchanters. Begone, I tell you! Leave my room in peace!"

A shout of laughter from all six was the only effect that my passionate speech produced. The men rolled on their couches, and their half-masks quivered with the convulsions of their mirth. The women shrieked, and tossed the slender wine-glasses wildly aloft, and turned to me and flung themselves on my bosom, fairly sobbing with laughter.

"Yes," I continued, as soon as the noisy mirth had subsided, "yes, I say, leave my room instantly! I will have none of your unnatural orgies here!"

"His room!" shrieked the woman on my right.

"His room!" echoed she on my left.

"His room! He calls it his room!" shouted the whole party, as they rolled once more into jocular convulsions.

"How know you that it is your room?" said one of the men who sat opposite to me, at length, after the laughter had once more somewhat subsided.

"How do I know?" I replied, indignantly. "How do I know my own room? How could I mistake it, pray? There's my furniture—my piano—"

"He calls that a piano!" shouted my neighbors, again in convulsions as I pointed to the corner where my huge piano, sacred to the memory of Blokeeta, used to stand. "Oh, yes! It is his room. There—there is his piano!"

The peculiar emphasis they laid on the word "piano" caused me to scrutinize the article I was indicating more thoroughly. Up to this time, though utterly amazed at the entrance of these people into my chamber, and connecting them somewhat with the wild stories I had heard in the garden, I still had a sort of indefinite idea that the whole thing was a masquerading freak got up in my absence, and that the bacchanalian orgy I was witnessing was nothing more than a portion of some elaborate hoax of which I was to be the victim. But when my eyes turned to the corner where I had left a huge and cumbrous piano, and beheld a vast and sombre organ lifting its fluted front to the very ceiling, and convinced myself, by a hurried process of memory, that it occupied the very spot in which I had left my own instrument, the little self-possession that I had left forsook me. I gazed around me bewildered.

In like manner every thing was changed. In the place of that old haftless dagger, connected with so many historic associations personal to myself, I beheld a Turkish yataghan dangling by its belt of crimson silk, while the jewels in the hilt blazed as the lamplight played upon them. In the spot where hung my cherished smoking-cap, memorial of a buried love, a knightly casque was suspended, on the crest of which a golden dragon stood in the act of springing. That strange lithograph by Calame was no longer a lithograph, but it seemed to me that the portion of the wall which it had covered, of the exact shape and size, had been cut out, and, in place of the picture, a *real* scene on the same scale, and with real actors, was distinctly visible. The old oak was there, and the stormy sky was there; but I saw the branches of the oak sway with the tempest, and the clouds drive before the wind. The wanderer in his cloak was gone; but in his place I beheld a circle of wild figures, men and women, dancing with linked hands around the bole of the great tree, chanting some wild fragment of a song, to which the winds roared an unearthly chorus. The snow-shoes, too, on whose sinewy woof I had sped for many days amidst Canadian wastes, had vanished, and in their place lay a pair of strange upcurled papooshes, that had, perhaps, been many a time shuffled off at the doors of mosques, beneath the steady blaze of an Orient sun.

All was changed. Wherever my eyes turned they missed familiar objects, yet encountered strange representatives. Still in all the substitutes there seemed to me a reminiscence of what they replaced. They seemed only for a time transmuted into other shapes, and there lingered around them the atmosphere of what they once had been. Thus I could have sworn the room to have been mine, yet there was nothing in it that I could rightly claim. Every thing reminded me of some former possession that it was not. I looked for the acacia at the window, and lo! long, silken palm-leaves swayed in through the open lattice; yet they had the same motion and the same air of my favorite tree, and seemed to murmur to me, "Though we seem to be palm-leaves, yet are we acacia-leaves; yes, those very ones on which you used to watch the butterflies alight and the rain patter while you smoked and dreamed!" So in all things. The room was, yet was not mine; and a sickening consciousness of my utter inability to reconcile its identity with its appearance overwhelmed me, and choked my reason.

"Well, have you determined whether or not this is your room?" asked the girl on my left, proffering me a huge tumbler creaming over with Champagne, and laughing wickedly as she spoke.

"It is mine," I answered, doggedly, striking the glass rudely with my hand, and dashing the aromatic wine over the white cloth. "I know that it is mine; and ye are jugglers and enchanters that want to drive me mad."

"Hush! hush!" she said, gently, not in the least angered at my rough treatment. "You are excited. Alf shall play something to soothe you."

At her signal one of the men arose and sat down at the organ. After a short, wild, spasmodic prelude, he began what seemed to me to be a symphony of recollections. Dark and sombre, and all through full of quivering and intense agony, it appeared to recall a dark and dismal night, on a cold reef, around which an unseen but terribly audible ocean broke with eternal fury. It seemed as if a lonely pair were on the reef, one living, the other dead; one clasping his arms around the tender neck and naked bosom of the other, striving to warm her into life, when his own vitality was being each moment sucked from him by the icy breath of the storm. Here and there a terrible wailing minor key would tremble through the chords like the shriek of sea-birds, or the warning of advancing death. While the man played I could scarce restrain myself. It seemed to be Blokeeta whom I listened to, and on whom I gazed. That wondrous night of pleasure and pain that I had once passed listening to him seemed to have been taken up again at the spot where it had broken off, and the same hand was continuing it. I stared at the man called Alf. There he sat with his cloak and doublet, and long rapier and mask of black velvet. But there was something in the air of the peaked beard, a familiar mystery in the wild mass of raven hair that fell as if wind-blown over his shoulders, which riveted my memory.

"Blokeeta! Blokeeta!"—I shouted, starting up furiously from the couch on which I was lying, and bursting the fair arms that were linked around my neck as if they had been hateful chains—"Blokeeta! my friend, speak to me I entreat you! Tell these horrid enchanters to leave me. Say that I hate them. Say that I command them to leave my room!"

The man at the organ stirred not in answer to my appeal. He ceased playing, and the dying sound of the last note he had touched faded off into a melancholy moan. The other men and the women burst once more into peals of mocking laughter.

"Why will you persist in calling this your room?" said the woman next me, with a smile meant to be kind, but to me inexpressibly loathsome. "Have we not shown you by the furniture, by the general appearance of the place, that you are mistaken, and that this can not be your apartment? Rest content, then, with us. You are welcome here, and need no longer trouble yourself about your room."

"Rest content!" I answered, madly; "live with ghosts! eat of awful meats, and see awful sights! Never, never! You have cast some enchantment over the place that has disguised it; but for all that I know it to be my room. You shall leave it!"

"Softly, softly!" said another of the sirens. "Let us settle this amicably. This poor gentleman seems obstinate and inclined to make an uproar. Now we do not want an uproar. We love the night and its quiet; and there is no night that we love so well as that on which the moon is coffined in clouds. Is it not so, my brothers?"

An awful and sinister smile gleamed on the countenances of her unearthly audience, and seemed to glide visibly from underneath their masks.

"Now," she continued, "I have a proposition to make. It would be ridiculous for us to surrender this room simply because this gentleman states that it is his; and yet I feel anxious to gratify, as far as may be fair, his wild assertion of ownership. A room, after all, is not much to us; we can get one easily enough, but still we would be loth to give this apartment up to so imperious a demand. We are willing, however, to *risk* its loss. That is to say"—turning to me—"I propose that we play for the room. If you win, we will immediately surrender it to you just as it stands; if, on the contrary, you lose, you shall bind yourself to depart and never molest us again."

Agonized at the ever-darkening mysteries that seemed to thicken around me, and despairing of being able to dissipate them by the mere exercise of my own will, I caught almost gladly at the chance thus presented to me. The idea of my loss or my gain scarce entered into my calculations. All I felt was an indefinite knowledge that I might, in the way proposed, regain, in an instant, that quiet chamber and that peace of mind which I had so strangely been deprived of.

"I agree!" I cried, eagerly; "I agree. Any thing to rid myself of such unearthly company!"

The woman touched a small golden bell that stood near her on the table, and it had scarce ceased to tinkle when a negro dwarf entered with a silver tray on which were dice-boxes and dice. A shudder passed over me as I thought in this stunted African I could trace a resemblance to the ghoul-like black servant to whose attendance I had been accustomed.

"Now," said my neighbor, seizing one of the dice-boxes and giving me the other, "the highest wins. Shall I throw first?"

I nodded assent. She rattled the dice, and I felt an inexpressible load lifted from my heart as she threw fifteen.

"It is your turn," she said, with a mocking smile; "but before you throw, I repeat the offer I made you before. Live with us. Be one of us. We will initiate you into our mysteries and enjoyments—enjoyments of which you can form no idea unless you experience them. Come; it is not too late yet to change your mind. Be with us!"

My reply was a fierce oath as I rattled the dice with spasmodic nervousness and flung them on the board. They rolled over and over again, and during that brief instant I felt a suspense, the intensity of which I have never known before or since. At last they lay before me. A shout of the same horrible, maddening laughter rang in my ears. I peered in vain at the dice, but my sight was so confused that I could not distinguish the amount of the cast. This lasted for a few moments. Then my sight grew clear, and I sank back almost lifeless with despair as I saw that I had thrown but *twelve!*

"Lost! lost!" screamed my neighbor, with a wild laugh. "Lost! lost!" shouted the deep voices of the masked men. "Leave us, coward!" they all cried; "you are not fit to be one of us. Remember your promise; leave us!"

Then it seemed as if some unseen power caught me by the shoulders and thrust me toward the door. In vain I resisted. In vain I screamed and shouted for help. In vain I implored them for pity. All the reply I had were those mocking peals of merriment, while, under the invisible influence, I staggered like a drunken man toward the door. As I reached the threshold the organ pealed out a wild triumphal strain. The power that impelled me concentrated itself into one vigorous impulse that sent me blindly staggering out into the echoing corridor, and, as the door closed swiftly behind me, I caught one glimpse of the apartment I had left forever. A change passed like a shadow over it. The lamps died out, the siren women and masked men vanished, the flowers, the fruits, the bright silver and bizarre furniture faded swiftly, and I saw again, for the tenth of a second, my own old chamber restored. There was the acacia waving darkly; there was the table littered with books; there was the ghostly lithograph, the dearly-beloved smoking cap, the Canadian snow-shoes, the ancestral dagger. And there, at the piano, organ no longer, sate Blokeeta playing.

The next instant the door closed violently, and I was left standing in the corridor stunned and despairing.

As soon as I had partially recovered my comprehension I rushed madly to the door with the dim idea of beating it in. My fingers beat against a cold and solid wall. There was no door! I felt all along the corridor for many yards on both sides. There was not even a crevice to give me hope. I rushed down stairs shouting madly. No one answered. In the vestibule I met the negro; I seized him by the collar, and demanded my room. The demon showed his white and awful teeth, which were filed into a saw-like shape, and extricating himself from my grasp with a sudden jerk, fled down the passage with a gibbering laugh. Nothing but echo answered to my despairing shrieks. The lonely garden resounded with my cries as I strode madly through the dark walks, and the tall funereal cypresses seemed to bury me beneath their heavy shadows. I met no one. Could find no one. I had to bear my sorrow and despair alone.

Since that awful hour I have never found my room. Everywhere I look for it, yet never see it. Shall I ever find it?

The Child That Loved a Grave

Far away in the deep heart of a lonely country there was an old solitary church-yard. People were no longer buried there, for it had fulfilled its mission long, long ago, and its rank grass now fed a few vagrant goats that clambered over its ruined wall and roamed through the sad wilderness of graves. It was bordered all round with willows and gloomy cypresses; and the rusty iron gate, seldom or ever opened, shrieked when the wind stirred it on its hinges as if some lost soul, condemned to wander in that desolate place forever, was shaking its bars and wailing at the terrible imprisonment.

In this church-yard there was one grave unlike all the rest. The stone which stood at the head bore no name, but instead the curious device, rudely sculptured, of a sun uprising out of the sea. The grave was very small and covered with a thick growth of dock and nettle, and one might tell by its size that it was that of a little child.

Not far from the old church-yard a young boy lived with his parents in a dreary cottage; he was a dreamy, dark-eyed boy, who never played with the children of the neighborhood, but loved to wander in the fields and lie by the banks of rivers, watching the leaves fall and the waters ripple, and the lilies sway their white heads on the bosom of the current. It was no wonder that his life was solitary and sad, for his parents were wild, wicked people who drank and quarreled all day and all night, and the noises of their quarrels were heard in calm summer nights by the neighbors that lived in the village under the brow of the hill.

The boy was terrified at all this hideous strife, and his young soul shrank within him when he heard the oaths and the blows echoing through the dreary cottage, so he used to fly out into the fields where every thing looked so calm and pure, and talk with the lilies in a low voice as if they were his friends.

In this way he came to haunt the old church-yard, roaming through its half-buried headstones, and spelling out upon them the names of people that had gone from earth years and years ago. The little grave, nameless and neglected however, attracted him more than all others. The strange device of the sun uprising out of the sea was to him a perpetual source of mystery and wonder; and so, whether by day or night, when the fury of his parents drove him from his home, he used to wander there and lie amidst the thick grass and think who was buried beneath it.

In time his love for the little grave grew so great that he adorned it after his childish fashion. He cleared away the docks and the nettles and the mulleins that grew so sombrely above it, and clipped the grass until it grew thick and soft as the carpet of heaven. Then he brought primroses from the green banks of dewy lanes where the hawthorn rained its white flowers, and red poppies from the corn-fields, and blue-bells from the shadowy heart of the forest, and planted them around the grave. With the supple twigs of the silver osier he hedged it round with a little simple fence, and scraped the creeping mosses from the gray head-stone until the little grave looked as if it might have been the grave of a good fairy.

Then he was content. All the long summer days he would lie upon it with his arms clasping its swelling mound, while the soft wind with wavering will would come and play about him and timidly lift his hair. From the hill-side he heard the shouts of the village boys at play, and sometimes one of them would come and ask him to join in their sports; but he would look at him with his calm, dark eyes and gently answer no; and the boy, awed and hushed, would steal back to his companions and speak in whispers about the child that loved a grave.

In truth, he loved the little grave better than all play. The stillness of the church-yard, the scent of the wild flowers, the golden checkers of the sunlight falling through the trees and playing over the grass were all delights to him. He would lie on his back for hours gazing up at the summer sky and watching the white clouds sailing across it, and wondering if they were the souls of good people sailing home to heaven. But when the black thunder-clouds came up bulging with passionate tears, and bursting with sound and fire, he would think of his bad parents at home, and, turning to the grave, lay his little cheek against it as if it were a brother.

So the summer went passing into autumn. The trees grew sad and shivered as the time approached when the fierce wind would strip them of their cloaks, and the rains and the storms buffet their naked limbs. The primroses grew pale and withered, but in their last moments seemed to look up at the child smilingly, as if to say, "Do not weep for us. We will come again next year." But the sadness of the season came over him as the winter approached, and he often wet the little grave with his tears, and kissed the gray head-stone, as one kisses a friend that is about to depart for years.

One evening toward the close of autumn, when the woods looked brown and grim, and the wind as it came over the hills had a fierce, wicked growl, the child heard, as he was sitting by the grave, the shriek of the old gate swinging upon its rusty hinges, and looking up he saw a strange procession enter. There were five men. Two bore between them what seemed to be a long box covered with black cloth, two more carried spades in their hands, while the fifth, a tall stern-faced man clad in a long cloak, walked at their head. As the child saw these men pass to and fro through the grave-yard, stumbling over half-buried head-stones, or stooping down and examining half-effaced inscriptions, his little heart almost ceased to beat, and he shrank behind the gray stone with the strange device in mortal terror.

The men walked to and fro, with the tall one at their head, searching steadily in the long grass, and occasionally pausing to consult. At last the leader turned and walked toward the little grave, and stooping down gazed at the gray stone. The moon had just risen, and its light fell on the quaint sculpture of the sun rising out of the sea. The tall man then beckoned to his companions. "I have found it," he said; "it is here." With that the four men came along, and all five stood by the grave. The child behind the stone could no longer breathe.

The two men bearing the long box laid it down in the grass, and taking off the black cloth, the child saw a little coffin of shining ebony covered with silver ornaments, and on the lid, wrought in silver, was the device of a sun uprising out of the sea, and the moon shone over all.

"Now to work!" said the tall man; and straightway the two that held the spades plunged them into the little grave. The child thought his heart would break; and, no longer able to restrain himself, he flung his body across the mound, and cried out to the strange leader.

"Oh, Sir!" he cried, sobbing, "do not touch my little grave! It is all I have to love in the world. Do not touch it; for all day long I lie here with my arms about it, and it seems like my brother. I tend it, and keep the grass short and thick, and I promise you, if you will leave it to me, that next year I will plant about it the finest flowers in the meadows."

"Tush, child, you are a fool!" answered the stern-faced man. "This is a sacred duty that I have to perform. He who is buried here was a child like you; but he was of royal blood, and his ancestors dwelt in palaces. It is not meet that bones like his should rest in common soil. Across the sea a grand mausoleum awaits them, and I have come to take them with me and lay them in vaults of porphyry and marble. Take him away, men, and to your work!"

So the men dragged the child from the grave by main force, and laid him near by in the grass, sobbing as if his heart would break; and then they dug up the grave. Through his tears he saw the small white bones gathered up and put in the ebony coffin, and heard the lid shut down, and saw the men shovel back the earth into the empty grave, and he felt as if they were robbers. Then they took up the coffin and retraced their steps. The gate shrieked once more on its hinges, and the child was alone.

He returned home silent, and tearless, and white as any ghost. When he went to his little bed he called his father, and told him he was going to die, and asked him to have him buried in the little grave that had a gray head-stone with a sun rising out of the sea carved upon it. The father laughed, and told him to go to sleep; but when morning came the child was dead!

They buried him where he wished; and when the sod was patted smooth, and the funeral procession departed, that night a new star came out in heaven and watched above the grave.

The Diamond Lens

I. THE BENDING OF THE TWIG

From a very early period of my life the entire bent of my inclinations had been towards microscopic investigations. When I was not more than ten years old, a distant relative of our family, hoping to astonish my inexperience, constructed a simple microscope for me, by drilling in a disk of copper a small hole, in which a drop of pure water was sustained by capillary attraction. This very primitive apparatus, magnifying some fifty diameters, presented, it is true, only indistinct and imperfect forms, but still sufficiently wonderful to work up my imagination to a preternatural state of excitement.

Seeing me so interested in this rude instrument, my cousin explained to me all that he knew about the principles of the microscope, related to me a few of the wonders which had been accomplished through its agency, and ended by promising to send me one regularly constructed, immediately on his return to the city. I counted the days, the hours, the minutes, that intervened between that promise and his departure.

Meantime I was not idle. Every transparent substance that bore the remotest semblance to a lens I eagerly seized upon and employed in vain attempts to realize that instrument, the theory of whose construction I as yet only vaguely comprehended. All panes of glass containing those oblate spheroidal knots familiarly known as "bull's eyes" were ruthlessly destroyed, in the hope of obtaining lenses of marvellous power. I even went so far as to extract the crystalline humor from the eyes of fishes and animals, and endeavored to press it into the microscopic service. I plead guilty to having stolen the glasses from my Aunt Agatha's spectacles, with a dim idea of grinding them into lenses of wondrous magnifying properties,—in which attempt it is scarcely necessary to say that I totally failed.

At last the promised instrument came. It was of that order known as Field's simple microscope, and had cost perhaps about fifteen dollars. As far as educational purposes went, a better apparatus could not have been selected. Accompanying it was a small treatise on the microscope,—its history, uses, and discoveries. I comprehended then for the first time the

"Arabian Nights' Entertainments." The dull veil of ordinary existence that hung across the world seemed suddenly to roll away, and to lay bare a land of enchantments. I felt towards my companions as the seer might feel towards the ordinary masses of men. I held conversations with Nature in a tongue which they could not understand. I was in daily communication with living wonders, such as they never imagined in their wildest visions. I penetrated beyond the external portal of things, and roamed through the sanctuaries. Where they beheld only a drop of rain slowly rolling down the window-glass, I saw a universe of beings animated with all the passions common to physical life, and convulsing their minute sphere with struggles as fierce and protracted as those of men. In the common spots of mould, which my mother, good housekeeper that she was, fiercely scooped away from her jam pots, there abode for me, under the name of mildew, enchanted gardens, filled with dells and avenues of the densest foliage and most astonishing verdure, while from the fantastic boughs of these microscopic forests hung strange fruits glittering with green and silver and gold.

It was no scientific thirst that at this time filled my mind. It was the pure enjoyment of a poet to whom a world of wonders has been disclosed. I talked of my solitary pleasures to none. Alone with my microscope, I dimmed my sight, day after day and night after night poring over the marvels which it unfolded to me. I was like one who, having discovered the ancient Eden still existing in all its primitive glory, should resolve to enjoy it in solitude, and never betray to mortal the secret of its locality. The rod of my life was bent at this moment. I destined myself to be a microscopist.

Of course, like every novice, I fancied myself a discoverer. I was ignorant at the time of the thousands of acute intellects engaged in the same pursuit as myself, and with the advantages of instruments a thousand times more powerful than mine. The names of Leeuwenhoek, Williamson, Spencer, Ehrenberg, Schultz, Dujardin, Schact, and Schleiden were then entirely unknown to me, or if known, I was ignorant of their patient and wonderful researches. In every fresh specimen of Cryptogamia which I placed beneath my instrument I believed that I discovered wonders of which the world was as yet ignorant. I remember well the thrill of delight and admiration that shot through me the first time that I discovered the common wheel animalcule *(Rotifera vulgaris)* expanding and contracting its flexible spokes, and seemingly rotating through the water. Alas! as I grew older, and obtained some works treating of my favorite study, I found that I was only on the threshold of a science to the investigation of which some of the greatest men of the age were devoting their lives and intellects.

As I grew up, my parents, who saw but little likelihood of anything practical resulting from the examination of bits of moss and drops of water through a brass tube and a piece of glass, were anxious that I should choose a profession. It was their desire that I should enter the counting-house of my uncle, Ethan Blake, a prosperous merchant, who carried on business in New York. This suggestion I decisively combated. I had no taste for trade; I should only make a failure; in short, I refused to become a merchant.

But it was necessary for me to select some pursuit. My parents were staid New England people, who insisted on the necessity of labor; and therefore, although, thanks to the bequest of my poor Aunt Agatha, I should, on coming of age, inherit a small fortune sufficient to place me above want, it was decided, that, instead of waiting for this, I should act the nobler part, and employ the intervening years in rendering myself independent.

After much cogitation I complied with the wishes of my family, and selected a profession. I determined to study medicine at the New York Academy. This disposition of my future suited me. A removal from my relatives would enable me to dispose of my time as I pleased, without fear of detection. As long as I paid my Academy fees, I might shirk attending the lectures, if I chose; and as I never had the remotest intention of standing an examination, there was no danger of my being "plucked." Besides, a metropolis was the place for me. There I could obtain excellent instruments, the newest publications, intimacy with men of pursuits kindred to my own,—in short, all things necessary to insure a profitable devotion of my life to my beloved science. I had an abundance of money, few desires that were not bounded by my illuminating mirror on one side and my object-glass on the other; what, therefore, was to prevent my becoming an illustrious investigator of the veiled worlds? It was with the most buoyant hopes that I left my New England home and established myself in New York.

II. The Longing of a Man of Science

My first step, of course, was to find suitable apartments. These I obtained, after a couple of days' search, in Fourth Avenue; a very pretty second-floor unfurnished, containing sitting-room, bedroom, and a smaller apartment which I intended to fit up as a laboratory. I furnished my lodgings simply, but rather elegantly, and then devoted all my energies to the adornment of the temple of my worship. I visited Pike, the celebrated optician, and passed in review his splendid collection of microscopes,— Field's Compound, Higham's, Spencer's, Nachet's Binocular, (that founded on the principles of the stereoscope,) and at length fixed upon that form known as Spencer's Trunnion Microscope, as combining the greatest number of improvements with an almost perfect freedom from tremor. Along with this I purchased every possible accessory,—draw-tubes, micrometers, a *camera-lucida,* lever-stage, achromatic condensers, white cloud illuminators, prisms, parabolic condensers, polarizing apparatus, forceps, aquatic boxes, fishing-tubes, with a host of other articles, all of which would have been useful in the hands of an experienced microscopist, but, as I afterwards discovered, were not of the slightest present value to me. It takes years of practice to know how to use a complicated microscope. The optician looked suspiciously at me as I made these wholesale purchases. He evidently was uncertain whether to set me down as some scientific celebrity or a madman. I think he inclined to the latter belief. I suppose I was mad. Every great genius is mad upon the subject in which he is greatest. The unsuccessful madman is disgraced, and called a lunatic.

Mad or not, I set myself to work with a zeal which few scientific students have ever equalled. I had everything to learn relative to the delicate study upon which I had embarked—a study involving the most earnest patience, the most rigid analytic powers, the steadiest hand, the most untiring eye, the most refined and subtle manipulation.

For a long time half my apparatus lay inactively on the shelves of my laboratory, which was now most amply furnished with every possible contrivance for facilitating my investigations. The fact was that I did not know how to use some of my scientific accessories,—never having been taught microscopics,—and those whose use I understood theoretically were of little avail, until by practice I could attain the necessary delicacy of handling. Still, such was the fury of my ambition, such the untiring perseverance of my experiments, that, difficult of credit as it may be, in the course of one year I became theoretically and practically an accomplished microscopist.

During this period of my labors, in which I submitted specimens of every substance that came under my observation to the action of my lenses, I became a discoverer,—in a small way, it is true, for I was very young, but still a discoverer. It was I who destroyed Ehrenberg's theory that the *Volcox globator* was an animal, and proved that his "monads" with stomachs and eyes were merely phases of the formation of a vegetable cell, and were, when they reached their mature state, incapable of the act of conjugation, or any true generative act, without which no organism rising to any stage of life higher than vegetable can be said to be complete. It was I who resolved the singular problem of rotation in the cells and hairs of plants into ciliary attraction, in spite of the assertions of Mr. Wenham and others, that my explanation was the result of an optical illusion.

But notwithstanding these discoveries, laboriously and painfully made as they were, I felt horribly dissatisfied. At every step I found myself stopped by the imperfections of my instruments. Like all active microscopists, I gave my imagination full play. Indeed, it is a common complaint against many such, that they supply the defects of their instruments with the creations of their brains. I imagined depths beyond depths in Nature which the limited power of my lenses prohibited me from exploring. I lay awake at night constructing imaginary microscopes of immeasurable power, with which I seemed to pierce through all the envelopes of matter down to its original atom. How I cursed those imperfect mediums which necessity through ignorance compelled me to use! How I longed to discover the secret of some perfect lens whose magnifying power should be limited only by the resolvability of the object, and which at the same time should be free from spherical and chromatic aberrations, in short from all the obstacles over which the poor microscopist finds himself continually stumbling! I felt convinced that the simple microscope, composed of a single lens of such vast yet perfect power, was possible of construction. To attempt to bring the compound microscope up to such a pitch would have been commencing at the wrong end; this latter being simply a partially successful endeavor to remedy those very defects of the simple instrument, which, if conquered, would leave nothing to be desired.

It was in this mood of mind that I became a constructive microscopist. After another year passed in this new pursuit, experimenting on every imaginable substance,—glass, gems, flints, crystals, artificial crystals formed of the alloy of various vitreous materials—in short, having constructed as many varieties of lenses as Argus had eyes, I found myself precisely where I started, with nothing gained save an extensive knowledge of glass-making. I was almost dead with despair. My parents were surprised at my apparent want of progress in my medical studies, (I had not attended one lecture since my arrival in the city.) and the expenses of my mad pursuit had been so great as to embarrass me very seriously.

I was in this frame of mind one day, experimenting in my laboratory on a small diamond,—that stone, from its great refracting power, having always occupied my attention more than any other,—when a young Frenchman, who lived on the floor above me, and who was in the habit of occasionally visiting me, entered the room.

I think that Jules Simon was a Jew. He had many traits of the Hebrew character: a love of jewelry, of dress, and of good living. There was something mysterious about him. He always had something to sell, and yet went into excellent society. When I say sell, I should perhaps have said peddle; for his operations were generally confined to the disposal of single articles,—a picture, for instance, or a rare carving in ivory, or a pair of duelling-pistols, or the dress of a Mexican *caballero*. When I was first furnishing my rooms, he paid me a visit, which ended in my purchasing an antique silver lamp, which he assured me was a Cellini,—it was handsome enough even for that,—and some other knick-knacks for my sitting-room. Why Simon should pursue this petty trade I never could imagine. He apparently had plenty of money, and had the *entrée* of the best houses in the city,—taking care, however, I suppose, to drive no bargains within the enchanted circle of the Upper Ten. I came at length to the conclusion that this peddling was but a mask to cover some greater object, and even went so far as to believe my young acquaintance to be implicated in the slave-trade. That, however, was none of my affair.

On the present occasion, Simon entered my room in a state of considerable excitement.

"*Ah! mon ami!*" he cried, before I could even offer him the ordinary salutation, "it has occurred to me to be the witness of the most astonishing things in the world. I promenade myself to the house of Madame —— How does the little animal—*le renard*—name himself in the Latin?"

"Vulpes," I answered.

"Ah! yes,—Vulpes. I promenade myself to the house of Madame Vulpes."

"The spirit medium?"

"Yes, the great medium. Great Heavens! what a woman! I write on a slip of paper many of questions concerning affairs the most secret,—affairs that conceal themselves in the abysses of my heart the most profound: and behold! by example! what occurs? This devil of a woman makes me replies the most truthful to all of them. She talks to me of things that I do not love to talk of to myself. What am I to think? I am fixed to the earth!"

"Am I to understand you, M. Simon, that this Mrs. Vulpes replied to questions secretly written by you, which questions related to events known only to yourself?"

"Ah! more than that, more than that," he answered, with an air of some alarm. "She related to me things—— But," he added, after a pause, and suddenly changing his manner, "why occupy ourselves with these follies? It was all the Biology, without doubt. It goes without saying that it has not my credence.—But why are we here, *mon ami?* It has occurred to me to discover the most beautiful thing as you can imagine.—a vase with green lizards on it, composed by the great Bernard Palissy. It is in my apartment: let us mount. I go to show it to you."

I followed Simon mechanically; but my thoughts were far from Palissy and his enamelled ware, although I, like him, was seeking in the dark after a great discovery. This casual mention of the spiritualist, Madame Vulpes, set me on a new track. What if this spiritualism should be really a great fact? What if, through communication with subtiler organisms than my own, I could reach at a single bound the goal, which perhaps a life of agonizing mental toil would never enable me to attain?

While purchasing the Palissy vase from my friend Simon, I was mentally arranging a visit to Madame Vulpes.

III. The Spirit of Leeuwenhoek

Two evenings after this, thanks to an arrangement by letter and the promise of an ample fee, I found Madame Vulpes awaiting me at her residence alone. She was a coarse-featured woman, with a keen and rather cruel dark eye, and an exceedingly sensual expression about her mouth and under jaw. She received me in perfect silence, in an apartment on the ground floor, very sparely furnished. In the centre of the room, close to where Mrs. Vulpes sat, there was a common round mahogany table. If I had come for the purpose of sweeping her chimney, the woman could not have looked more indifferent to my appearance. There was no attempt to inspire the visitor with any awe. Everything bore a simple and practical aspect. This intercourse with the spiritual world was evidently as familiar an occupation with Mrs. Vulpes as eating her dinner or riding in an omnibus.

"You come for a communication, Mr. Linley?" said the medium, in a dry, business-like tone of voice.

"By appointment,—yes."

"What sort of communication do you want?—a written one?"

"Yes,—I wish for a written one."

"From any particular spirit?"

"Yes."

"Have you ever known this spirit on this earth?"

"Never. He died long before I was born. I wish merely to obtain from him some information which he ought to be able to give better than any other."

"Will you seat yourself at the table, Mr. Linley," said the medium, "and place your hands upon it?"

I obeyed,—Mrs. Vulpes being seated opposite me, with her hands also on the table. We remained thus for about a minute and a half, when a violent succession of raps came on the table, on the back of my chair, on the floor immediately under my feet, and even on the window-panes. Mrs. Vulpes smiled composedly.

"They are very strong to-night," she remarked. "You are fortunate." She then continued, "Will the spirits communicate with this gentleman?"

Vigorous affirmative.

"Will the particular spirit he desires to speak with communicate?"

A very confused rapping followed this question.

"I know what they mean," said Mrs. Vulpes, addressing herself to me; "they wish you to write down the name of the particular spirit that you desire to converse with. Is that so?" she added, speaking to her invisible guests.

That it was so was evident from the numerous affirmatory responses. While this was going on, I tore a slip from my pocket-book, and scribbled a name under the table.

"Will this spirit communicate in writing with this gentleman?" asked the medium once more.

After a moment's pause her hand seemed to be seized with a violent tremor, shaking so forcibly that the table vibrated. She said that a spirit had seized her hand and would write. I handed her some sheets of paper that were on the table, and a pencil. The latter she held loosely in her hand, which presently began to move over the paper with a singular and seemingly involuntary motion. After a few moments had elapsed she handed me the paper, on which I found written, in a large, uncultivated hand, the words, "He is not here, but has been sent for." A pause of a minute or so now ensued, during which Mrs. Vulpes remained perfectly silent, but the raps continued at regular intervals. When the short period I mention had elapsed, the hand of the medium was again seized with its convulsive tremor, and she wrote, under this strange influence, a few words on the paper, which she handed to me. They were as follows:—

I am here. Question me.

Leeuwenhoek

I was astounded. The name was identical with that I had written beneath the table, and carefully kept concealed. Neither was it at all probable that an uncultivated woman like Mrs. Vulpes should know even the name of the great father of microscopics. It may have been Biology; but this theory was soon doomed to be destroyed. I wrote on my slip—still concealing it from Mrs. Vulpes—a series of questions, which, to avoid tediousness, I shall place with the responses in the order in which they occurred.

I.—Can the microscope be brought to perfection?

SPIRIT.—Yes.

I.—Am I destined to accomplish this great task?

SPIRIT.—You are.

I.—I wish to know how to proceed to attain this end. For the love which you bear to science, help me!

SPIRIT.—A diamond of one hundred and forty carats, submitted to electromagnetic currents for a long period, will experience a rearrangement of its atoms *inter se*, and from that stone you will form the universal lens.

I.—Will great discoveries result from the use of such a lens?

SPIRIT.—So great, that all that has gone before is as nothing.

I.—But the refractive power of the diamond is so immense, that the image will be formed within the lens. How is that difficulty to be surmounted?

SPIRIT.—Pierce the lens through its axis, and the difficulty is obviated. The image will be formed in the pierced space, which will itself serve as a tube to look through. Now I am called. Good night!

I cannot at all describe the effect that these extraordinary communications had upon me. I felt completely bewildered. No biological theory could account for the *discovery* of the lens. The medium might, by means of biological *rapport* with my mind, have gone so far as to read my questions, and reply to them coherently. But Biology could not enable her to discover that magnetic currents would so alter the crystals of the diamond as to remedy its previous defects, and admit of its being polished into a perfect lens. Some such theory may have passed through my head, it is true; but if so, I had forgotten it. In my excited condition of mind there was no course left but to become a convert, and it was in a state of the most painful nervous exaltation that I left the medium's house that evening. She accompanied me to the door, hoping that I was satisfied. The raps followed us as we went through the hall, sounding on the balusters, the flooring, and even the lintels of the door. I hastily expressed my satisfaction, and escaped hurriedly into the cool night air. I walked home with but one thought possessing me,—how to obtain a diamond of the immense size required. My entire means multiplied a hundred times over would have been inadequate to its purchase. Besides, such stones are rare, and become historical. I could find such only in the regalia of Eastern or European monarchs.

IV. THE EYE OF MORNING

There was a light in Simon's room as I entered my house. A vague impulse urged me to visit him. As I opened the door of his sitting-room unannounced, he was bending, with his back toward me, over a carvel lamp, apparently engaged in minutely examining some object which he held in his hands. As I entered, he started suddenly, thrust his hand into his breast pocket, and turned to me with a face crimson with confusion.

"What!" I cried, "poring over the miniature of some fair lady? Well, don't blush so much; I won't ask to see it."

Simon laughed awkwardly enough, but made none of the negative protestations usual on such occasions. He asked me to take a seat.

"Simon," said I, "I have just come from Madame Vulpes."

This time Simon turned as white as a sheet, and seemed stupefied, as if a sudden electric shock had smitten him. He babbled some incoherent words, and went hastily to a small closet where he usually kept his liquors. Although astonished at his emotion, I was too preoccupied with my own idea to pay much attention to anything else.

"You say truly when you call Madame Vulpes a devil of a woman," I continued. "Simon, she told me wonderful things tonight, or rather was the means of telling me wonderful things. Ah! if I could only get a diamond that weighed one hundred and forty carats!"

Scarcely had the sigh with which I uttered this desire died upon my lips, when Simon, with the aspect of a wild beast, glared at me savagely, and rushing to the mantel-piece, where some foreign weapons hung on the wall, caught up a Malay creese, and brandished it furiously before him.

"No!" he cried in French, into which he always broke when excited. "No! you shall not have it! You are perfidious! You have consulted with that demon, and desire my treasure! But I will die first! Me! I am brave! You cannot make me fear!"

All this, uttered in a loud voice trembling with excitement, astounded me. I saw at a glance that I had accidentally trodden upon the edges of Simon's secret, whatever it was. It was necessary to reassure him.

"My dear Simon," I said, "I am entirely at a loss to know what you mean. I went to Madame Vulpes to consult with her on a scientific problem, to the solution of which I discovered that a diamond of the size I just mentioned was necessary. You were never alluded to during the evening, nor, so far as I was concerned, even thought of. What can be the meaning of this outburst? If you happen to have a set of valuable diamonds in your possession, you need fear nothing from me. The diamond which I require you could not possess; or if you did possess it, you would not be living here."

Something in my tone must have completely reassured him, for his expression immediately changed to a sort of constrained merriment, combined, however, with a certain suspicious attention to my movements. He laughed, and said that I must bear with him; that he was at certain moments subject to a species of vertigo, which betrayed itself in incoherent speeches, and that the attacks passed off as rapidly as they came. He put his weapon aside while making this explanation, and endeavored, with some success, to assume a more cheerful air.

All this did not impose on me in the least. I was too much accustomed to analytical labors to be baffled by so flimsy a veil. I determined to probe the mystery to the bottom.

"Simon," I said, gayly, "let us forget all this over a bottle of Burgundy. I have a case of Lausseure's *Clos Vougeot* down-stairs, fragrant with the odors and ruddy with the sunlight of the Côte d'Or. Let us have up a couple of bottles. What say you?"

"With all my heart," answered Simon, smilingly.

I produced the wine and we seated ourselves to drink. It was of a famous vintage, that of 1848, a year when war and wine throve together, —and its pure, but powerful juice seemed to impart renewed vitality to the system. By the time we had half finished the second bottle, Simon's hand, which I knew was a weak one, had begun to yield, while I remained calm as ever, only that every draught seemed to send a flush of vigor through my limbs. Simon's utterance became more and more indistinct. He took to singing French *chansons* of a not very moral tendency. I rose suddenly from the table just at the conclusion of one of those incoherent verses, and fixing my eyes on him with a quiet smile, said:

"Simon, I have deceived you. I learned your secret this evening. You may as well be frank with me. Mrs. Vulpes, or rather, one of her spirits, told me all."

He started with horror. His intoxication seemed for the moment to fade away, and he made a movement towards the weapon that he had a short time before laid down. I stopped him with my hand.

"Monster!" he cried, passionately, "I am ruined! What shall I do? You shall never have it! I swear by my mother!"

"I don't want it," I said; "rest secure, but be frank with me. Tell me all about it."

The drunkenness began to return. He protested with maudlin earnestness that I was entirely mistaken,—that I was intoxicated; then asked me to swear eternal secrecy, and promised to disclose the mystery to me. I pledged myself, of course, to all. With an uneasy look in his eyes, and hands unsteady with drink and nervousness, he drew a small case from his breast and opened it. Heavens! How the mild lamp-light was shivered into a thousand prismatic arrows, as it fell upon a vast rose-diamond that glittered in the case! I was no judge of diamonds, but I saw at a glance that this was a gem of rare size and purity. I looked at Simon with wonder, and —must I confess it?—with envy. How could he have obtained this treasure? In reply to my questions, I could just gather from his drunken statements (of which, I fancy, half the incoherence was affected) that he had been superintending a gang of slaves engaged in diamond-washing in Brazil; that he had seen one of them secrete a diamond, but, instead of informing his employers, had quietly watched the negro until he saw him bury his treasure; that he had dug it up, and fled with it, but that as yet he was afraid to attempt to dispose of it publicly,—so valuable a gem being almost certain to attract too much attention to its owner's antecedents,— and he had not been able to discover any of those obscure channels by which such matters are conveyed away safely. He added, that, in accordance with Oriental practice, he had named his diamond by the fanciful title of "The Eye of Morning."

While Simon was relating this to me, I regarded the great diamond attentively. Never had I beheld anything so beautiful. All the glories of light, ever imagined or described, seemed to pulsate in its crystalline chambers. Its weight, as I learned from Simon, was exactly one hundred and forty carats. Here was an amazing coincidence. The hand of Destiny seemed in it. On the very evening when the spirit of Leeuwenhoek communicates to me the great secret of the microscope, the priceless means which he directs me to employ start up within my easy reach! I determined, with the most perfect deliberation, to possess myself of Simon's diamond.

I sat opposite him while he nodded over his glass, and calmly revolved the whole affair. I did not for an instant contemplate so foolish an act as a common theft, which would of course be discovered, or at least necessitate flight and concealment, all of which must interfere with my scientific plans. There was but one step to be taken,—to kill Simon. After all, what was the life of a little peddling Jew, in comparison with the interests of science? Human beings are taken every day from the condemned prisons to be experimented on by surgeons. This man, Simon, was by his own confession a criminal, a robber, and I believed on my soul a murderer. He deserved death quite as much as any felon condemned by the laws; why should I not, like government, contrive that his punishment should contribute to the progress of human knowledge?

The means for accomplishing everything I desired lay within my reach. There stood upon the mantel-piece a bottle half full of French laudanum. Simon was so occupied with his diamond, which I had just restored to him, that it was an affair of no difficulty to drug his glass. In a quarter of an hour he was in a profound sleep.

I now opened his waistcoat, took the diamond from the inner pocket in which he had placed it, and removed him to the bed, on which I laid him so that his feet hung down over the edge. I had possessed myself of the Malay creese, which I held in my right hand, while with the other I discovered as accurately as I could by pulsation the exact locality of the heart. It was essential that all the aspects of his death should lead to the surmise of self-murder. I calculated the exact angle at which it was proba- ble that the weapon, if levelled by Simon's own hand, would enter his breast; then with one powerful blow I thrust it up to the hilt in the very spot which I desired to penetrate. A convulsive thrill ran through Simon's limbs. I heard a smothered sound issue from his throat, precisely like the bursting of a large air-bubble, sent up by a diver, when it reaches the surface of the water; he turned half round on his side, and as if to assist my plans more effectually, his right hand, moved by some mere spasmodic impulse, clasped the handle of the creese, which it remained holding with extraordinary muscular tenacity. Beyond this there was no apparent strug- gle. The laudanum, I presume, paralyzed the usual nervous action. He must have died instantaneously.

There was yet something to be done. To make it certain that all suspi- cion of the act should be diverted from any inhabitant of the house to Simon himself, it was necessary that the door should be found in the morning *locked on the inside.* How to do this, and afterwards escape myself? Not by the window; that was a physical impossibility. Besides, I was determined that the windows *also* should be found bolted. The solu- tion was simple enough. I descended softly to my own room for a peculiar instrument which I had used for holding small slippery substances, such as minute spheres of glass, etc. This instrument was nothing more than a long slender hand-vice, with a very powerful grip, and a considerable lever- age, which last was accidentally owing to the shape of the handle. Nothing was simpler than, when the key was in the lock, to seize the end of its stem in this vice, through the keyhole, from the outside, and so lock the door. Previously, however, to doing this, I burned a number of papers on Simon's hearth. Suicides almost always burn papers before they destroy themselves. I also emptied some more laudanum into Simon's glass,— having first removed from it all traces of wine,—cleaned the other wine- glass, and brought the bottles away with me. If traces of two persons drinking had been found in the room, the question naturally would have arisen, Who was the second? Besides, the wine-bottles might have been identified as belonging to me. The laudanum I poured out to account for its presence in his stomach, in case of a *post-mortem* examination. The theory naturally would be, that he first intended to poison himself, but, after swallowing a little of the drug, was either disgusted with its taste, or changed his mind from other motives, and chose the dagger. These arrangements made, I walked out, leaving the gas burning, locked the door with my vice, and went to bed.

Simon's death was not discovered until nearly three in the afternoon. The servant, astonished at seeing the gas burning,—the light streaming on the dark landing from under the door,—peeped through the keyhole and saw Simon on the bed. She gave the alarm. The door was burst open, and the neighborhood was in a fever of excitement.

Every one in the house was arrested, myself included. There was an inquest; but no clue to his death, beyond that of suicide, could be obtained. Curiously enough, he had made several speeches to his friends the preceding week, that seemed to point to self-destruction. One gentleman swore that Simon had said in his presence that "he was tired of life." His landlord affirmed, that Simon, when paying him his last month's rent, remarked that "he would not pay him rent much longer." All the other evidence corresponded,—the door locked inside, the position of the corpse, the burnt papers. As I anticipated, no one knew of the possession of the diamond by Simon, so that no motive was suggested for his murder. The jury, after a prolonged examination, brought in the usual verdict, and the neighborhood once more settled down into its accustomed quiet.

V. ANIMULA

The three months succeeding Simon's catastrophe I devoted night and day to my diamond lens. I had constructed a vast galvanic battery, composed of nearly two thousand pairs of plates,—a higher power I dared not use, lest the diamond should be calcined. By means of this enormous engine I was enabled to send a powerful current of electricity continually through my great diamond, which it seemed to me gained in lustre every day. At the expiration of a month I commenced the grinding and polishing of the lens, a work of intense toil and exquisite delicacy. The great density of the stone, and the care required to be taken with the curvatures of the surfaces of the lens, rendered the labor the severest and most harassing that I had yet undergone.

At last the eventful moment came; the lens was completed. I stood trembling on the threshold of new worlds. I had the realization of Alexander's famous wish before me. The lens lay on the table, ready to be placed upon its platform. My hand fairly shook as I enveloped a drop of water with a thin coating of oil of turpentine, preparatory to its examination,—a process necessary in order to prevent the rapid evaporation of the water. I now placed the drop on a thin slip of glass under the lens, and throwing upon it, by the combined aid of a prism and a mirror, a powerful stream of light. I approached my eye to the minute hole drilled through the axis of the lens. For an instant I saw nothing save what seemed to be an illuminated chaos, a vast luminous abyss. A pure white light, cloudless and serene, and seemingly limitless as space itself, was my first impression. Gently, and with the greatest care, I depressed the lens a few hairs' breadths. The wondrous illumination still continued, but as the lens approached the object, a scene of indescribable beauty was unfolded to my view.

I seemed to gaze upon a vast space, the limits of which extended far beyond my vision. An atmosphere of magical luminousness permeated the entire field of view. I was amazed to see no trace of animalculous life. Not a living thing, apparently, inhabited that dazzling expanse. I comprehended instantly, that, by the wondrous power of my lens, I had penetrated beyond the grosser particles of aqueous matter, beyond the realms of Iufusoria and Protozoa, down to the original gaseous globule, into whose luminous interior I was gazing, as into an almost boundless dome filled with a supernatural radiance.

It was, however, no brilliant void into which I looked. On every side I beheld beautiful inorganic forms, of unknown texture, and colored with the most enchanting hues. These forms presented the appearance of what might be called, for want of a more specific definition, foliated clouds of the highest rarity; that is, they undulated and broke into vegetable formations, and were tinged with splendors compared with which the gilding of our autumn woodlands is as dross compared with gold. Far away into the illimitable distance stretched long avenues of these gaseous forests, dimly transparent, and painted with prismatic hues of unimaginable brilliancy. The pendant branches waved along the fluid glades until every vista seemed to break through half-lucent ranks of many-colored drooping silken pennons. What seemed to be either fruits or flowers, pied with a thousand hues lustrous and ever varying, bubbled from the crowns of this fairy foliage. No hills, no lakes, no rivers, no forms animate or inanimate were to be seen, save those vast auroral copses that floated serenely in the luminous stillness, with leaves and fruits and flowers gleaming with unknown fires, unrealizable by mere imagination.

How strange, I thought, that this sphere should be thus condemned to solitude! I had hoped, at least, to discover some new form of animal life,—perhaps of a lower class than any with which we are at present acquainted,—but still, some living organism. I find my newly discovered world, if I may so speak, a beautiful chromatic desert.

While I was speculating on the singular arrangements of the internal economy of Nature, with which she so frequently splinters into atoms our most compact theories, I thought I beheld a form moving slowly through the glades of one of the prismatic forests. I looked more attentively, and found that I was not mistaken. Words cannot depict the anxiety with which I awaited the nearer approach of this mysterious object. Was it merely some inanimate substance, held in suspense in the attenuated atmosphere of the globule? or was it an animal endowed with vitality and motion? It approached, flitting behind the gauzy, colored veils of cloud-foliage, for seconds dimly revealed, then vanishing. At last the violet pennons that trailed nearest to me vibrated; they were gently pushed aside, and the Form floated out into the broad light.

It was a female human shape. When I say "human," I mean it possessed the outlines of humanity,—but there the analogy ends. Its adorable beauty lifted it illimitable heights beyond the loveliest daughter of Adam.

I cannot, I dare not, attempt to inventory the charms of this divine revelation of perfect beauty. Those eyes of mystic violet, dewy and serene, evade my words. Her long lustrous hair following her glorious head in a golden wake, like the track sown in heaven by a falling star, seems to quench my most burning phrases with its splendors. If all the bees of Hybla nestled upon my lips, they would still sing but hoarsely the wondrous harmonies of outline that enclosed her form.

She swept out from between the rainbow-curtains of the cloud-trees into the broad sea of light that lay beyond. Her motions were those of some graceful Naiad, cleaving, by a mere effort of her will, the clear, unruffled waters that fill the chambers of the sea. She floated forth with the serene grace of a frail bubble ascending through the still atmosphere of a June day. The perfect roundness of her limbs formed suave and enchanting curves. It was like listening to the most spiritual symphony of Beethoven the divine, to watch the harmonious flow of lines. This, indeed, was a pleasure cheaply purchased at any price. What cared I, if I had waded to the portal of this wonder through another's blood? I would have given my own to enjoy one such moment of intoxication and delight.

Breathless with gazing on this lovely wonder, and forgetful for an instant of everything save her presence, I withdrew my eye from the microscope eagerly,—alas! As my gaze fell on the thin slide that lay beneath my instrument, the bright light from mirror and from prism sparkled on a colorless drop of water! There, in that tiny bead of dew, this beautiful being was forever imprisoned. The planet Neptune was not more distant from me than she. I hastened once more to apply my eye to the microscope.

Animula (let me now call her by that dear name which I subsequently bestowed on her) had changed her position. She had again approached the wondrous forest, and was gazing earnestly upwards. Presently one of the trees—as I must call them—unfolded a long ciliary process, with which it seized one of the gleaming fruits that glittered on its summit, and sweeping slowly down, held it within reach of Animula. The sylph took it in her delicate hand, and began to eat. My attention was so entirely absorbed by her, that I could not apply myself to the task of determining whether this singular plant was or was not instinct with volition.

I watched her, as she made her repast, with the most profound attention. The suppleness of her motions sent a thrill of delight through my frame; my heart beat madly as she turned her beautiful eyes in the direction of the spot in which I stood. What would I not have given to have had the power to precipitate myself into that luminous ocean, and float with her through those groves of purple and gold! While I was thus breathlessly following her every movement, she suddenly started, seemed to listen for a moment, and then cleaving the brilliant ether in which she was floating, like a flash of light, pierced through the opaline forest, and disappeared.

Instantly a series of the most singular sensations attacked me. It seemed as if I had suddenly gone blind. The luminous sphere was still before me, but my daylight had vanished. What caused this sudden disappearance? Had she a lover, or a husband? Yes, that was the solution! Some signal from a happy fellow-being had vibrated through the avenues of the forest, and she had obeyed the summons.

The agony of my sensations, as I arrived at this conclusion, startled me. I tried to reject the conviction that my reason forced upon me. I battled against the fatal conclusion,—but in vain. It was so. I had no escape from it. I loved an animalcule!

It is true, that, thanks to the marvelous power of my microscope, she appeared of human proportions. Instead of presenting the revolting aspect of the coarser creatures, that live and struggle and die, in the more easily resolvable portions of the water-drop, she was fair and delicate and of surpassing beauty. But of what account was all that? Every time that my eye was withdrawn from the instrument, it fell on a miserable drop of water, within which, I must be content to know, dwelt all that could make my life lovely.

Could she but see me once! Could I for one moment pierce the mystical walls that so inexorably rose to separate us, and whisper all that filled my soul, I might consent to be satisfied for the rest of my life with the knowledge of her remote sympathy. It would be something to have established even the faintest personal link to bind us together,—to know that at times, when roaming through those enchanted glades, she might think of the wonderful stranger, who had broken the monotony of her life with his presence, and left a gentle memory in her heart!

But it could not be. No invention, of which human intellect was capable, could break down the barriers that Nature had erected. I might feast my soul upon her wondrous beauty, yet she must always remain ignorant of the adoring eyes that day and night gazed upon her, and, even when closed, beheld her in dreams. With a bitter cry of anguish I fled from the room, and, flinging myself on my bed, sobbed myself to sleep like a child.

VI. The Spilling of the Cup

I arose the next morning almost at daybreak, and rushed to my microscope. I trembled as I sought the luminous world in miniature that contained my all. Animula was there. I had left the gas-lamp, surrounded by its moderators, burning, when I went to bed the night before. I found the sylph bathing, as it were, with an expression of pleasure animating her features, in the brilliant light which surrounded her. She tossed her lustrous golden hair over her shoulders with innocent coquetry. She lay at full length in the transparent medium, in which she supported herself with ease, and gambolled with the enchanting grace that the Nymph Salmacis might have exhibited when she sought to conquer the modest Hermaphroditus. I tried an experiment to satisfy myself if her powers of reflection were developed. I lessened the lamp-light considerably. By the dim light that remained, I could see an expression of pain flit across her face. She looked upward suddenly, and her brows contracted. I flooded the stage of the microscope again with a full stream of light, and her whole expression changed. She sprang forward like some substance deprived of all weight. Her eyes sparkled, and her lips moved. Ah! if science had only the means of conducting and reduplicating sounds, as it does the rays of light, what carols of happiness would then have entranced my ears! what jubilant hymns to Adonaïs would have thrilled the illumined air!

I now comprehended how it was that the Count de Gabalis peopled his mystic world with sylphs,—beautiful beings whose breath of life was lambent fire, and who sported forever in regions of purest ether and purest light. The Rosicrucian had anticipated the wonder that I had practically realized.

How long this worship of my strange divinity went on thus I scarcely know. I lost all note of time. All day from early dawn, and far into the night, I was to be found peering through that wonderful lens. I saw no one, went nowhere, and scarce allowed myself sufficient time for my meals. My whole life was absorbed in contemplation as rapt as that of any of the Romish saints. Every hour that I gazed upon the divine form strengthened my passion,—a passion that was always overshadowed by the maddening conviction, that, although I could gaze on her at will, she never, never could behold me!

At length I grew so pale and emaciated, from want of rest, and continual brooding over my insane love and its cruel conditions, that I determined to make some effort to wean myself from it. "Come," I said, "this is at best but a fantasy. Your imagination has bestowed on Animula charms which in reality she does not possess. Seclusion from female society has produced this morbid condition of mind. Compare her with the beautiful women of your own world, and this false enchantment will vanish."

I looked over the newspapers by chance. There I beheld the advertisement of a celebrated *danseuse* who appeared nightly at Niblo's. The Signorina Caradolce had the reputation of being the most beautiful as well as the most graceful woman in the world. I instantly dressed and went to the theatre.

The curtain drew up. The usual semicircle of fairies in white muslin were standing on the right toe around the enamelled flower-bank, of green canvas, on which the belated prince was sleeping. Suddenly a flute is heard. The fairies start. The trees open, the fairies all stand on the left toe, and the queen enters. It was the Signorina. She bounded forward amid thunders of applause, and lighting on one foot remained poised in air. Heavens! was this the great enchantress that had drawn monarchs at her chariot-wheels? Those heavy muscular limbs, those thick ankles, those cavernous eyes, that stereotyped smile, those crudely painted cheeks! Where were the vermeil blooms, the liquid expressive eyes, the harmonious limbs of Animula?

The Signorina danced. What gross, discordant movements! The play of her limbs was all false and artificial. Her bounds were painful athletic efforts; her poses were angular and distressed the eye. I could bear it no longer; with an exclamation of disgust that drew every eye upon me, I rose from my seat in the very middle of the Signorina's *pas-de-fascination,* and abruptly quitted the house.

I hastened home to feast my eyes once more on the lovely form of my sylph. I felt that henceforth to combat this passion would be impossible. I applied my eye to the lens. Animula was there,—but what could have happened? Some terrible change seemed to have taken place during my absence. Some secret grief seemed to cloud the lovely features of her I gazed upon. Her face had grown thin and haggard; her limbs trailed heavily; the wondrous lustre of her golden hair had faded. She was ill!—ill, and I could not assist her! I believe at that moment I would have gladly forfeited all claims to my human birthright, if I could only have been dwarfed to the size of an animalcule, and permitted to console her from whom fate had forever divided me.

I racked my brain for the solution of this mystery. What was it that afflicted the sylph? She seemed to suffer intense pain. Her features contracted, and she even writhed, as if with some internal agony. The wondrous forests appeared also to have lost half their beauty. Their hues were dim and in some places faded away altogether. I watched Animula for hours with a breaking heart, and she seemed absolutely to wither away under my very eye. Suddenly I remembered that I had not looked at the water-drop for several days. In fact, I hated to see it; for it reminded me of the natural barrier between Animula and myself. I hurriedly looked down on the stage of the microscope. The slide was still there,—but, great heavens! the water-drop had vanished! The awful truth burst upon me; it had evaporated, until it had become so minute as to be invisible to the naked eye; I had been gazing on its last atom, the one that contained Animula,—and she was dying!

I rushed again to the front of the lens, and looked through. Alas! the last agony had seized her. The rainbow-hued forests had all melted away, and Animula lay struggling feebly in what seemed to be a spot of dim light. Ah! the sight was horrible: the limbs once so round and lovely shrivelling up into nothings; the eyes—those eyes that shone like heaven —being quenched into black dust; the lustrous golden hair now lank and discolored. The last throe came. I beheld that final struggle of the blackening form—and I fainted.

When I awoke out of a trance of many hours, I found myself lying amid the wreck of my instrument, myself as shattered in mind and body as it. I crawled feebly to my bed, from which I did not rise for months.

They say now that I am mad; but they are mistaken. I am poor, for I have neither the heart nor the will to work; all my money is spent, and I live on charity. Young men's associations that love a joke invite me to lecture on Optics before them, for which they pay me, and laugh at me while I lecture. "Linley, the mad microscopist," is the name I go by. I suppose that I talk incoherently while I lecture. Who could talk sense when his brain is haunted by such ghastly memories, while ever and anon among the shapes of death I behold the radiant form of my lost Animula!

The Pot of Tulips

Twenty-eight years ago I went to spend the summer at an old Dutch villa which then lifted its head from the wild country that, in present days, has been tamed down into a site for a Crystal Palace. Madison Square was then a wilderness of fields and scrub oak, here and there diversified with some tall and stately elm. Worthy citizens who could afford two establishments rusticated in the groves that then flourished where ranks of brownstone porticoes now form the landscape; and the locality of Fortieth Street, where my summer palace stood, was justly looked upon as at an enterprising distance from the city.

I had an imperious desire to live in this house ever since I can remember. I had often seen it when a boy, and its cool verandas and quaint garden seemed, whenever I passed, to attract me irresistibly. In after years, when I grew up to man's estate, I was not sorry, therefore, when one summer, fatigued with the labors of my business, I beheld a notice in the papers intimating that it was to be let furnished. I hastened to my dear friend, Jasper Joye, painted the delights of this rural retreat in the most glowing colors, easily obtained his assent to share the enjoyments and the expense with me, and in a month afterward we were taking our ease in this new paradise.

Independent of early associations other interests attached me to this house. It was somewhat historical, and had given shelter to George Washington on the occasion of one of his visits to the city. Furthermore, I knew the descendants of the family to whom it had originally belonged. Their history was strange and mournful, and it seemed to me as if their individuality was somehow shared by the edifice. It had been built by a Mr. Van Koeren, a gentleman of Holland, the younger son of a rich mercantile firm in the Hague, who had emigrated to this country in order to establish a branch of his father's business in New York, which even then gave indications of the prosperity it has since reached with such marvelous rapidity. He had brought with him a fair young Belgian wife; a loving girl—if I may believe her portrait—with soft brown eyes, chestnut hair, and a deep, placid contentment spreading over her fresh and innocent features. Her son, Alain Van Koeren, had her picture—an old miniature in a red gold frame—as well as that of his father; and in truth, when looking on the two, one could not conceive a greater contrast than must have existed between husband and wife. Mr. Van Koeren must have been a man of terrible will and gloomy temperament. His face—in the picture—is dark and austere, his eyes deep-sunken, and burning as if with a slow, inward fire. The lips are thin and compressed, with much determination of purpose; and his chin, boldly salient, is brimful of power and resolution. When first I saw those two pictures I sighed inwardly, and thought, "Poor child! you must often have sighed for the sunny meadows of Brussels, in the long gloomy nights spent in the company of that terrible man!"

I was not far wrong, as I afterward discovered. Mr. and Mrs. Van Koeren were very unhappy. Jealousy was his monomania, and he had scarcely been married before his girl-wife began to feel the oppression of a gloomy and ceaseless tyranny. Every man under fifty, whose hair was not white and whose form was erect, was an object of suspicion to this Dutch Bluebeard. Not that he was vulgarly jealous. He did not frown at his wife before strangers, or attack her with reproaches in the midst of her festivities. He was too well-bred a man to bare his private woes to the world. But at night, when the guests had departed and the dull light of the quaint old Flemish lamps but half-illuminated the nuptial chamber, then it was that with monotonous invective Mr. Van Koeren crushed his wife. And Marie, weeping and silent, would sit on the edge of the bed listening to the cold trenchant irony of her husband, who, pacing up and down the room, would now and then stop in his walk to gaze with his burning eyes upon the pallid face of his victim. Even the evidences that Marie gave of becoming a mother did not check him. He saw in that coming event that most husbands anticipate with mingled joy and fear, only an approaching incarnation of his dishonor. He watched with a horrible refinement of suspicion for the arrival of that being in whose features he madly believed he would but too surely trace the evidences of his wife's crime.

Whether it was that these ceaseless attacks wore out her strength, or that Providence wished to add another chastening misery to her burden of woe, I dare not speculate; but it is certain that one luckless night Mr. Van Koeren learned with fury that he had become a father two months before the allotted time. During his first paroxysm of rage on the receipt of intelligence which seemed to confirm all his previous suspicions, it was, I believe, with difficulty that he was prevented from slaying both the innocent causes of his resentment. The caution of his race and the presence of the physicians induced him, however, to put a curb upon his furious will until reflection suggested quite as criminal, if not as dangerous a vengeance. As soon as his poor wife had recovered from her illness, unnaturally prolonged by the delicacy of constitution induced by previous mental suffering, she was astonished to find, instead of increasing his persecutions, that her husband had changed his tactics and treated her with studied neglect. He rarely spoke to her except on occasions when the decencies of society demanded that he should address her. He avoided her presence, and no longer inhabited the same apartment. He seemed, in short, to strive as much as possible to forget her existence. But if she did not suffer from personal ill-treatment it was because a punishment more acute was in store for her. If Mr. Van Koeren had chosen to affect to consider her beneath his vengeance, it was because his hate had taken another direction, and seemed to have derived increased intensity from the alteration. It was upon the unhappy boy, the cause of all this misery, that the father lavished a terrible hatred. Mr. Van Koeren seemed determined, that if this child sprang from other loins than his, that the mournful destiny which he forced upon him would amply avenge his own existence and the infidelity of his mother. While the child was an infant his plan seemed to have been formed. Ignorance and neglect were the two deadly influences with which he sought to assassinate the moral nature of this boy; and his terrible campaign against the virtue of his own son, was, as he grew up, carried into execution with the most consummate generalship. He gave him money, but debarred him from education. He allowed him liberty of action, but withheld advice. It was in vain that his mother, who foresaw the frightful consequences of such a training, sought in secret by every means in her power to nullify her husband's attempts. She strove in vain to seduce her son into an ambition to be educated. She beheld with horror all her agonized efforts frustrated, and saw her son, and only child, becoming, even in his youth, a drunkard and a libertine. In the end it proved too much for her strength; she sickened, and went home to her sunny Belgian plains. There she lingered for a few months in a calm but rapid decay, whose calmness was broken but by the one grief; until one autumn day, when the leaves were falling from the limes, she made a little prayer for her son to the Good God, and died. Vain orison. Spendthrift, gamester, libertine, and drunkard by turns, Alain Van Koeren's earthly destiny was unchangeable, The father, who should have been his guide, looked on each fresh depravity of his son's with a species of grim delight. Even the death of his wronged wife had no effect upon his fatal purpose. He still permitted the young man to run blindly to destruction by the course into which he himself had led him.

As years rolled by, and Mr. Van Koeren himself approached to that time of life when he might soon expect to follow his persecuted wife, he relieved himself of the hateful presence of his son altogether. Even the link of a systematic vengeance, which had hitherto united them, was severed, and Alain was cast adrift without either money or principle. The occasion of this final separation between father and son was the marriage of the latter with a girl of humble, though honest extraction. This was a good excuse for the remorseless Van Koeren, so he availed himself of it by turning his son out of doors. From that time forth they never met. Alain lived a life of meagre dissipation, and soon died, leaving behind him one child, a daughter. By a coincidence natural enough, Mr. Van Koeren's death followed his son's almost immediately. He died as he had lived, sternly. But those who were around his couch in his last moments, mentioned some singular facts connected with the manner of his death. A few moments before he expired he raised himself in the bed, and seemed as if conversing with some person invisible to the spectators. His lips moved as if in speech, and immediately afterward he sank back, bathed in a flood of tears. "Wrong! wrong!" he was heard to mutter, feebly; then he implored passionately the forgiveness of some one who he said was present. The death struggle ensued almost immediately, and in the midst of his agony he seemed wrestling for speech. All that could be heard, however, were a few broken words. "I was wrong. My—unfounded— For God's sake look in— You will find—" Having uttered these fragmentary sentences, he seemed to feel that the power of speech had passed away forever. He fixed his eyes piteously on those around him, and, with a great sigh of grief, expired. I gathered these facts from his granddaughter, and Alain's daughter, Alice Van Koeren, who had been summoned by some friend to her grandfather's dying couch when it was too late. It was the first time she had seen him, and then she saw him die.

The results of Mr. Van Koeren's death were nine days wonder to all the merchants in New York. Beyond a small sum in the bank, and the house in which he lived, which was mortgaged for its full value, Mr. Van Koeren had died a pauper! To those who knew him, and knew his affairs, this seemed inexplicable. Five or six years before his death he had retired from business with a fortune of over a hundred thousand dollars. He had lived quietly since then; was known not to have speculated, and could not have gambled. The question then was, where had his wealth vanished to? Search was made in every secretary, in every bureau, for some document which might throw a light on the mysterious distribution that he had made of his property. None were found. Neither will, nor certificates of stock, nor title deeds, nor bank accounts, were any where discernible. Inquiries were made at the offices of companies in which Mr. Van Koeren was known to be largely interested; he had sold out his stock years ago.

Real estate that had been believed to be his, was found, on investigation, to have passed into other hands. There could be no doubt but that for some years past Mr. Van Koeren had been steadily converting all his immense property into money, and what he had done with that money no one knew. Alice Van Koeren and her mother, who at the old gentleman's death were at first looked on as millionaires, discovered, when all was over, that they were no better off than before. It was evident that the old man, determined that one who, though bearing his name, he believed not to be of his blood, should never inherit his wealth, or any share of it, had made away with his fortune before his death—a posthumous vengeance, which was the only one by which the laws of the State of New York, relative to inheritance, could be successfully evaded.

I took a peculiar interest in the case, and even helped to make some researches after the lost property, not so much, I confess, from a spirit of general philanthropy, as from certain feelings which I experienced toward Alice Van Koeren, the heir to this invisible estate. I had long known both her and her mother when they were living in an honest poverty, and earning a scanty subsistence by their own labor; Mrs. Van Koeren working as an embroideress, and Alice turning to account, as a preparatory governess, the education which her good mother, spite of her limited means, had bestowed on her.

In a few words, then, I loved Alice Van Koeren, and was determined to make her my wife, as soon as my means would allow me to support a fitting establishment. My passion had never been declared. I was content for the time with the secret consciousness of my own love, and the no less grateful certainty that Alice returned it, all unuttered as it was. I had, therefore, a double interest in passing the summer at the old Dutch villa, for I felt it to be connected somehow with Alice, and I could not forget the singular desire to inhabit it which I had so often experienced as a boy.

It was a lovely day in June when Jasper Joye and myself took up our abode in our new residence, and as we smoked our cigars on the piazza in the evening, we felt, for the first time, the unalloyed pleasure with which a townsman breathes the pure air of the country.

The house and grounds had a quaint sort of beauty that to me were eminently pleasing. Landscape gardening, in the modern acceptation of the term, was then almost unknown in this country, and the "laying out" of the garden that surrounded our new home would doubtless have shocked Mr. Loudon, the late Mr. Downing, or Sir Thomas Dick Lauder. It was formal and artificial to the last degree. The beds were cut into long parallelograms, rigid and severe of aspect, and edged with prim rows of stiff, dwarf box. The walks, of course, crossed always at right angles, and the laurel and cypress trees that grew here and there were clipped into cones, and spheres, and rhomboids. It is true, that at the time my friend and I hired the house some years of neglect had restored to this formal garden somewhat of the raggedness of nature. The box edgings were rank and wild. The clipped trees, forgetful of geometric propriety, flourished off into unauthorized boughs and rebel offshoots. The walks were green with moss, and the beds of Dutch tulips, which had been planted in the shape of certain gorgeous birds, whose colors were represented by masses of blossoms, each of a single hue, had transgressed their limits, and the purple of a parrot's wings might have been seen running recklessly into the crimson of his head; while as bulbs, however well-bred, *will* create other bulbs, the flower-birds of this queer old Dutch garden became in time abominably distorted in shape. Flamingoes with humps; golden pheasants with legs preternaturally elongated; macaws afflicted with an attack of hydrocephalus, each species of deformity being proportioned to the rapidity with which the roots had spread in some particular direction. Still, this strange mixture of raggedness and formality—this conglomerate of nature and art, had its charms. It was pleasant to watch the struggle, as it were, between the opposing elements, and to see nature triumphing by degrees in every direction.

Then the house itself was pleasant and commodious. Rooms that, though not lofty, were spacious. Wide windows and cool piazzas extending over the four sides of the building; and a collection of quaint old carved furniture, some of which, from its elaborateness, might well have come from the chisel of Master Grinling Gibbons. There was a mantlepiece in the dining-room with which I remember being very much struck when first I came to take possession. It was a most singular and fantastical piece of carving. It was a perfect tropical garden, menagerie, and aviary in one. Birds, beasts, and flowers were sculptured on the wood with exquisite correctness of detail, and painted with the hues of nature. The Dutch taste for color was here fully gratified. Parrots, love-birds, scarlet lorys, blue-faced baboons, crocodiles, passion-flowers, tigers, Egyptian lilies, and Brazilian butterflies, were all mixed up in the most gorgeous confusion. The artist, whoever he was, must have been an admirable naturalist, for the ease and freedom of his carving was only equaled by the wonderful accuracy with which the different animals were represented. Altogether it was one of those oddities of Dutch conception whose strangeness was, in this instance, redeemed by the excellence of the execution.

Such was the establishment that Jasper Joye and myself were to inhabit for the summer months.

"What a strange thing it was," said Jasper, as we lounged on the piazza together the night of our arrival, "that old Van Koeren's property should never have turned up!"

"It is a question with some people whether he had any at his death," I answered.

"Pshaw! every one knows that he did not or could not have lost that with which he retired from business."

"It is strange," said I thoughtfully; "yet every possible search has been made for any documents that might throw some light on the mystery. I have myself sought in every quarter for the traces of this lost wealth, but in vain."

"Perhaps he buried it?" suggested Jasper, laughing; "if so, we may find it here in some hole one fine morning."

"I think it much more likely that he destroyed it," I replied. "You know he never could be got to believe that Alain Van Koeren was his son, and I believe him quite capable of having flung all his money into the sea, in order to prevent those whom he considered not of his blood inheriting it, which they must have done under our laws."

"I am sorry that Alice did not become an heiress, both for your sake and hers. She is a charming girl."

Jasper, from whom I concealed nothing, knew of my love.

"As to that," I answered, "it is little matter. I shall in a year or two be independent enough to marry, and can afford to let Mr. Van Koeren's cherished gold sleep wherever he has concealed it."

"Well, I'm off to bed," said Jasper, yawning. "This country air makes one sleepy early. Be on the look-out for trap-doors and all that sort of thing, old fellow. Who knows but the old chap's dollars will turn up. Good-night!"

"Good-night, Jasper!"

So we parted for the night. He to his room, which lay on the west side of the building, I to mine on the east, situated at the end of a long corridor, and exactly opposite to Jasper's.

The night was very still and warm. The clearness with which I heard the song of the katydid, and the croak of the bull-frog, seemed to make the silence more distinct. The air was dense and breathless, and although longing to throw wide my windows, I dared not, for without the ominous trumpetings of a whole army of mosquitoes sounded threateningly.

I tossed on my bed oppressed with the heat; kicked the blankets into every spot where they ought not to be; gradually got the sheets twisted into a rope; turned my pillow every two minutes in the hope of finding a cool side; in short, did every thing that a man does when he lies awake on a very hot night, and can not open his window.

Suddenly, in the midst of my miseries, and when I had made up my mind to fling open the casement in spite of the legion of mosquitoes that I knew were hungrily waiting outside, suddenly I felt a continuous stream of cold air blowing upon my face. Luxurious as the sensation was, I could not help starting as I felt it. Where could this draught come from? The door was closed—so were the windows. It did not come from the direction of the fire-place; and even if it did, the air without was too still to produce so strong a current. I got up in my bed and gazed round the room, the whole of which, though only lit by a dim twilight, was still sufficiently visible. I thought at first it was a trick of Jasper's, who might have provided himself with a bellows or a long tube; but a careful investigation of the apartment convinced me that no one was there. Besides, I had locked the door, and it was not likely that any one had been concealed in the room before I entered it. It was exceedingly strange: but still the draught of cool wind blew on my face and chest, every now and then changing its direction— sometimes on one side, sometimes on the other. I am not constitutionally nervous, and had been too long accustomed to reflect on philosophical subjects to become the prey of fear in the presence of mysterious phenomena. I had devoted much of my leisure time to the investigation of what are popularly called supernatural matters by those who have not reflected or examined sufficiently to discover that none of these apparent miracles are *super*natural, but all, however singular, directly dependent on certain natural laws. I became speedily convinced therefore, as I sat up in my bed peering into the dim recesses of my chamber, that this mysterious wind was the effect or forerunner of a supernatural visitation, and I mentally determined to investigate it as it developed itself with a philosophical calmness.

"Is any one in this room?" I asked, as distinctly as I could. No reply; while the cool wind still swept over my cheek. I knew, in the case of Elizabeth Eslinger, who was visited by an apparition while in the Weinsberg jail, and whose singular and apparently authentic experiences were made the subject of a book by Dr. Kerner, that the manifestation of the spirit was invariably accompanied by such a breezy sensation as I now experienced. I therefore gathered my will, as it were, into a focus, and endeavored, as much as lay in my power, to put myself *en rapport* with the disembodied spirit, if such there was, knowing that on such conditions alone would it be enabled to manifest itself to me.

Presently it seemed to me as if a luminous cloud was gathering in one corner of the room—a sort of dim phosphoric vapor, shadowy and ill-defined. It changed its position frequently, sometimes coming nearer, and at others retreating to the farthest end of the room. As it grew intenser and more radiant, I observed a sickening and corpse-like odor diffuse itself through the chamber, and despite my anxiety to witness this phenomenon undisturbed, I could with difficulty conquer the feeling of faintness which oppressed me.

The luminous cloud now began to grow brighter and brighter as I gazed. The horrible odor of which I have spoken did not cease to oppress me, and gradually I could discover certain lines making themselves visible in the midst of this lambent radiance. These lines took the form of a human figure—a tall man, dressed in a long dressing-robe, with a pale countenance, burning eyes, and a very bold and prominent chin. At a glance I recognized the original of the picture of old Van Koeren that I had seen with Alice. My interest was now aroused to the highest point; I felt that I stood face to face with a spirit, and doubted not that I should learn the fate of the old man's mysteriously-concealed wealth.

The spirit presented a very strange appearance. He himself was not luminous, except some tongues of fire that seemed to proceed from the tips of his fingers, but was completely surrounded by a thin gauze of light, so to speak, through which his outlines were visible. His head was bare, and his white hair fell in huge masses around his stern, saturnine face. As he moved on the floor, I distinctly heard a strange crackling sound, such as one hears when a substance has been overcharged with electricity. But the circumstance that seemed to me most incomprehensible connected with the apparition, was that Mr. Van Koeren held in both hands a curiously-painted flower-pot, out of which sprang a number of the most beautiful tulips in full blossom. He seemed very uneasy and agitated, and moved about the room as if in pain, frequently bending over the pot of tulips as if to inhale their odor, then holding it out to me, seemingly in the hope of attracting my attention to it. I was, I confess, very much puzzled. I knew that Mr. Van Koeren had in his lifetime devoted much of his leisure to the cultivation of flowers, importing from Holland the most expensive and rarest bulbs; but how this innocent fancy could trouble him after death, I could not imagine. I felt assured, however, that some important reason lay at the bottom of this spectral eccentricity, and determined to fathom it if I could.

"What brings you here?" I asked audibly; directing mentally, however, at the same time, the question to the spirit with all the power of my will. He did not seem to hear me, but still kept moving uneasily about, with the crackling noise I mentioned, and holding the pot of tulips toward me.

"It is evident," I said to myself, "that I am not sufficiently *en rapport* with this spirit in order for him to make himself understood by speech. He has, therefore, recourse to symbols. The pot of tulips is a symbol. But of what?"

While reflecting on these things, I continued to gaze upon the spirit. While observing him attentively, he approached my bedside by a rapid movement, and laid one hand on my arm. The touch was icy cold, and pained me at the moment. Next morning my arm was swollen, and marked with a round blue spot. Then passing to my bedroom-door, the spirit opened it noisily and went out, shutting it behind him. Catching for a moment at the idea that I was the dupe of a trick, I jumped out of bed and ran to the door. It was locked, with the key on the inside, and a brass safety-bolt, which lay above the lock, shot safely home. All was as I had left it on going to bed. Yet I declare most solemnly, that as the ghost made his exit, I not alone saw the door open, but *I saw the corridor outside,* and *distinctly observed a large picture of William of Orange that hung just opposite to my room.* This to me was the most curious portion of the phenomena I had witnessed. Either the door had been opened by the ghost, and the resistance of physical obstacles overcome in some amazing manner—because in this case the bolts must have been replaced when the ghost was *outside* the door—or he must have had a sufficient magnetic *rapport* with my mind to impress upon it the belief that the door was opened, and also to conjure up in my brain the vision of the corridor and the picture, features that I would have seen if the door had been opened by any ordinary physical agency.

The next morning at breakfast I suppose my manner must have betrayed me, for Jasper said to me, after staring at me for some time,

"Why, Harry Escott, what's the matter with you? You look as if you had seen a ghost!"

"So I have, Jasper."

Jasper, of course, burst into a loud fit of laughter, and said he'd shave my head and give me a shower-bath.

"Well, you may laugh," I answered; "but you shall see it to-night, Jasper."

He became serious in a moment—I suppose there was something earnest in my manner that convinced him that my words were not idle—and asked me to explain. I described my interview as accurately as I could.

"How did you know that it was old Van Koeren?" he asked.

"Because I have seen his picture a hundred times with Alice," I answered, "and this apparition was as like it as it was possible for a ghost to be like a miniature."

"You must not think I'm laughing at you, Harry," he continued, "but I wish you would answer this. We have all heard of ghosts—ghosts of men, women, children, dogs, horses, in fact every living animal; but hang me of ever I heard of the ghost of a flower-pot before.

"My dear Jasper, you would have heard of such things if you had studied such branches of learning. All the phenomena I witnessed last night are supportable by well-authenticated facts. The cool wind has attended the appearance of more than one ghost, and Baron Reichenbach asserts that his patients, who you know are for the most part sensitive to apparitions, invariably feel this wind when a magnet is brought close to their bodies. With regard to the flower-pot about which you make so merry, it is to me the least wonderful portion of the apparitions. When a ghost is unable to find a person of sufficient receptivity, in order to communicate with him by speech, he is obliged to have recourse to symbols to express his wishes. These he either creates by some mysterious power out of the surrounding atmosphere, or he impresses, by magnetic force on the mind of the person he visits, the form of the symbol he is anxious to have represented. There is an instance mentioned by Jung Stilling of a student at Brunswick, who appeared to a professor of his college with a picture in his hands, which picture had a hole in it that the ghost thrust his head through. For a long time this symbol was a mystery; but the student was persevering, and appeared every night with his head through the picture, until at last it was discovered that, before he died, he had gotten some painted slides for a magic lantern from a shop-keeper in the town, which had not been paid for at his death; and when the debt had been discharged, he and his picture vanished forevermore. Now here was a symbol distinctly bearing on the question at issue. This poor student could find no better way of expressing his uneasiness at the debt for the painted slides than by thrusting his head through a picture. How he conjured up the picture I can not pretend to explain, but that it was used as a symbol is evident."

"Then you think the flower-pot of old Van Koeren is a symbol?"

"Most assuredly, the pot of tulips he held was intended to express that which he could not speak. I think it must have had some reference to his missing property, and it is our business to discover in what manner."

"Let us go and dig up all the tulip beds," said Jasper, "who knows but he may have buried his money in one of them?"

I grieve to say that I assented to Jasper's proposition, and on that eventful day every tulip in that quaint old garden was ruthlessly uprooted. The gorgeous macaws, and ragged parrots, and long-legged pheasants so cunningly formed by those brilliant flowers, were that day exterminated. Jasper and I had a regular *battue* amidst this floral preserve, and many a splendid bird fell before our unerring spades. We, however, dug in vain.

No secret coffer turned up out of the deep mould of the flower-beds. We evidently were not on the right scent. Our researches for that day terminated, and Jasper and myself waited impatiently for the night.

It was arranged that Jasper should sleep in my room. I had a small bed rigged up for him near my own, and I was to have the additional assistance of his senses in the investigation of the strange phenomena that we so confidently expected to appear.

The night came. We retired to our respective couches, after carefully bolting the doors, and subjecting the entire apartment to the strictest scrutiny, rendering it totally impossible that a secret entrance should exist unknown to us. We then put out the lights and awaited the apparition.

We did not remain in suspense long. About twenty minutes after we retired to bed Jasper called out,

"Harry," said he, "I feel the cool wind!"

"So do I," I answered, for at that moment a light breeze seemed to play across my temples.

"Look, look, Harry!" continued Jasper in a tone of painful eagerness, "I see a light—there in the corner!"

It was the phantom. As before, the luminous cloud appeared to gather in the room, growing more and more intense each minute. Presently the dark lines mapped themselves out, as it were, in the midst of this pale, radiant vapor, and there stood Mr. Van Koeren, ghastly and mournful as ever, with the pot of tulips in his hands.

"Do you see it?" I asked Jasper.

"My God! yes," said Jasper, in a low voice. "How terrible he looks!"

"Can you speak to me, to-night?" I said, addressing the apparition, and again concentrating my will upon my question. "If so, unburden yourself. We will assist you, if we can."

There was no reply. The ghost preserved the same sad, impassive countenance; he had heard me not. He seemed in great distress on this occasion, moving up and down, and holding out the pot of tulips imploringly toward me, each motion of his being accompanied by the crackling noise and the corpse-like odor. I felt sorely troubled myself to see this poor spirit torn by an endless grief; so anxious to communicate to me what lay on his soul, and yet debarred by some occult power from the privilege.

"Why, Harry," cried Jasper after a silence, during which we both watched the motions of the ghost intently, "why, Harry, my boy, there are *two* of them!"

Astonished by his words I looked around, and became immediately aware of the presence of a second luminous cloud, in the midst of which I could distinctly trace the figure of a pale but lovely woman. I needed no second glance to assure me that it was the unfortunate wife of Mr. Van Koeren.

"It is his wife, Jasper," I replied; "I recognize her, as I have recognized her husband, by the portrait."

"How sad she looks!" exclaimed Jasper in a low voice.

She did indeed look sad. Her face, pale and mournful in its cast, did not, however, seem convulsed with sorrow, as was her husband's. She seemed to be oppressed with a calm grief, and gazed with a look of interest that was painful in its intensity, on Mr. Van Koeren. It struck me, from his air, that though she saw him, he did not see her. His whole attention was concentrated on the pot of tulips, while Mrs. Van Koeren, who floated at an elevation of about three feet from the floor, and thus overtopped her husband, seemed equally absorbed in the contemplation of his slightest movement. Occasionally she would turn her eyes on me, as if to call my attention to her companion, and then returning, gaze on him with a sad womanly, half-eager smile, that to me was inexpressibly mournful.

There was something exceedingly touching in this strange sight. These two spirits so near, yet so distant. The sinful husband torn with grief and weighed down with some terrible secret, and so blinded by the grossness of his being as to be unable to see the wife-angel who was watching over him; while she, forgetting all her wrongs, and attracted to earth by perhaps the same human sympathies, watched from a greater spiritual height, and with a tender interest, the struggles of her suffering spouse.

"By Jove!" exclaimed Jasper, jumping from his bed, "I know what it means now."

"What does it mean?" I asked, as eager to know as he was to communicate.

"Well, that flower-pot that the old chap is holding—" Jasper, I grieve to say, was rather profane.

"Well! what of that flower-pot?"

"Observe the pattern. It has two handles made of red snakes, whose tails twist round the top and form a rim. It contains tulips of three colors, yellow, red, and purple."

"I see all that as well as you do. Let us have the solution."

"Well, Harry, my boy! don't you remember that there is just such a flower-pot, tulips, snakes and all, carved on the queer old painted mantle-piece in the dining-room."

"So there is!" and a gleam of hope shot across my brain, and my heart beat quicker.

"Now, as sure as you are alive, Harry, the old fellow has concealed something important behind that mantle-piece."

"Jasper, if ever I am Emperor of France, I will make you chief of police; your inductive reasoning is magnificent."

Actuated by the same impulse, and without another word, we both sprang out of bed and lit a candle. The apparitions, if they remained, were no longer visible in the strong light. Hastily throwing on some clothes, we rushed down stairs to the dining-room, determined to have the old mantle-piece down, without loss of time. We had scarce entered the room when we felt the cool wind blowing on our faces.

"Jasper," said I, "they are here!"

"Well," answered Jasper, "that only confirms my suspicions that we are on the right track this time. Let us go to work. See! here's the pot of tulips."

This pot of tulips occupied the centre of the mantle-piece, and served as a nucleus round which all the fantastic animals sculptured elsewhere might be said to gather. It was carved on a species of raised shield, or boss, of wood, that projected some inches beyond the plane of the remainder of the mantle-piece. The pot itself was painted a brick-color. The snakes were of bronze color, gilt, and the tulips—yellow, red, and purple—were painted after nature with the most exquisite accuracy.

For some time Jasper and myself tugged away at this projection without any avail. We were convinced that it was a movable panel of some kind, but yet were totally unable to move it. Suddenly it struck me that we had not yet twisted it. I immediately proceeded to apply all my strength, and after a few seconds of vigorous exertion, I had the satisfaction of finding it move slowly round. After giving it half a dozen turns, to my astonishment the long upper panel of the mantle-piece fell out toward us, apparently on concealed hinges, after the manner of the portion of escritoirs that is used for writing upon. Within were several square cavities sunk in the wall, and lined with wood, like the pigeon-holes of a desk. In one of these was a bundle of papers.

We seized these papers with avidity, and hastily glanced over them. They proved to be documents vouching for property to the amount of nearly two hundred thousand dollars, invested in the name of Mr. Van Koeren in a certain firm at Bremen, who, no doubt, thought by this time that the money would remain unclaimed forever. The desires of these poor troubled spirits were accomplished. Justice to the child had been given through the instrumentality of the erring father.

The formulas necessary to prove Alice and her mother sole heirs to Mr. Van Koeren's estate were briefly gone through, and the poor governess leaped suddenly from the task of teaching stupid children to the envied position of a great heiress. I had ample reason afterward for thinking that her heart did not change with her position.

That Mr. Van Koeren became aware of his wife's innocence, just before he died, I have no doubt. How this was manifested, I can not of course say, but I think it highly probable that his poor wife herself was enabled at the critical moment of dissolution, when the link that binds body and soul together is attenuated to the last thread, to put herself *en rapport* with her unhappy husband. Hence his sudden starting up in his bed, his apparent conversation with some invisible being, and his fragmentary disclosures, too broken, however, to be comprehended.

The question of apparitions has been so often discussed, that I feel no inclination to enter here upon the truth or fallacy of the ghostly theory. I myself believe in ghosts. Alice, my wife—for we are married, dear reader —believes in them firmly; and if it suited me to do so, I could overwhelm you with a scientific theory of my own on the subject, reconciling ghosts and natural phenomena. I will spare you, however, for I intend to deliver a lecture on the subject at Hope Chapel this winter, and if I disclosed my theory now, some one of our "gifted lecturers" would perhaps forestall me, and make "his arrangements for the season" on the strength of my ideas. Any one, however, who wishes to investigate this subject, will find an opportunity by addressing a note to Mr. Harry Escott, care of the publishers of this Magazine.

The Bohemian

I was launched into the world when I reached twenty-one, at which epoch I found myself in possession of health, strength, physical beauty, and boundless ambition. I was poor. My father had been an unsuccessful operator in Wall Street. Had passed through the various vicissitudes of fortune common to his profession, and ended by being left a widower, with barely enough to live upon and give me a collegiate education. As I was aware what strenuous exertions he had made to accomplish this last; how he had pinched himself in a thousand ways to endow me with intellectual capital, I immediately felt, on leaving college, the necessity of burdening him no longer. The desire for riches entirely possessed me. I had no dream but wealth. Like those poor wretches so lately starving on the Darien Isthmus, who used to beguile their hunger with imaginary banquets, I consoled my pangs of present poverty with visions of boundless treasure. A friend of mine, who was paying teller in one of our New York banks, once took me into the vaults when he was engaged in depositing his specie, and as I beheld the golden coins falling in yellow streams from his hands, a strange madness seemed to possess me. I became from that moment a prey to a morbid disorder, which, if we had a psychological pathology, might be classed as the *mania aurabilis*. I literally saw gold. Nothing but gold. Walking out in the country my eyes involuntarily sought the ground, as if hoping to pierce the sod and discover some hidden treasure. Coming home late at nights, through the silent New York streets, every stray piece of mud, or loose fragment of paper that lay upon the side-walk, was carefully scanned, for, in spite of my better reason, I cherished the vague hope that some time or other I should light upon a splendid treasure, which, for want of a better claimant, would remain mine. It seemed, in short, as if one of those gold gnomes of the Hartz Mountains had taken possession of me, and ruled me like a master. I dreamed such dreams as would cast Sinbad's valley of diamonds into the shade. The very sunlight itself never shone upon me but the wish crossed my brain that I could solidify its splendid beams and coin them into "eagles."

I was by profession a lawyer. Like the rest of my fraternity I had my

little office, a small room on the fourth story in Nassau Street, with magnificent painted tin labels announcing my rank and title all the way up the
stairs. Despite the fact that I had nine of these labels fixed to the walls,
and in every available corner, my legal threshold was virgin. No client
gladdened my sight. Many and many a time my heart beat as I heard
heavy footsteps ascending the stairs, but the half-dawning hope of employment was speedily crushed. They always stopped on the floor below, where
a disgusting conveyancer, with a large practice, had put up his shingle. So
I passed day after day alone with my "Code" and "Blackstone," and my
"Chitty," writing articles for the magazines on legal-looking paper—so
that in case a client entered he might imagine I was engaged at my
profession—by which I earned a scanty and precarious subsistence.

I was, of course, at this period in love. That a young man should be very
ambitious, very poor, and very unhappy, and not in love, would be too
glaring a contradiction of the usual course of worldly destinies. I was,
therefore, entirely and hopelessly in love. My life was divided between two
passions. The desire of becoming wealthy, and my love for Annie Deane.

Annie was an author's daughter. Need I add, after this statement, that
she was as poor as myself? This was the only point in my theory of the
conquest of wealth on which I contradicted myself. To be consistent I
should have devoted myself to some of those young ladies, about whom it
is whispered before you are introduced, that "she will have a hundred and
fifty thousand dollars." But though I had made up my mind to devote my
life to the acquisition of wealth, and though I verily believe I might have
parted with my soul for the same end, I had yet too much of the natural
man in my composition to sacrifice my heart.

Annie Deane was, however, such a girl as to make this infraction of my
theory of life less remarkable. She was, indeed, marvelously beautiful. Not
of that insipid style of beauty which one sees in Greek statues and London
annuals. Her nose did *not* form a grand line with her forehead. Her mouth
would scarcely have been claimed by Cupid as his bow; but then, her
upper lip was so short, and the teeth within so pearly. The brow was so
white and full, and the throat so round, slender, and pliant; and when,
above all this, a pair of wondrous dark-gray eyes reigned in supreme and
tender beauty, I felt that a portion of the wealth of my life had already
been accomplished when I gained the love of Annie Deane.

Our love affair ran as smoothly as if the old adage never existed. Probably for the reason that there was no goal in sight, we were altogether too
poor to dream of marriage as yet, and there did not seem very much
probability of my achieving the success necessary to the fulfillment of our
schemes. Annie's constitutional delicacy, however, was a source of some

uneasiness to me. She evidently possessed a very highly-strung nervous organization, and was, to the extremest degree, what might be termed *impressionable*. The slightest change in the weather affected her strangely. Certain atmospheres appeared to possess an influence over her for the better or the worse; but it was in connection with social instincts, so to speak, that the peculiarities of her organism were so strikingly developed. These instincts, for I can not call them any thing else, guided her altogether in her choice of acquaintances. She was accustomed to declare that by merely touching a person's hand, she could tell whether she would like or dislike them. Upon the entrance of certain persons into a room where she was, even if she had never seen them before, her frame would sink and shiver like a dying flower, and she would not recover until they had left the apartment. For these strange affections she could not herself account, and they on more than one occasion were the source of very bitter annoyances to herself and her parents.

Well, things were in this state when one day, in the early part of June, I was sitting alone in my little office. The beginning of a story which I was writing for Harper's lay upon the table. The title was elaborately written out at the top of the page, but it seemed as if I had stuck in the middle of the second paragraph. In the first—for it was an historical tale after the most approved model—I had described the month, the time of day, and the setting sun. In the second I introduced my three horsemen, who were riding slowly down a hill. The nose of the first and elder horseman, however, upset me. I could not for the life of me determine whether it was to be aquiline or Roman.

While I was debating this important point, and swaying between a multitude of suggestions, there came a sharp, decisive knock at my door. I think if the knock had come upon the nose about which I was thinking, or on my own, I could scarcely be more surprised. "A client!" I cried to myself. "Huzza! the gods have at last laid on a pipe from Pactolus for my especial benefit." In reality, between ourselves, I did not say any thing half so good, but the exclamation as I have written it will convey some idea at the vague exultation that filled my soul when I heard that knock.

"Come in!" I cried, when I had reached down a Chitty, and concealed my story under a second-hand brief which I had borrowed from a friend in the profession. "Come in!" and I arranged myself in a studious and absorbed attitude.

The door opened and my visitor entered. I had a sort of instinct that he was no client from the first moment. Rich men—and who but a rich man goes to law—may sometimes be seedy in their attire, but it is always a peculiar and respectable seediness. The air of wealth is visible, I know not by what magic, beneath the most threadbare coat. You see at a glance that the man who wears it might, if he chose, be clad in fine linen. The seediness of the poor man is, on the other hand, equally unmistakable. You seem to discern at a glance that his coat is poor from necessity. My visitor it was easy to perceive was of this latter class. My hopes of profit sank at the sight of his pale, unshorn face—his old shapeless boots—his shabby Kossuth hat—his over-coat shining with long wear, which, though buttoned, I could see no longer merited its name, for it was plain that no other coat lurked beneath it. Withal this man had an air of conscious power as he entered. You could see that he had nothing in his pockets, but then he looked as if he had a great deal in his brain.

He saluted me with a sort of careless respect as he entered. I bowed in return, and offered him the other chair. I had but two.

"Can I do any thing for you, Sir?" I inquired blandly, still clinging to the hope of clientage.

"Yes," said he, shortly; "I never make purposeless visits."

"Hem! If you will be so kind as to state your case"—for his rudeness rather shook my faith in his poverty—"I will give it my best attention."

"I've no doubt of that, Mr. Cranstoun," he replied; "for you are as much interested in it as I am."

"Indeed!" I exclaimed, not without some surprise and much interest at this sudden disclosure. "To whom have I the honor of speaking, then?"

"My name is Philip Brann."

"Brann?—Brann? A resident of this city?"

"No. I am by birth an Englishman, but I never reside any where."

"Oh! you are a commercial agent, then, perhaps?"

"I am a Bohemian!"

"A what?"

"A Bohemian," he repeated, coolly removing the papers with which I had concealed my magazine story, and glancing over the commencement; "you see, my habits are easy."

"I see it perfectly, Sir," I answered, indignantly.

"When I say that I am a Bohemian, I do not wish you to understand that I am a Zingaro. I don't steal chickens, tell fortunes, or live in a camp. I am a social Bohemian, and fly at higher game."

"But what has all this got to do with me?" I asked, sharply; for I was not a little provoked at the disappointment I experienced in the fellow's not having turned out to be a client.

"Much. It is necessary that you should know something about me before you do that which you will do."

"Oh, I am to do something, then!"

"Certainly. Have you read Henri Murger's 'Scènes de la Vie de Bohéme?'"

"Yes."

"Well, then, you can comprehend my life. I am clever, learned, witty, and tolerably good looking. I can write brilliant magazine articles"—here his eye rested contemptuously on my historical tale—"I can paint pictures, and, what is more, sell the pictures I paint. I can compose songs, make comedies, and captivate women."

"On my word, Sir, you have a choice of professions," I said, sarcastically; for the scorn with which the Bohemian had eyed my story humiliated me.

"That's it," he answered; "I don't want a profession. I could make plenty of money if I chose to work, but I don't choose to work. I will never work. I have a contempt for labor."

"Probably you despise money equally," I replied, with a sneer.

"No, I don't. To acquire money without trouble is the great object of my life, as to acquire it in any way, or by any means, is the great object of yours."

"And pray, Sir, how do you know that I have any such object?" I asked, in a haughty tone.

"Oh, I know it. You dream only of wealth. You intend to try and obtain it by industry. You will never succeed."

"Your prophecies, Sir, are more dogmatical than pleasant."

"Don't be angry," he replied, smiling at my frowns. "You shall be wealthy. I can show you the road to wealth. We will follow it together!"

The sublime assurance of this man astounded me. His glance, penetrating and vivid, seemed to pierce into my very heart. A strange and uncontrollable interest in him and his plans filled my breast. I burned to know more.

"What is your proposal?" I asked, severely; for a thought at the moment flashed across me that some unlawful scheme might be the aim of this singular being.

"You need not be alarmed," he answered, as if reading my thoughts. "The road I wish to lead you is an honest one. I am too wise a man ever to become a criminal."

"Then, Mr. Philip Brann, if you will explain your plans, I shall feel more assured on that point."

"Well, in the first place," he began, crossing his legs and taking a cigar out of a bundle that lay in one of the pigeon-holes of my desk, "in the first place, you must introduce me to the young lady to whom you are engaged, Miss Annie Deane."

"Sir!" I exclaimed, starting to my feet, and quivering with indignation at such a proposal; "what do you mean? Do you think it likely that I would introduce to a young lady in whom I am interested a man whom I never saw before to-day, and who has voluntarily confessed to being a vagabond? Sir, in spite of your universal acquirements, I think Providence forgot to endow you with sense."

"I'll trouble you for one of those matches. Thank you. So you refuse to introduce me! I knew you would. But I also know that ten minutes from this time you will be very glad to do it. Look at my eyes!"

The oddity of this request, and the calm assurance with which it was made, were too much for me. In spite of my anger, I burst into a fit of loud laughter. He waited patiently until my mirth had subsided.

"You need not laugh," he resumed; "I am perfectly serious. Look at my eyes attentively, and tell me if you see any thing strange in them."

At such a proposition from any other man, I should have taken for granted that he was mocking me, and kicked him down stairs. This Bohemian, however, had an earnestness of manner that staggered me. I became serious, and I did look at his eyes.

They were certainly very singular eyes. The most singular eyes that I had ever beheld. They were long, gray, and of a very deep hue. Their steadiness was wonderful. They never moved. One might fancy that they were gazing into the depths of one of those Italian lakes on an evening when the waters are so calm as to seem solid. But it was the interior of these organs—if I may so speak—that was so marvelous. As I gazed, I seemed to behold strange things passing in the deep gray distance which seemed to stretch infinitely away. I could have sworn that I saw figures moving, and landscapes wonderfully real. My gaze seemed to be fastened to his by some inscrutable power; and the outer world gradually passing off like a cloud, left me literally living in that phantom region which I beheld in those mysterious eyes.

I was aroused from this curious lethargy by the Bohemian's voice. It seemed to me at first as if muffled by distance, and sounded drowsily on my ear. I made a powerful effort and recalled my senses, which seemed to be wandering in some far-off places.

"You are more easily affected than I imagined," remarked Brann, as I stared heavily at him with a half-stupefied air.

"What have you done? What is this lethargy that I feel upon me?" I stammered out.

"Ah! you believe now," replied Brann, coldly; "I thought you would. Did you observe nothing strange in my eyes?"

"Yes. I saw landscapes, and figures, and many strange things. I almost thought I could distinguish Miss—Miss—Deane!"

"Well, it is not improbable. People can behold whatever they wish in my eyes."

"But will you not explain? I no longer doubt the fact that you are possessed of extraordinary powers, but I must know more of you. Why do you wish to be introduced to Miss Deane?"

"Listen to me, Cranstoun," answered the Bohemian, placing his hand on my shoulder; "I do not wish you to enter into any blindfold compact. I will explain all my views to you; for though I have learned to trust no man, I know you can not avail yourself of any information I may give you without my assistance."

"So much the better," said I; "for then you will not suspect me."

"As you have seen," continued the Bohemian, "I possess some remarkable powers—the origin, the causes of these endowments, I do not care to investigate. The scientific men of France and Germany have wearied themselves in reducing the psychological phenomena of which I am a practical illustration to a system. They have failed. An arbitrary nomenclature, and a few interesting and suggestive experiments made by Reichenbach, are all the results of years of the intellectual toil of our greatest minds. As you will have guessed by this time, I am what is vulgarly called 'a Mesmerist.' I can throw people into trances, deaden the nervous susceptibilities, and do a thousand things by which, if I chose to turn exhibitor, I could realize a fortune. But while possessing those qualities which exhibit merely a commonplace superiority of psychical force, and which are generally to be found in men of a highly sympathetic organization, I yet can boast of unique powers such as I have never known to be granted to another being besides myself. What these powers are I have now no need to inform you. You will very soon behold them practically illustrated.

"Now, to come to my objects. Like you, I am ambitious, but I have, unlike you, a constitutional objection to labor. It is sacrilege to expect men with minds like yours and mine to work. Why should we—who are expressly and evidently created by Nature to enjoy—why should we, with our delicate tastes, our refined susceptibilities, our highly-wrought organizations, spend our lives in ministering to the enjoyment of others? In short, my friend, I do not wish to row the boat in the great voyage in life. I prefer sitting at the stern, with purple awnings and ivory couches around me, and my hand upon the golden helm. I wish to achieve fortune at a single stroke. With your assistance I can do it. You will join me!"

"Under certain conditions."

I was not yet entirely carried away by the earnest eloquence of this strange being.

"I will grant what conditions you like," he continued, fervently. "Above all, I will set your mind at rest by swearing to you, whatever may be my power, never in any way to interfere between you and the young girl whom you love. I will respect her as I would a sister."

This last promise cleared away many of my doubts. The history which this man gave of himself, and the calm manner with which he asserted his wondrous power over women, I confess rendered me somewhat cautious about introducing him to Annie. His air was, however, now so frank and manly; he seemed to be so entirely absorbed by his one idea of wealth, that I had no hesitation in declaring to him that I accepted his strange proposals.

"Good!" he exclaimed. "You are, I see, a man of resolution. We will succeed. I will now let you into my plans. Your *fiancée*, Miss Annie Deane, is a *clairvoyante* of the first water. I saw her the other day at the Academy of Design. I stood near her as she examined a picture, and my physiognomical and psychological knowledge enabled me to ascertain beyond a doubt that her organization was the most nervous and sympathetic I had ever met. It is to her pure and piercing instincts that we will owe our success."

Without regarding my gestures of astonishment and alarm, he continued:

"You must know that this so-called science of Mesmerism is in its infancy. Its professors are, for the most part, incapables, its pupils credulous fools. As a proof of this, endeavor to recall, if you can, any authentic instance in which this science has been put to any practical use. Have these mesmeric professors and their instruments, ever been able to predict or foresee the rise of stocks, the course of political events, the approaches of disaster. Never, my friend, save in the novels of Alexandre Dumas and Sir Edward Bulwer Lytton. The reason of this is very simple. The professors were limited in their power, and the *somnambules* limited in their susceptibilities. When two such people as Miss Deane and myself labor together, every thing is possible!"

"Oh! I see. You propose to operate in the stocks. My dear Sir, you are mad. Where is the money?"

"Bah! who said any thing about operating in stocks? That involves labor and an office. I can afford neither. No, Cranstoun, we will take a shorter road to wealth than that. A few hours' exertion are all we need to make us *millionaires.*"

"For Heaven's sake explain! I am wearied with curiosity deferred."

"It is thus: This island and its vicinity abounds in concealed treasure. Much has been deposited by the early Dutch settlers during their wars with the Indians. Captain Kyd and other buccaneers have made numberless *cachés* containing their splendid spoils, which a violent death prevented their ever reclaiming. Poor Poe, you know, who was a Bohemian, like myself, made a story on the tradition, but, poor fellow! *he* only dug up his treasure on paper. There was also a considerable quantity of plate, jewels, and coin concealed by the inhabitants of New York and the neighborhood during the war with England. You may wonder at my asserting this so confidently. Let it suffice for you that I know it to be so. It is my intention to discover some of this treasure."

Having calmly made this announcement, he folded his arms and gazed at me with the air of a god prepared to receive the ovations of his worshipers.

"How is this to be accomplished?" I inquired earnestly, for I had begun to put implicit faith in this man, who seemed equally gifted and audacious.

"There are two ways by which we can arrive at our desires. The first is by the command of that power common to *somnambules,* who, having their faculties concentrated on a certain object during the magnetic trance, become possessed of the power of inwardly beholding and verbally describing it, as well as the locality where it is situated. The other is peculiar to myself, and as you have seen, consists in rendering my eyes a species of *camera obscura* to the *clairvoyante,* in which she vividly perceives all that we would desire. This mode I have greater faith in than in any other, and I believe that our success will be found there."

"How is it," I inquired, "that you have not before put this wondrous power to a like use? Why did you not enrich yourself long since through this means?"

"Because I have never been able to find a *somnambule* sufficiently impressionable to be reliable in her evidence. I have tried many, but they have all deceived me. You confess to having beheld certain shadowy forms in my eyes, but you could not define them distinctly. The reason is simply that your magnetic organization was not perfect. This faculty of mine, which has so much astonished you, is nothing new. It is practiced by the Egyptians, who use a small glass mirror where I use my eyes. The testimony of M. Leon Laborde, who practiced the art himself, Lord Prudhoe, and a host of other witnesses have recorded their experience of the truth of the science which I preach. However, I need discourse no further on it. I will prove to you its verity. Now that you have questioned me sufficiently, will you introduce me to your lady-love, Mr. Henry Cranstoun?"

"And will you promise me, Mr. Philip Brann, on your honor as a man, that you will respect my relations with that lady?"

"I promise, upon my honor!"

"Then, I yield. When shall it be?"

"To-night. I hate delays."

"This evening, then, I will meet you at the Astor House, and we will go together to Mr. Deane's house."

That night, accompanied by my new friend, the Bohemian, I knocked at the door of Mr. Deane's house in Amity Place. A modest neighborhood fit for a man who earned his living by writing novels for cheap publishers, and correspondence for Sunday newspapers. Annie was, as usual, in the sitting-room on the first floor, and the lamps had not yet been lighted, so that the apartment seemed filled with a dull gloom as we entered.

"Annie dear," said I, as she ran to meet me, "let me present to you my particular friend, Mr. Philip Brann, whom I have brought with me for a special purpose, which I will presently explain."

She did not reply.

Piqued by this strange silence, and feeling distressed about the Bohemian, who stood calmly upright with a faint smile on his lips, I repeated my introduction rather sharply.

"Annie," I reiterated, "you could not have heard me. I am anxious to introduce to you my friend, Mr. Brann."

"I heard you," she answered, in a low voice, catching at my coat as if to support herself, "but I feel very ill."

"Good Heavens! what's the matter, darling? Let me get you a glass of wine, or water."

"Do not be alarmed," said the Bohemian, arresting my meditated rush to the door, "I understand Miss Deane's indisposition thoroughly. If she will permit me, I will relieve her at once."

A low murmur of assent seemed to break involuntarily from Annie's lips. The Bohemian led her calmly to an arm-chair near the window, held her hands in his for a few moments, and spoke a few words to her in a low tone. In less than a minute she declared herself quite recovered.

"It was you who caused my illness," she said to him, in a tone whose vivacity contrasted strangely with her previous languor. "I felt your presence in the room like a terrible electrical shock."

"And I have cured what I caused," answered the Bohemian; "you are very sensitive to magnetic impressions. So much the better."

"Why so much the better?" she asked anxiously.

"Mr. Cranstoun will explain," replied Brann carelessly; and, with a slight bow, he moved to another part of the dusky room, leaving Annie and myself together.

"Who is this Mr. Brann, Henry?" asked Annie, as soon as the Bohemian was out of earshot. "His presence affects me strangely."

"He is a strange person, who possesses wonderful powers," I answered; "he is going to be of great service to us, Annie!"

"Indeed! how so?"

I then related to her what had passed between the Bohemian and myself at my office, and explained his object in coming hither on this evening. I painted in glowing colors the magnificent future that opened for her and myself, if his scheme should prove successful, and ended by entreating her, for my sake, to afford the Bohemian every facility for arriving at the goal of his desires.

As I finished, I discovered that Annie was trembling violently. I caught her hand in mine. It was icy cold, and quivered with a sort of agitated and intermittent tremor.

"Oh, Henry!" she exclaimed, "I feel a singular presentiment that seems to warn me against this thing. Let us rest content in our poverty. Have a true heart, and learn to labor and to wait. You will be rich in time; and then we will live happily together, secure in the consciousness that our means have been acquired by honest industry. I fear those secret treasure-seekings."

"What nonsense!" I cried; "these are a timid girl's fears. It would be folly to pine patiently for years in poverty when we can achieve wealth at a stroke. The sooner we are rich the sooner we will be united, and to postpone that moment would be to make me almost doubt your love. Let us try this man's power. There will be nothing lost if he fails."

"Do with me as you will, Henry," she answered, "I will obey you in all things; only I can not help feeling a vague terror that seems to forbode misfortune."

I laughed and bade her be of good cheer, and rang for lights in order that the experiment might be commenced at once. We three were alone. Mrs. Deane was on a visit at Philadelphia; Mr. Deane was occupied with his literary labors in another room, so that we had every thing necessary to insure the quiet which the Bohemian insisted should reign during his experiments.

The Bohemian did not magnetize in the common way with passes and manipulations. He sat a little in the shade, with his back to the strong glare of the chandeliers, while Annie sat opposite to him, looking full in his face. I sat at a little distance at a small table, with a pencil and notebook, with which I was preparing to register such revelations as our *clairvoyante* should make.

The Bohemian commenced operations by engaging Miss Deane in a light and desultory conversation. He seemed conversant with all the topics of the town, and talked of the opera, and the annual exhibition at the Academy of Design, as glibly as if he had never done any thing but cultivate small talk. Imperceptibly but rapidly, however, he gradually led the conversation to money matters. From these he glided into a dissertation on the advantages of wealth, touched on the topic of celebrated misers, thence slid smoothly into a discourse on concealed treasures, about which he spoke in so eloquent and impressive a manner as to completely fascinate both his hearers.

Then it was that I observed a singular change take place in Annie Deane's countenance. Hitherto pale and somewhat listless, as if suffering from mental depression, she suddenly became illumined as if by an inward fire. A rosy flush mounted to her white cheeks; her lips, eagerly parted as if drinking in some intoxicating atmosphere, were ruddy with a supernatural health, and her eyes dilated as they gazed upon the Bohemian with a piercing intensity. The latter ceased to speak, and after a moment's silence, he said gently,

"Miss Deane, do you see?"

"I see!" she murmured, without altering the fixity of her gaze for an instant.

"Mark what you observe well," continued the Bohemian; "describe it with all possible accuracy;" then turning to me, he said rapidly, "Take care and note every thing."

"I see," pursued Annie, speaking in a measured monotone, and gazing into the Bohemian's eyes, while she waved her hand gently as if keeping time to the rhythm of her words, "I see a sad and mournful island on which the ocean beats forever. The sandy ridges are crowned with manes of bitter grass that wave and wave sorrowfully in the wind. No trees or shrubs are rooted in that salt and sterile soil. The burning breath of the Atlantic has seared the surface and made it always barren. The surf that whitens on the shore drifts like a shower of snow across its bleak and storm-blown plains. It is the home of the sea-gull and the crane."

"It is called Coney Island?" the Bohemian half inquired, half asserted.

"It is the name," pursued the Seeress, but in so even a tone that one would scarce imagine she had heard the question. She then continued to speak as before, still keeping up that gentle oscillation of her hand, which, in spite of my reason, seemed to me to have something terrible in its monotony.

"I see the spot," she continued, "where that you love lies buried. My gaze pierces through the shifting soil until it finds the gold that burns in the gloom. And there are jewels, too, of regal size and priceless value hidden so deeply in the barren sand! No sunlight has reached them for many years, but they burn for me as if they were set in the glory of an eternal day!"

"Describe the spot accurately!" cried the Bohemian in a commanding tone, making for the first time a supremely imperative gesture.

"There is a spot upon that lonely island," the Seeress continued, in that unimpassioned monotone that seemed more awful than the thunder of an army, "where three huge sandy ridges meet. At the junction of these three ridges a stake of locust-wood is driven deeply down. When by the sun it is six o'clock a shadow falls westward on the sand. Where this shadow ends the treasure lies."

"Can you draw?" asked the Bohemian.

"She can not," I answered hastily. The Bohemian raised his hand to enjoin silence.

"I can draw *now*," the Seeress replied firmly, never for an instant removing her eyes from the Bohemian's.

"Will you draw the locality you describe, if I give you the materials?" pursued the magnetizer.

"I will."

Brann drew a sheet of Bristol board and a pencil from his pocket, and presented them to her in silence. She took them, and still keeping her eyes immovably fixed on those of the magnetizer, she commenced sketching rapidly. I was thunderstruck. Annie, I knew, possessed no accomplishments, and had never made even the rudest sketch before.

"It is done!" she said, after a few minutes silence, handing the Bristol board back to the Bohemian. Moved by an inexpressible curiosity I rose and looked over his shoulder. It was wonderful! There was a masterly sketch of such a locality as she described executed on the paper. But its vividness, its desolation, its evident truth were so singularly given that I could scarcely believe my senses. I could almost hear the storms of the Atlantic howling over the barren sands.

"There is something wanting yet," said the Bohemian, handing the sketch back to her, and smiling at my amazement.

"I know it," she remarked, calmly. Then giving a few rapid strokes with her pencil, she handed it to him once more.

The points of the compass had been added in the upper right hand corner of the drawing. Nothing more was needed to establish the perfect accuracy of the sketch.

"This is truly wonderful!" I could not help exclaiming.

"It is finished!" cried the Bohemian, exultingly, and dashing his hand-kerchief two or three times across Annie's face. Under this new influence her countenance underwent a rapid change. Her eyes, a moment before dilated to their utmost capabilities, now suddenly became dull, and the eyelids drooped heavily over them. Her form, that during the previous scene had been rigidly erect, and strung to its highest point of tension, seemed to collapse like one of those strips of gold-leaf that electricians experiment with, when the subtle fluid has ceased to course through its pores. Without uttering a word, and before the Bohemian or myself could stir, she sank like a corpse on the floor.

"Wretch!" I cried, rushing forward, "what have you done?"

"Secured the object of our joint ambition," replied the fellow with that imperturbable calmness that so distinguished him. "Do not be alarmed at this fainting fit, my friend. Exhaustion is always the consequence of such violent psychological phenomena. Miss Deane will be perfectly recovered by to-morrow evening, and by that time we will have returned *million-aires.*"

"I will not leave her until she is recovered," I answered sullenly, while I tried to restore the dear girl to consciousness.

"Yes, but you will," asserted Brann, lighting his cigar as coolly as if nothing very particular had happened. "By dawn, to-morrow, you and I will have embarked for Coney Island."

"You cold-blooded savage!" I cried passionately, "will you assist me to restore your victim to consciousness? If you do not, by Heaven, I will blow your brain out!"

"What with? The fire-shovel?" he answered with a laugh. Then care-lessly approaching he took Annie's hand in his, and blew with his mouth gently upon her forehead. The effect was almost instantaneous. Her eyes gradually unclosed, and she made a feeble effort to sustain herself.

"Call the housekeeper," said the Bohemian, "have Miss Deane con-ducted to bed, and by to-morrow evening all will be tranquil."

I obeyed his directions almost mechanically, little dreaming how bit-terly his words would be realized. Yes! truly. All *would* be tranquil by to-morrow evening!

I sat up all night with Brann. I did not leave Mr. Deane's until a late hour, when I saw Annie apparently wrapped in a peaceful slumber, and betook myself to a low tavern that remained open all night, where the Bohemian awaited me. There we arranged our plan. We were to take a boat at the Battery at the earliest glimpse of dawn, then, provided with a spade and shovel, a pocket compass, and a small valise in which to transport our treasure, we were to row down to our destination. I was feverish and troubled. The strange scene I had witnessed, and the singular adventure that awaited, seemed in combination to have set my brain on fire. My temples throbbed; the cold perspiration stood upon my forehead, and it was in vain that I allowed myself to join the Bohemian in the huge draughts of brandy which he continually gulped down, and which seemed to produce little or no effect on his iron frame. How madly, how terribly I longed for the dawn!

At last the hour came. We took our implements in a carriage down to the Battery, hired a boat, and in a short time were out in the stream pulling lustily down the foggy harbor. The exercise of rowing seemed to afford me some relief. I pulled madly at my oar, until the sweat rolled in huge drops from my brow, and hung in trembling beads on the curls of my hair. After a long and wearisome pull we landed on the island at the most secluded spot we could find, taking particular care that it was completely sheltered from the view of the solitary hotel, where doubtless many inquisitive idlers would be found. After beaching our boat carefully, we struck toward the centre of the island, Brann seeming to possess some wonderful instinct for the discovery of localities, for almost without any trouble he walked nearly straight to the spot we were in search of.

"This is the place," said he, dropping the valise which he carried. "Here are the three ridges, and the locust stake, lying exactly due north. Let us see what the true time is."

So saying he unlocked the valise and drew forth a small sextant, with which he proceeded to take an observation. I could not help admiring the genius of this man, who seemed to think of and foresee every thing. After a few moments engaged in making calculations on the back of a letter, he informed me that exactly twenty-one minutes would elapse before the shadow of the locust-stake would fall on the precise spot indicated by the Seeress. "Just time enough," said he, "to enjoy a cigar."

Never did twenty-one minutes appear so long to a human being as these did to me. There was nothing in the landscape to arrest my attention. All was a wild waste of sand, on which a few patches of salt grass waved mournfully. My heart beat until I could hear its pulsations. A thousand times I thought that my strength must give way beneath the weight of my emotions, and that death would overtake me ere I had realized my dreams. I was obliged at length to dip my handkerchief in a marshy pool that was near me, and bind it about my burning temples.

At length the shadow from the locust log fell upon the enchanted spot. Brann and myself seized the spades wildly, and dug with the fury of ghouls who were rooting up their loathsome repast. The light sand flew in heaps on all sides. The sweat rolled from our bodies. The hole grew deeper and deeper!

At last—oh Heavens!—a metallic sound! my spade struck some hollow sonorous substance. My limbs fairly shook as I flung myself into the pit, and scraped the sand away with my nails. I laughed like a madman and burrowed like a mole. The Bohemian, always calm, with a few strokes of his shovel laid bare an old iron pot with a loose lid. In an instant this was dashed with a frantic blow of my fist, and my hands were buried in a heap of shining gold! Red glittering coins; bracelets that seemed to glow like the stars in heaven; goblets, rings, jewels in countless profusion flashed before my eyes for an instant like the sparkles of an Aurora—then came a sudden darkness—and I remember no more!

How long I lay in this unconscious state I know not. It seemed to me that I was aroused by a sensation similar to that of having water poured upon me, and I was some moments before I could summon up sufficient strength to raise myself on one elbow. I looked bewilderedly around. I was alone! I then strove to remember something that I seemed to have forgotten, when my eye fell on the hole in the sand, on the edge of which I found I was lying. A dull-red gleam as of gold seemed to glimmer from out the bottom. This talismanic sight restored to me every thing—my memory and my strength. I sprang to my feet. I gazed around. The Bohemian was nowhere visible. Had he fled with the treasure? My heart failed me for a moment at the thought; but no! there lay the treasure gleaming still in the depths of the hole, with a dull-red light, like the distant glare of hell. I looked at the sun; he had sank low in the horizon, and the dews already falling, had, with the damp sea-air, chilled me to the bone. While I was brushing the moisture from my coat, wondering at this strange conduct of the Bohemian, my eye caught sight of a slip of paper pinned upon my sleeve. I tore it off eagerly. It contained these words:

I leave you. I am honest though I am selfish, and have divided with you the treasure which you have helped me to gain. You are now rich, but it may be that you will not be happy. Return to the city, but return in doubt.

The Bohemian

What terrible enigma was this that the last sentence of this note enshrouded? what vailed mystery was it that rose before my inward vision in shapeless horror? I knew not. I could not guess, but a foreboding of some unknown and overwhelming disaster rushed instantly upon me, and seemed to crush my very soul. Was it Annie, or was it my father? One thing was certain, there was no time to be lost in penetrating the riddle. I seized the valise, which the Bohemian had charitably left me—how he bore away his own share of the treasure I know not—and poured the gold and jewels into it with trembling hands. Then scarce able to travel with the weight of the treasure, I staggered toward the beach, where we had left the boat. She was gone. Without wasting an instant I made my way as rapidly as I could to the distant pier, where a thin stream of white smoke informed me that the steamer for New York was waiting for the bathers. I reached her just as she was about to start, and staggering to an obscure corner sat down upon my treasure sorrowfully.

With what different feelings to those which I anticipated was I returning to the city. My dream of wealth had been realized beyond my wildest hopes. All that I had thought necessary to yield me the purest happiness was mine, and yet there was not a more miserable wretch in existence. Those fatal words—"Return to the city, but return in doubt!" were ever before me. Oh! how I counted every stroke of the engine that impelled me to the city.

There was a poor blind humpbacked fiddler on board, who played all along the way. He played execrably, and his music made my flesh creep. As we neared the city he came round with his hat soliciting alms. In my recklessness, I tumbled all the money I had in my pockets into his hands. I never shall forget the look of joy that flashed over his poor old seared and sightless face at the touch of these few dollars. "Good Heavens!" I groaned, "here am I, sitting on the wealth of a kingdom, which is all mine, and dying of despair; while this old wretch has extracted from five dollars enough of happiness to make a saint envious!" Then my thoughts wandered back to Annie and the Bohemian, and there always floated before me in the air the agonizing words—"Return to the city, but return in doubt!"

The instant I reached the pier, I dashed through the crowd with my valise, and jumping into the first carriage I met, promised a liberal bounty to the driver if he would drive me to Amity Place in the shortest possible space of time. Stimulated by this, we flew through the streets, and in a few moments I was standing at Mr. Deane's door. Even then it seemed to me as if a dark cloud seemed to hang over that house above all others in the city. I rang; but my hand had scarcely left the bell-handle when the door opened, and Doctor Lott, the family physician, appeared on the threshold. He looked grave and sad.

"We were expecting you, Mr. Cranstoun," he said, very mournfully.

"Has—has any thing—happened?" I stammered, catching at the railings for support.

"Hush! come in." And the kind Doctor took me by the arm and led me like a child into the parlor.

"Doctor, for Heaven's sake, tell me what is the matter? I know something has happened. Is Annie dead? Oh! my brain will burst unless you end this suspense!"

"No—not dead. But tell me, Mr. Cranstoun, did Miss Deane experience any uncommon excitement lately?"

"Yes—yes—last night," I groaned wildly, "she was mesmerized by a wretch. Oh! fool that I was to suffer it!"

"Ah! that explains all," answered the Doctor. Then he took my hand gently in his—"Prepare yourself, Mr. Cranstoun," he continued, with deep pity in his voice, "prepare yourself for a terrible shock."

"She *is* dead, then!" I murmured. "Is she not?"

"She is. She died this morning of the effects of over-excitement, the cause of which I was ignorant of until now. Calm yourself, my dear Sir. She expired blessing you."

I tore myself from his grasp, and rushed up stairs. The door of her room was open, and, in spite of myself, my agitated tramp softened to a stealthy footfall as I entered. There were two figures in the room. One was an old man, who knelt by the bedside of my lost love, sobbing bitterly. It was her father. The other lay upon the bed, with marble face, crossed hands, and sealed eyelids. All was tranquil and serene in the chamber of death. Even the sobbings of the father, though bitter, were muffled and subdued. And she lay on the couch, with closed eyes, the calmest of all! Oh! the Seeress now saw more than earthly science could show her.

I felt, as I knelt by her father and kissed her cold hand in the agony of my heart, that I was justly rewarded.

Below stairs, in the valise, lay the treasure I had gained. Here, in her grave-clothes, lay the treasure I had lost!

Seeing the World

The hall reverberated with plaudits. The *improvisatore* surpassed himself. Scarcely was a subject given to him by the spectators than grand ideas, profound sentiments, clad in majestic verse, rolled from his lips, as if evoked by some magic. The artist did not reflect for an instant. In the twinkling of an eye his newly-born thoughts ran through all the phases of growth, and appeared clothed in the most exact expression. Ingenuity of form, splendor of imagery, harmony of rhythm, all were exhibited at the same moment. But this was a trifle. People gave him two or three subjects at the same time. The *improvisatore* dictated a poem on one, wrote a second, and improvised a third; and each production was, in its way, perfect. The first excited enthusiasm; the second called the tears into the eyes of the listeners; and the third was so humorous that none could restrain their laughter. In the midst of this the *improvisatore* did not seem to be in the least preoccupied with his subject. He talked and laughed with his neighbors. All the elements of poetical composition seemed to be at his disposal, as the pieces on a chess-board, which he used when he needed them, with the most superb indifference.

At last the attention and admiration of the spectators were exhausted. They were more wearied than the *improvisatore*. He was calm and cold. One could not trace on his countenance the slightest of fatigue; his features, in place of expressing the lofty joy of the poet content with his labor, displayed only the vulgar satisfaction of the conjuror who astonishes a stupid crowd. He listened to the laughter, and watched the tears tremble on the cheeks, with a sort of disdain; he alone neither laughed nor wept; he alone had no belief in his utterances. In the moments of divinest inspiration he had the air of a faithless priest, whom long habit has familiarized with the mysteries of the temple. The last of the audience had scarcely issued from the apartment when the *improvisatore* flung himself upon the pile of money received at the door, and commenced counting it with the avidity of Harpagon. The sum was large. He had never received so large a one in a single evening, and he was enchanted.

His joy was very pardonable. From his infancy upward poverty, cold and hard, had crushed him in its stony arms. He had not been born amidst songs, but amidst the dolorous sighs of his mother. When his intellect began to awaken, he beheld no rose-gardens in life; his young imagination encountered every where the icy smile of indigence. Nature was a little more generous to him than Fate. She gave him the creative faculty, but she condemned him to seek with the sweat of his brow the expression of his poetical conceptions. The editors and publishers paid him for his poetry prices that would have enabled him to live in comfort, if he was not obliged to spend an eternity of time on the composition of the smallest verse. It sometimes occurred, but very rarely, that in a moment of inspiration his intellect—always vailed in clouds—shone out with clearness; but if, on such occasions, this nebulous star showed itself clear and brilliant, it was only for an instant, and the poor poet had to make superhuman efforts to profit by the fleeting light.

Here again the labor recommenced: the expression fled before the words; the words would not come, or, if they did, were the wrong ones; the metre was rebellious; hideous prepositions came at the end of each line, interminable verbs became entangled in a web of substantives, and the rhymes—the accursed rhymes—always appeared in the shape of some barbarous and discordant words. Every verse cost the unhappy poet broken pens, finger-nails bitten to the quick, and locks of hair torn from his head in moments of agony. All his efforts were impotent. A thousand times he vowed to abandon poesy, and adopt some honest profession. But without having all the gifts, he had all the faults of a poet—the innate passion for independence, the incorrigible aversion to manual labor, the habit of awaiting inspiration, the radical want of punctuality. Add to this, the irritability which always accompanies poetic natures, an instinctive tendency to luxury, and an aristocratic craving for distinction. He could neither translate nor work by the page or column; and while his brother authors made considerable sums by compositions that were frequently insignificant, he saw himself universally neglected by editors and publishers. The little that he did receive for works that often cost him years of labor, went to pay usurious interest on money borrowed of the Jews, and poor Cipriano—as the poet was named—found his necessitous condition as hard and cheerless as ever.

In the town in which Cipriano resided lived also a physician named Segelius. Thirty years previously he had earned the reputation of being a skillful and learned practitioner; but he was poor, and had so small a practice, that he resolved to abandon medicine and take to commerce. After remaining a long time in India he returned to his native country with ingots of gold, and an immense quantity of precious stones. He built a magnificent mansion surrounded by a vast park, and hired numberless servants. His old acquaintances remarked with astonishment that neither the years he had spent, nor the long voyages he had made in tropical countries, had produced the slightest change in him. On the contrary, he appeared more young, more elastic, more sprightly than before. Not less surprising was the fact that the plants of every country in the world grew and prospered in his park, without any care being bestowed on them. Beyond this Segelius had nothing extraordinary about him. He was a man of good figure and excellent manners, with black mustaches. His clothes were simple, but elegant. He received the best society, but himself scarcely ever went beyond his huge park. He lent money to young men without interest; had a capital cook, the best wines, and liked to remain a long time at table. He went to bed early, and rose late. In fact, he led a superbly aristocratic existence.

Segelius had not entirely abandoned his practice as a physician, yet followed it but seldom, and then with a sort of repugnance, as if he did not wish to be troubled with it. But when he did practice he performed miracles. However grave the disease or the wound, and although the invalid was yielding up his last sigh, Segelius took no pains whatever, and would not even go to see him. After putting two or three questions to the relatives, more as a matter of form than any thing else, he took a small bottle from a box, and ordered them to give it to the patient, who, without fail, was as well as ever next morning. Segelius took no pay for these services. His disinterestedness, added to his marvelous good-nature, would have drawn patients to him from every corner of the earth, if he had not imposed on the invalids the most singular and fantastic conditions. For instance, to throw a certain sum of money into the sea; to perform some very disagreeable task; to burn one's house, etc. Rumor increased the singularity of these actions, and prevented even the most despairing invalids from coming to him. It was remarked that since a certain time no one had come to consult him; and it was further noticed, that if any of his patients did not comply with the conditions of his prescriptions, they infallibly died. The same happened, people said, to those who went to law with him, spoke evil of him, or displeased him.

It was natural after this that Segelius should have a great number of enemies. The physicians and apothecaries were, of course, his bitterest foes, and denied his right to make use of secret remedies; the most natural deaths were attributed to his poisons. They did not stop even there. They hinted suspiciously at the origin of his great fortune, and accused him of all species of crime. These public clamors obliged the police to visit his house, and institute a rigorous search. His servants were taken aside and interrogated. Segelius favored the inquisition, left the field free to his inquisitors, whom he scarcely honored with a glance, and retired smiling disdainfully at their attempts.

Their search was, indeed, vain. Nothing was discovered in the house but vases of gold, pipes ornamented with diamonds, delightfully luxurious beds and lounges, exquisite tables, and secret boudoirs fitted up with perfumed furniture, and concealing harmonious instruments. In short, the doctor's house inclosed all the comforts and luxuries of life, but nothing more; nothing that could awaken the suspicions of justice. His correspondence revealed naught beyond his many relations with the bankers and chief merchants in every quarter of the globe. Some Arabian manuscripts, and packets of papers covered with writing in cipher excited at first some suspicion, but on examination they proved to be nothing more than commercial letters, as the doctor had before stated. Finally, this inquiry justified the doctor on every point, and recoiled upon the heads of his enemies, every one of whom met shortly after with some misfortune.

It was to this man, strange and mysterious, that Cipriano, in a paroxysm of despair, came one day to solicit aid.

"Doctor," said he, casting himself on his knees, "relieve the most unfortunate man in the world. Nature has given me the passion for poesy, but refused me the boon of words and the faculty of expressing my thoughts. I think deeply, but when I wish to speak words fail me. If I wish to write, it is still worse. My sufferings are more horrible, I swear to you, than any you have ever alleviated. O God, can it be that it is you who have cast a spell over me, and condemned me to this eternal pain?"

"Son of Adam," said the doctor—this was his phrase in his gayer moments—"Son of Adam, behold the privilege of thy race! Thou canst obtain nothing but by the sweat of thy brow! It is destiny. Nevertheless," he added, after a moment's pause, "I can give thee a remedy for thy fate; but on one condition."

"I will consent to all that you wish, doctor, rather than die a thousand deaths every day."

"What they say of me, then, in the town does not frighten you?"

"No, doctor, because I can be in no worse plight than that in which you see me."

The doctor smiled.

"I will be frank with you," continued Cipriano. "It is not alone the love of poesy, nor the love of glory that has brought me to you. I nurse another sentiment more tender than either. Could I be but assured of facility of composition, I would be able to earn a living, and Charlotte would be mine. You understand me, doctor."

"That's what I like," cried Segelius; "I love nothing better than frankness. Evil lights alone on those who play a double game. You are, I see, a man free and open, and you merit a reward. I consent willingly to grant your prayer, and give you the faculty of producing without labor; but my first condition is, that the gift shall always remain with you."

"You mock me, Doctor Segelius."

"Not at all. I am also a frank man, and conceal nothing from those who have confidence in me. Listen, and take good heed of what I say. The faculty I give you will become a part of yourself; will grow, live, and die with you. You consent?"

"Can you doubt it?"

"Very good. My second condition is, that you will see every thing, know every thing, and comprehend every thing. Do you accept?"

"You certainly jest, doctor. I know not how to thank you. In place of one faculty, you give me four. Why should I not accept?"

"But understand me well. *You will see, you will know, and you will comprehend every thing.*"

"You are the most generous of men, Doctor Segelius."

"You accept then?"

"Certainly. Do you want a written engagement?"

"It is not needed. Your word suffices. A promise can not be torn like a piece of paper. Know that in this world nothing is lost, nothing perishes."

At these words Segelius placed his hand on the head of the poet, and another on his heart, and pronounced the following words in a solemn voice:

"Receive from the mysterious spheres the gift of knowing all things, of reading every thing in the world, of speaking and writing nobly, in a gay or serious vein, in verse or prose, for heat or for cold, in sleeping and waking, on wood and on sand, in joy as in pain, and in every language of the earth."

Segelius then put a manuscript in the poet's hand and dismissed him.

When Cipriano was gone, the doctor burst into a fit of laughter, and cried,

"Pepe! my cloak of frieze!"

And, as in *Freyschutz*, all the panels of the library replied by a diabolical echo, "Ahou! Ahou!"

Cipriano imagined these words to be an order given by Segelius to his *valet de chambre*, and was astonished that so elegant a man as the doctor would wear so common a garment. He peeped through the keyhole of the door and beheld a singular occurrence.

All the books in the library were in motion. From one of the manuscripts the figure 8 came out, from another the letter *aleph*, from a third the Greek delta, and so through all. At last the room was filled with animated figures and letters, that bowed and straightened themselves, and again closed themselves convulsively; dancing, leaping on their deformed feet, and falling on the floor. The commas, the periods, the marks of accentuation, glided through the midst of the band, like the infusoria seen through a solar microscope; and an old Chaldean volume beat time to the infernal dance with such vigor that the window-panes trembled with fear. Cipriano fled.

When he was somewhat more calm, he opened the manuscript which Segelius had given him. It was a huge roll covered with unknown characters. But scarcely had Cipriano cast his eyes, illumined with superior light, upon the paper than he understood the mysterious writing. There all the forces of nature were enumerated—the systematic life of the crystal, the fantastic will of the poet, the magnetic oscillations of the globe, the passions of the infusoria, the nervous laws of the language, the capricious wanderings of rivers. Every thing appeared to him arranged in mathematical progression—things of the mind as those of the heart. Cipriano beheld creation naked, and the lofty mystery of the conception and birth of thoughts seemed to him commonplace and easy. There existed for him a miraculous bridge, cast across the abyss that separates thought from expression—he spoke in verse.

We have seen at the commencement of this narrative the prodigious success which Cipriano enjoyed in his *rôle* of *improvisatore*. The first time that he tested this astonishing faculty he returned home with a full purse and a gay heart, but a little fatigued. Having taken a glass of water to appease his thirst, he suddenly started while he was carrying it to his lips. He looked at it. The tumbler did not contain water, but was full of something horrible and revolting. Two gases in a perpetual struggle were filled with myriads of microscopic insects that swam in them. Cipriano emptied his glass and filled another. There was the same odious mixture. He ran to the stream from which the water had been brought. Afar off he beheld its waves pure and silvery, rolling calmly; but when he drew near, there was the same frightful fluid, full of busy animalcules. The unhappy *improvisatore* shivered, and his blood seemed to freeze. In his despair he flung himself on the grass, and sought to forget his sufferings in sleep. Scarcely had he lain down when he heard grinding noises, blows, hisses, as if thousands of hammers were striking on an anvil, as if iron hoofs trampled upon a stone pavement, as if steel files were tearing some hard and polished surface. He rose and looked around him. The moon lit the garden. The shadow of the railings fell in dark bands across the foliage of the shrubs. All was calm and silent. He lay down again, and the noise recommenced. He could not sleep, and passed the night without closing his eyes. In the morning Cipriano ran to Charlotte's house, to confide to her his joy and grief, and to find repose by her side. Charlotte, who had heard of his success, awaited him with impatience. She was elegantly dressed, with bows of red ribbon in her beautiful fair hair, and from time to time she admired herself in her mirror, with innocent coquetry. Cipriano entered, ran toward Charlotte, holding out his hand smilingly, but suddenly he stopped and gazed at her with eyes of terror.

He beheld—what? Through the garments and the flesh he saw the triangular artery called the heart beating in the young girl's bosom. He saw the blood coursing up to the roots of the hair, and forming the delicate blush upon the cheeks that he had loved so much. Wretched man! In those eyes so beautiful and full of love he found nothing more than a species of *camera obscura*, made of a reticulated membrane and a drop of liquid. In that graceful walk, he saw only the play of ingenious mechanism. Alas! Charlotte was no longer an angel upon earth for him, and the object of his purest hopes. She was nothing more in his eyes than an anatomical preparation. Cipriano fled with terror.

Not far from this was a portrait of the Madonna to which Cipriano had often had recourse in his hours of suffering and despair, and whose radiant face had always ravished and soothed him. He fell on his knees before the holy picture and prayed. Scarcely had he lifted his eyes in adoration than all disappeared. There was no longer a picture before the penetrating eyes of the *improvisatore*, but a piece of canvas and a blotch of colors; the work of the artist seemed nothing more than a chemical amalgam.

Who can tell how Cipriano suffered? Sight, taste, smell, hearing—all the senses had acquired in him a frightful acuteness. An insect, a grain of dust, that did not exist to the rest of mankind, was to him a cause of anguish and suffering. The flapping of the wing of a butterfly almost deafened him. *He saw every thing—comprehended every thing.* But between him and mankind there was an abyss always. Nothing in the world of nature harmonized with him.

When he wished to seek forgetfulness in the perusal of some great poetical work, or in burying himself in historical studies, or in employing his intellect in the subtleties of some system of philosophy, all was in vain. His tongue babbled the words, but his mind saw other things.

Beneath the varnish of poetical expression he discovered all the artifices of the poet. In the consoling truths, in the eternal progress that history deduces from events, he saw nothing but an arbitrary arrangement of facts. The invention of a system of philosophy was nothing in his eyes but the desire of saying something new. For him there was no more music; the majestic harmonies of Haydn and Mozart struck him as only physical phenomena, as peculiar vibrations of the molecules of air. When he was among his relatives and intimate friends he read the evil thoughts in their hearts, and the criminal designs that each nourished against the other.

Cipriano went mad. He left his country, and sought to fly from himself, traveling through distant lands, but always, as of old, *seeing every thing— knowing every thing.*

He still retained the fatal gift of poesy. If the cruel faculty of seeing and knowing all slumbered for an instant, the passion for verse replaced it, and the stanzas rolled from his lips like water from a fountain. With what bitter regret he recalled that time of sweet suffering, when inspiration came to him seldom, or objects appeared to him under a doubtful form, waveringly and in slow succession. To-day he sees all—all simultaneously in a melancholy nudity. Then, from another world, a buzzing swarm of poetic inspirations descends incessantly on his head.

For many years Cipriano wandered from country to country, and necessity obliged him often to have recourse to the fatal gift of Segelius. This procured him all the luxuries of life—all the material enjoyments. But each one of those joys contained a poison the sting of which was more acute after each success. At last he resolved to use this accursed faculty no more; to stifle it, to crush it, even if it were at the price of starvation and death. But it was too late. In this savage struggle against himself Cipriano gave way. His reason trembled. The delicate links that united the mysterious elements of thought and sentiment were broken. Sentiment remained to him no longer, nor ideas; only vertigos of sensibility, fragments of thoughts, that he clad still in confused words that he himself did not understand. Misery and hunger had crushed his frame. He wandered for a long time, living on public charity, and not knowing himself whither he went.

I saw him once, when, in my capacity of American engineer on a Russian railroad, I traveled through the Steppes. He was living in the house of a Russian gentleman of small means, where he played the part of the old court fool. He wore a caftan of thick cloth, belted round the waist with a band of red leather. He babbled verses incessantly, in an incomprehensible language composed of all the idioms of the earth. He related his story to me himself, and complained bitterly of his poverty; but above all, his sorest affliction was that of not being comprehended, and being beaten every time that he, in one of his poetic inspirations, not having any paper, wrote his verses on the walls and tables. That, however, which pained him more than all was the fact that the family and servants laughed at the only happy memory which the fatal gifts of Segelius had not destroyed—his first verses to Charlotte.

What Was It?

A Mystery

It is, I confess, with considerable diffidence that I approach the strange narrative which I am about to relate. The events which I propose detailing are of so extraordinary and unheard-of a character that I am quite prepared to meet with an unusual amount of incredulity and scorn. I accept all such beforehand. I have, I trust, the literary courage to face unbelief. I have, after mature consideration, resolved to narrate, in as simple and straightforward a manner as I can compass, some facts that passed under my observation in the month of July last, and which, in the annals of the mysteries of physical science, are wholly unparalleled.

I live at No. — Twenty-sixth Street, in this city. The house is in some respects a curious one. It has enjoyed for the last two years the reputation of being haunted. It is a large and stately residence, surrounded by what was once a garden, but which is now only a green inclosure used for bleaching clothes. The dry basin of what has been a fountain, and a few fruit-trees, ragged and unpruned, indicate that this spot, in past days, was a pleasant, shady retreat, filled with fruits and flowers and the sweet murmur of waters.

The house is very spacious. A hall of noble size leads to a vast spiral staircase winding through its centre; while the various apartments are of imposing dimensions. It was built some fifteen or twenty years since by Mr. A——, the well-known New York merchant, who five years ago threw the commercial world into convulsions by a stupendous bank fraud. Mr. A——, as every one knows, escaped to Europe, and died not long after of a broken heart. Almost immediately after the news of his decease reached this country, and was verified, the report spread in Twenty-sixth Street that No. — was haunted. Legal measures had dispossessed the widow of its former owner, and it was inhabited merely by a care-taker and his wife, placed there by the house-agent into whose hands it had passed for purposes of renting or sale. These people declared that they were troubled with unnatural noises. Doors were opened without any visible agency. The remnants of furniture scattered through the various rooms were, during the night, piled one upon the other by unknown hands. Invisible feet passed up and down the stairs in broad daylight, accompanied by the rustle of unseen silk dresses and the gliding of viewless hands along the massive balusters. The caretaker and his wife declared they would live there no longer. The house-agent laughed, dismissed them, and put others in their place. The noises and supernatural manifestations continued. The neighborhood caught up the story, and the house remained untenanted for three years. Several parties negotiated for it; but somehow, always before the bargain was closed, they heard the unpleasant rumors, and declined to treat any further.

It was in this state of things that my landlady—who at that time kept a boarding-house in Bleecker Street, and who wished to move farther up town—conceived the bold idea of renting No. — Twenty-sixth Street. Happening to have in her house rather a plucky and philosophical set of boarders, she laid her scheme before us, stating candidly every thing she had heard respecting the ghostly qualities of the establishment to which she wished to remove us. With the exception of one or two timid persons —a sea-captain and a returned Californian, who immediately gave notice that they would leave—every one of Mrs. Moffat's guests declared that they would accompany her in her chivalric incursion into the abode of spirits.

Our removal was effected in the month of May, and we were all charmed with our new residence. The portion of Twenty-sixth Street where our house is situated—between Seventh and Eighth Avenues—is one of the pleasantest localities in New York. The gardens back of the houses, running down nearly to the Hudson, form, in the summer time, a perfect avenue of verdure. The air is pure and invigorating, sweeping, as it does, straight across the river from the Weehawken heights, and even the ragged garden which surrounded the house on two sides, although display-ing on washing-days rather too much clothes-line, still gave us a piece of green sward to look at, and a cool retreat in the summer evenings, where we smoked our cigars in the dusk, and watched the fire-flies flashing their dark-lanterns in the long grass.

Of course we had no sooner established ourselves at No. — than we began to expect the ghosts. We absolutely awaited their advent with ea-gerness. Our dinner conversation was supernatural. One of the boarders, who had purchased Mrs. Crowe's "Night Side of Nature" for his own private delectation, was regarded as a public enemy by the entire house-hold for not having bought twenty copies. The man led a life of supreme wretchedness while he was perusing the volume. A system of espionage was established, of which he was the victim. If he incautiously laid the book down for an instant and left the room, it was immediately seized and read aloud in secret places to a select few. I found myself a person of immense importance, it having leaked out that I was tolerably well versed in the history of supernaturalism, and had once written a story, entitled "The Pot of Tulips," for *Harper's Monthly,* the foundation of which was a ghost. If a table or a wainscot panel happened to warp when we were assembled in the large drawing-room, there was an instant silence, and every one was prepared for an immediate clanking of chains and a spectral form.

After a month of psychological excitement, it was with the utmost dissatisfaction that we were forced to acknowledge that nothing in the remotest degree approaching the supernatural had manifested itself. Once the black butler asseverated that his candle had been blown out by some invisible agency while in the act of undressing himself for the night; but as I had more than once discovered this colored gentleman in a condition when one candle must have appeared to him like two, I thought it possible that, by going a step farther in his potations, he might have reversed this phenomenon, and seen no candle at all where he ought to have beheld one.

Things were in this state when an incident took place so awful and inexplicable in its character that my reason fairly reels at the bare memory of the occurrence. It was the 10th of July. After dinner was over I repaired, with my friend Dr. Hammond, to the garden to smoke my evening pipe. Independent of certain mental sympathies which existed between the Doctor and myself, we were linked together by a secret vice. We both smoked opium. We knew each other's secret, and respected it. We enjoyed together that wonderful expansion of thought; that marvelous intensifying of the perceptive faculties; that boundless feeling of existence when we seem to have points of contact with the whole universe; in short, that unimaginable spiritual bliss, which I would not surrender for a throne, and which I hope you, reader, will never—never taste.

Those hours of opium happiness which the Doctor and I spent together in secret were regulated with a scientific accuracy. We did not blindly smoke the drug of Paradise, and leave our dreams to chance. While smoking we carefully steered our conversation through the brightest and calmest channels of thought. We talked of the East, and endeavored to recall the magical panorama of its glowing scenery. We criticised the most sensuous poets, those who painted life ruddy with health, brimming with passion, happy in the possession of youth, and strength, and beauty. If we talked of Shakespeare's "Midsummer Night's Dream," we lingered over

Ariel and avoided Caliban. Like the Gebers, we turned our faces to the East, and saw only the sunny side of the world.

This skillful coloring of our train of thought produced in our subsequent visions a corresponding tone. The splendors of Arabian fairy-land dyed our dreams. We paced that narrow strip of grass with the tread and port of kings. The song of the *Rana arborea* while he clung to the bark of the ragged plum-tree sounded like the strains of divine orchestras. Houses, walls, and streets melted like rain-clouds, and vistas of unimaginable glory stretched away before us. It was a rapturous companionship. We each of us enjoyed the vast delight more perfectly because, even in our most ecstatic moments, we were ever conscious of each other's presence. Our pleasures, while individual, were still twin, vibrating and moving in musical accord.

On the evening in question, the 10th of July, the Doctor and myself found ourselves in an unusually metaphysical mood. We lit our large meer-schaums, filled with fine Turkish tobacco; in the core of which burned a little black nut of opium, that, like the nut in the fairy tale, held within its narrow limits wonders beyond the reach of kings; we paced to and fro, conversing. A strange perversity dominated the currents of our thought. They would *not* flow through the sun-lit channels into which we strove to divert them. For some unaccountable reason they constantly diverged into dark and lonesome beds, where a continual gloom brooded. It was in vain that, after our old fashion, we flung ourselves on the shores of the East, and talked of its gay bazaars, of the splendors of the time of Haroun, of harems and golden palaces. Black afreets continually arose from the depths of our talk, and expanded, like the one the fisherman released from the copper vessel, until they blotted every thing bright from our vision. Insensibly we yielded to the occult force that swayed us, and indulged in gloomy speculation. We had talked some time upon the proneness of the human mind to mysticism and the almost universal love of the Terrible, when Hammond suddenly said to me:

"What do you consider to be the greatest element of Terror?"

The question, I own, puzzled me. That many things were terrible, I knew. Stumbling over a corpse in the dark; beholding, as I once did, a woman floating down a deep and rapid river, with wildly-lifted arms and awful, upturned face, uttering, as she sank, shrieks that rent one's heart, while we, the spectators, stood frozen at a window which overhung the river at a height of sixty feet, unable to make the slightest effort to save her, but dumbly watching her last supreme agony and her disappearance. A shattered wreck, with no life visible, encountered floating listlessly on the ocean, is a terrible object, for it suggests a huge terror, the proportions of which are vailed. But it now struck me for the first time that there must be one great and ruling embodiment of fear, a King of Terrors to which all others must succumb. What might it be? To what train of circumstances would it owe its existence?

"I confess, Hammond," I replied to my friend, "I never considered the subject before. That there must be one Something more terrible than any other thing, I feel. I can not attempt, however, even the most vague definition."

"I am somewhat like you, Harry," he answered. "I feel my capacity to experience a terror greater than any thing yet conceived by the human mind. Something combining in fearful and unnatural amalgamation hitherto supposed incompatible elements. The calling of the voices in Brockden Brown's novel of 'Wieland' is awful; so is the picture of the Dweller of the Threshold in Bulwer's 'Zanoni;' but," he added, shaking his head gloomily, "there is something more horrible still than these."

"Look here, Hammond," I rejoined; "let us drop this kind of talk for Heaven's sake. We shall suffer for it, depend on it."

"I don't know what's the matter with me tonight," he replied, "but my brain is running upon all sorts of weird and awful thoughts. I feel as if I could write a story like Hoffman tonight, if I were only master of a literary style."

"Well, if we are going to be Hoffmanesque in our talk I'm off to bed. Opium and nightmares should never be brought together. How sultry it is! Good-night, Hammond."

"Good-night, Harry. Pleasant dreams to you."

"To you, gloomy wretch, afreets, ghouls, and enchanters."

We parted, and each sought his respective chamber. I undressed quickly and got into bed, taking with me, according to my usual custom, a book, over which I generally read myself to sleep. I opened the volume as soon as I had laid my head upon the pillow, and instantly flung it to the other side of the room. It was Goudon's "History of Monsters"—a curious French work, which I had lately imported from Paris, but which, in the state of mind I was then in, was any thing but an agreeable companion. I resolved to go to sleep at once; so turning down my gas until nothing but a little blue point of light glimmered on the top of the tube, I composed myself to rest once more.

The room was in total darkness. The atom of gas that still remained lighted did not illuminate a distance of three inches round the burner. I desperately drew my arm across my eyes, as if to shut out even the darkness, and tried to think of nothing. It was in vain. The confounded themes touched on by Hammond in the garden kept obtruding themselves on my brain. I battled against them. I erected ramparts of would-be blankness of intellect to keep them out. They still crowded upon me. While I was lying still as a corpse, hoping that by a perfect physical inaction I would hasten mental repose, an awful incident occurred. A Something dropped, as it seemed, from the ceiling, plumb upon my chest, and the next instant I felt two bony hands encircling my throat, endeavoring to choke me.

I am no coward, and am possessed of considerable physical strength. The suddenness of the attack instead of stunning me strung every nerve to its highest tension. My body acted from instinct, before my brain had time to realize the terrors of my position. In an instant I wound two muscular arms around the creature, and squeezed it, with all the strength of despair, against my chest. In a few seconds the bony hands that had fastened on my throat loosened their hold, and I was free to breathe once more. Then commenced a struggle of awful intensity. Immersed in the most profound darkness, totally ignorant of the nature of the Thing by which I was so suddenly attacked, finding my grasp slipping every moment by reason, it seemed to me, of the entire nakedness of my assailant, bitten with sharp teeth in the shoulder, neck, and chest, having every moment to protect my throat against a pair of sinewy, agile hands, which my utmost efforts could not confine—these were a combination of circumstances to combat which required all the strength and skill and courage that I possessed.

At last, after a silent, deadly, exhausting struggle, I got my assailant under by a series of incredible efforts of strength. Once pinned, with my knee on what I made out to be its chest, I knew that I was victor. I rested for a moment to breathe. I heard the creature beneath me panting in the darkness, and felt the violent throbbing of a heart. It was apparently as exhausted as I was, that was one comfort. At this moment I remembered that I usually placed under my pillow, before going to bed, a large, yellow silk pocket-handkerchief, for use during the night. I felt for it instantly; it was there. In a few seconds more I had, after a fashion, pinioned the creature's arms.

I now felt tolerably secure. There was nothing more to be done but to turn on the gas, and having first seen what my midnight assailant was like, arouse the household. I will confess to being actuated by a certain pride in not giving the alarm before; I wished to make the capture alone and unaided.

Never loosing my hold for an instant, I slipped from the bed to the floor, dragging my captive with me. I had but a few steps to make to reach the gas-burner; these I made with the greatest caution, holding the creature in a grip like a vice. At last I got within arm's-length of the tiny speck of blue light, which told me where the gas-burner lay. Quick as lightning I released my grasp with one hand and let on the full flood of light. Then I turned to look at my captive.

I can not even attempt to give any definition of my sensations the instant after I turned on the gas. I suppose I must have shrieked with terror, for in less than a minute afterward my room was crowded with the inmates of the house. I shudder now as I think of that awful moment. *I saw nothing!* Yes; I had one arm firmly clasped round a breathing, panting, corporeal shape, my other hand gripped with all its strength a throat as warm, and apparently fleshly, as my own; and yet, with this living substance in my grasp, with its body pressed against my own, and all in the bright glare of a large jet of gas, I absolutely beheld nothing! Not even an outline—a vapor!

I do not, even at this hour, realize the situation in which I found myself. I can not recall the astounding incident thoroughly. Imagination in vain tries to compass the awful paradox.

It breathed. I felt its warm breath upon my cheek. It struggled fiercely. It had hands. They clutched me. Its skin was smooth, just like my own. There it lay, pressed close up against me, solid as stone—and yet utterly invisible!

I wonder that I did not faint or go mad on the instant. Some wonderful instinct must have sustained me; for, absolutely, in place of loosening my hold on the terrible Enigma, I seemed to gain an additional strength in my moment of horror, and tightened my grasp with such wonderful force that I felt the creature shivering with agony.

Just then Hammond entered my room at the head of the household. As soon as he beheld my face—which, I suppose, must have been an awful sight to look at—he hastened forward, crying,

"Great Heaven, Harry! what has happened?"

"Hammond! Hammond!" I cried, "come here. Oh! this is awful! I have been attacked in bed by something or other, which I have hold of; but I can't see it—I can't see it!"

Hammond, doubtless struck by the unfeigned horror expressed in my countenance, made one or two steps forward with an anxious yet puzzled expression. A very audible titter burst from the remainder of my visitors. This suppressed laughter made me furious. To laugh at a human being in my position! It was the worst species of cruelty. *Now,* I can understand why the appearance of a man struggling violently, as it would seem, with an airy nothing, and calling for assistance against a vision, should have appeared ludicrous. *Then,* so great was my rage against the mocking crowd that had I the power I would have stricken them dead where they stood.

"Hammond! Hammond!" I cried again, despairingly, "for God's sake come to me. I can hold the—the Thing but a short while longer. It is overpowering me. Help me. Help me!"

"Harry," whispered Hammond, approaching me, "you have been smoking too much opium."

"I swear to you Hammond that this is no vision," I answered, in the same low tone. "Don't you see how it shakes my whole frame with its struggles? If you don't believe me convince yourself. Feel it—touch it."

Hammond advanced and laid his hand in the spot I indicated. A wild cry of horror burst from him. He had felt it!

In a moment he had discovered somewhere in my room a long piece of cord, and was the next instant winding it, and knotting it about the body of the unseen being that I clasped in my arms.

"Harry," he said, in a hoarse, agitated voice, for, though he preserved his presence of mind, he was deeply moved. "Harry, it's all safe now. You may let go, old fellow, if you're tired. The Thing can't move."

I was utterly exhausted, and I gladly loosed my hold.

Hammond stood holding the ends of the cord that bound the Invisible, twisted round his hand, while before him, self-supporting, as it were, he beheld a rope laced and interlaced, and stretching tightly around a vacant space. I never saw a man look so thoroughly stricken with awe. Nevertheless his face expressed all the courage and determination which I knew him to possess. His lips, although white, were set firmly, and one could perceive at a glance that, although stricken with fear, he was not daunted.

The confusion that ensued among the guests of the house, who were witnesses of this extraordinary scene between Hammond and myself—who beheld the pantomime of binding this struggling Something—who beheld me almost sinking from physical exhaustion when my task of jailer was over—the confusion and terror that took possession of the by-standers, when they saw all this, was beyond description. Many of the weaker ones fled from the apartment. The few who remained behind clustered near the door, and could not be induced to approach Hammond and his Charge. Still incredulity broke out through their terror. They had not the courage to satisfy themselves, and yet they doubted. It was in vain that I begged of some of the men to come near and convince themselves by touch of the existence of a living being in that room which was invisible. They were incredulous, but did not dare to undeceive themselves. How could a solid, living, breathing body be invisible? they asked. My reply was this. I gave a sign to Hammond, and both of us—conquering our fearful repugnance to touching the invisible creature—lifted it from the ground, manacled as it was, and took it to my bed. Its weight was about that of a boy of fourteen.

"Now my friends," I said, as Hammond and myself held the creature suspended over the bed, "I can give you self-evident proof that here is a solid, ponderable body which, nevertheless, you can not see. Be good enough to watch the surface of the bed attentively."

I was astonished at my own courage in treating this strange event so calmly; but I had recovered from my first terror, and felt a sort of scientific pride in the affair which dominated every other feeling.

The eyes of the by-standers were immediately fixed on my bed. At a given signal Hammond and I let the creature fall. There was the dull sound of a heavy body alighting on a soft mass. The timbers of the bed creaked. A deep impression marked itself distinctly on the pillow, and on the bed itself. The crowd who witnessed this gave a sort of low, universal cry, and rushed from the room. Hammond and I were left alone with our Mystery.

We remained silent for some time, listening to the low, irregular breathing of the creature on the bed, and watching the rustle of the bedclothes as it impotently struggled to free itself from confinement. Then Hammond spoke.

"Harry, this is awful."

"Ay, awful."

"But not unaccountable."

"Not unaccountable! What do you mean? Such a thing has never occurred since the birth of the world. I know not what to think, Hammond. God grant that I am not mad, and that this is not an insane fantasy!"

"Let us reason a little, Harry. Here is a solid body which we touch, but which we can not see. The fact is so unusual that it strikes us with terror. Is there no parallel, though, for such a phenomenon? Take a piece of pure glass. It is tangible and transparent. A certain chemical coarseness is all that prevents its being so entirely transparent as to be totally invisible. It is not *theoretically impossible*, mind you, to fabricate a glass which shall not reflect a single ray of light—a glass so pure and homogeneous in its atoms that the rays from the sun shall pass through it as they do through the air, refracted but not reflected. We do not see the air, and yet we feel it."

"That's all very well, Hammond, but these are inanimate substances. Glass does not breathe, air does not breathe. *This* thing has a heart that palpitates. A will that moves it. Lungs that play and inspire and respire."

"You forget the strange phenomena of which we have so often heard of late," answered the Doctor, gravely. "At the meetings called 'spirit circles,' invisible hands have been thrust into the hands of those persons round the table—warm, fleshly hands that seemed to pulsate with mortal life."

"What? Do you think, then, that this thing is—"

"I don't know what it is," was the solemn reply; "but please the gods I will, with your assistance, thoroughly investigate it."

We watched together, smoking many pipes, all night long by the bedside of the unearthly being that tossed and panted until it was apparently wearied out. Then we learned by the low, regular breathing that it slept.

The next morning the house was all astir. The boarders congregated on the landing outside my room, and Hammond and myself were lions. We had to answer a thousand questions as to the state of our extraordinary prisoner, for as yet not one person in the house except ourselves could be induced to set foot in the apartment.

The creature was awake. This was evidenced by the convulsive manner in which the bedclothes were moved in its efforts to escape. There was something truly terrible in beholding, as it were, those second-hand indications of the terrible writhings and agonized struggles for liberty, which themselves were invisible.

Hammond and myself had racked our brains during the long night to discover some means by which we might realize the shape and general appearance of the Enigma. As well as we could make out by passing our hands over the creature's form, its outlines and lineaments were human. There was a mouth; a round, smooth head without hair; a nose, which, however, was little elevated above the cheeks; and its hands and feel felt like those of a boy. At first we thought of placing the being on a smooth surface and tracing its outline with chalk, as shoemakers trace the outline of the foot. This plan was given up as being of no value. Such an outline would give not the slightest idea of its conformation.

A happy thought struck me. We would take a cast of it in plaster of Paris. This would give us the solid figure, and satisfy all our wishes. But how to do it? The movements of the creature would disturb the setting of the plastic covering, and distort the mould. Another thought. Why not give it chloroform? It had respiratory organs—that was evident by its breathing. Once reduced to a state of insensibility, we could do with it what we would. Doctor X—— was sent for; and after the worthy physician had recovered from the first shock of amazement, he proceeded to administer the chloroform. In three minutes afterward we were enabled to remove the fetters from the creature's body, and a well-known modeler of this city was busily engaged in covering the invisible form with the moist clay. In five minutes more we had a mould, and before evening a rough *fac-simile* of the Mystery. It was shaped like a man. Distorted, uncouth, and horrible, but still a man. It was small, not over four feet and some inches in height, and its limbs betrayed a muscular development that was unparalleled. Its face surpassed in hideousness any thing I had ever seen. Gustave Dore, or Callot, or Tony Johannot never conceived any thing so horrible. There is a face in one of the latter's illustrations to *"Un voyage ou il vous plaira,"* which somewhat approaches the countenance of this creature, but does not equal it. It was the physiognomy of what I should have fancied a ghoul to be. It looked as if it was capable of feeding on human flesh.

Having satisfied our curiosity, and bound every one in the house over to secrecy, it became a question what was to be done with our Enigma? It was impossible that we should keep such a horror in our house; it was equally impossible that such an awful being should be let loose upon the world. I confess that I would have gladly voted for the creature's destruction. But who would shoulder the responsibility? Who would undertake the execution of this horrible semblance of a human being? Day after day this question was deliberated gravely. The boarders all left the house. Mrs. Moffat was in despair, and threatened Hammond and myself with all sorts of legal penalties if we did not remove the Horror. Our answer was, "We will go if you like, but we decline taking this creature with us. Remove it yourself if you please. It appeared in your house. On you the responsibility rests." To this there was, of course, no answer. Mrs. Moffat could not obtain for love or money a person who would even approach the Mystery.

The most singular part of the transaction was, that we were entirely ignorant of what the creature habitually fed on. Every thing in the way of nutriment that we could think of was placed before it, but was never touched. It was awful to stand by, day after day, and see the clothes toss and hear the hard breathing, and know that it was starving.

Ten, twelve days, a fortnight passed, and it still lived. The pulsations of the heart, however, were daily growing fainter, and had now nearly ceased altogether. It was evident that the creature was dying for want of sustenance. While this terrible life-struggle was going on I felt miserable. I could not sleep of nights. Horrible as the creature was, it was pitiful to think of the pangs it was suffering.

At last it died. Hammond and I found it cold and stiff one morning in the bed. The heart had ceased to beat, the lungs to inspire. We hastened to bury it in the garden. It was a strange funeral, the dropping of that viewless corpse into the damp hole. The cast of its form I gave to Doctor X——, who keeps it in his museum in Tenth Street.

As I am on the eve of a long journey from which I may not return, I have drawn up this narrative of an event the most singular that has ever come to my knowledge.

Harry Escott

[Note: It is rumored that the proprietors of a well-known museum in this city have made arrangements with Dr. X—— to exhibit to the public the singular cast which Mr. Escott deposited with him. So extraordinary a history can not fail to attract universal attention.]

The Wondersmith

I. GOLOSH STREET AND ITS PEOPLE

A small lane, the name of which I have forgotten, or do not choose to remember, slants suddenly off from Chatham Street, (before that head-long thoroughfare reaches into the Park,) and retreats suddenly down towards the East River, as if it were disgusted with the smell of old clothes, and had determined to wash itself clean. This excellent intention it has, however, evidently contributed towards the making of that imaginary pavement mentioned in the old adage; for it is still emphatically a dirty street. It has never been able to shake off the Hebraic taint of filth which it inherits from the ancestral thoroughfare. It is slushy and greasy, as if it were twin brother of the Roman Ghetto.

I like a dirty slum; not because I am naturally unclean,—I have not a drop of Neapolitan blood in my veins,—but because I generally find a certain sediment of philosophy precipitated in its gutters. A clean street is terribly prosaic. There is no food for thought in carefully swept pavements, barren kennels, and vulgarly spotless houses. But when I go down a street which has been left so long to itself that it has acquired a distinct outward character, I find plenty to think about. The scraps of sodden letters lying in the ash-barrel have their meaning: desperate appeals, perhaps, from Tom, the baker's assistant, to Amelia, the daughter of the dry-goods retailer, who is always selling at a sacrifice in consequence of the late fire. That may be Tom himself who is now passing me in a white apron, and I look up at the windows of the house (which does not, however, give any signs of a recent conflagration) and almost hope to see Amelia wave a white pocket-handkerchief. The bit of orange-peel lying on the sidewalk inspires thought. Who will fall over it? who but the industrious mother of six children, the eldest of which is only nine months old, all of whom are dependent on her exertions for support? I see her slip and tumble. I see the pale face convulsed with agony, and the vain struggle to get up; the pitying crowd closing her off from all air; the anxious young doctor who happened to be passing by; the manipulation of the broken limb, the shake of the head, the moan of the victim, the litter borne on men's shoulders, the gates of the New York Hospital unclosing, the subscription taken up on the spot. There is some food for speculation in that three-year-old, tattered child, masked with dirt, who is throwing a brick at another three-year-old, tattered child, masked with dirt. It is not difficult to perceive that he is destined to lurk, as it were, through life. His bad, flat face—or, at least, what can be seen of it—does not look as if it were made for the light of day. The mire in which he wallows now is but a type of the moral mire in which he will wallow hereafter. The feeble little hand lifted at this instant to smite his companion, half in earnest, half in jest, will be raised against his fellow-beings forevermore.

Golosh Street—as I will call this nameless lane before alluded to—is an interesting locality. All the oddities of trade seem to have found their way thither and made an eccentric mercantile settlement. There is a bird-shop at one corner, wainscoted with little cages containing linnets, waxwings, canaries, blackbirds, Mino-birds, with a hundred other varieties, known only to naturalists. Immediately opposite is an establishment where they sell nothing but ornaments made out of the tinted leaves of autumn, varnished and gummed into various forms. Farther down is a second-hand book-stall, which looks like a sentry-box mangled out flat, and which is remarkable for not containing a complete set of any work. There is a small chink between two ordinary-sized houses, in which a little Frenchman makes and sells artificial eyes, specimens of which, ranged on a black velvet cushion, stare at you unwinkingly through the window as you pass, until you shudder and hurry on, thinking how awful the world would be, if every one went about without eyelids. There are junk-shops in Golosh Street that seem to have got hold of all the old nails in the Ark and all the old brass of Corinth. Madame Filomel, the fortune-teller, lives at No. 12 Golosh Street, second story front, pull the bell on the left-hand side. Next door to Madame is the shop of Herr Hippe, commonly called the Wondersmith.

Herr Hippe's shop is the largest in Golosh Street, and to all appearance is furnished with the smallest stock. Beyond a few packing-cases, a turner's lathe, and a shelf laden with dissected maps of Europe, the interior of the shop is entirely unfurnished. The window, which is lofty and wide, but much begrimed with dirt, contains the only pleasant object in the place. This is a beautiful little miniature theatre,—that is to say, the orchestra and stage. It is fitted with charmingly painted scenery and all the appliances for scenic changes. There are tiny traps, and delicately constructed "lifts," and real footlights fed with burning-fluid, and in the orchestra sits a diminutive conductor before his desk, surrounded by musical manikins, all provided with the smallest of violoncellos, flutes, oboes, drums, and such like. There are characters also on the stage. A Templar in a white cloak is dragging a fainting female form to the parapet of a ruined bridge, while behind a great black rock on the left one can see a man concealed, who, kneeling, levels an arquebuse at the knight's heart. But the orchestra is silent; the conductor never beats the time, the musicians never play a note. The Templar never drags his victim an inch nearer to the bridge, the masked avenger takes an eternal aim with his weapon. This repose appears unnatural; for so admirably are the figures executed, that they seem replete with life. One is almost led to believe, in looking on them, that they are resting beneath some spell which hinders their motion. One expects every moment to hear the loud explosion of the arquebuse,—to see the blue smoke curling, the Templar falling,—to hear the orchestra playing the requiem of the guilty.

Few people knew what Herr Hippe's business or trade really was. That he worked at something was evident; else why the shop? Some people inclined to the belief that he was an inventor, or mechanician. His workshop was in the rear of the store, and into that sanctuary no one but himself had admission. He arrived in Golosh Street eight or ten years ago, and one fine morning, the neighbors, taking down their shutters, observed that No. 13 had got a tenant. A tall, thin, sallow-faced man stood on a ladder outside the shop-entrance, nailing up a large board, on which "Herr Hippe, Wondersmith," was painted in black letters on a yellow ground. The little theatre stood in the window, where it stood ever after, and Herr Hippe was established.

But what was a Wondersmith? people asked each other. No one could reply. Madame Filomel was consulted, but she looked grave, and said that it was none of her business. Mr. Pippel, the bird-fancier, who was a German, and ought to know best, thought it was the English for some singular Teutonic profession; but his replies were so vague, that Golosh Street was as unsatisfied as ever. Solon, the little humpback, who kept the odd-volume book-stall at the lowest corner, could throw no light upon it. And at length people had to come to the conclusion, that Herr Hippe was either a coiner or a magician, and opinions were divided.

II. A BOTTLEFUL OF SOULS

It was a dull December evening. There was little trade doing in Golosh Street, and the shutters were up at most of the shops. Hippe's store had been closed at least an hour, and the Mino-birds and Bohemian waxwings at Mr. Pippel's had their heads tucked under their wings in their first sleep.

Herr Hippe sat in his parlor, which was lit by a pleasant wood-fire. There were no candles in the room, and the flickering blaze played fantastic tricks on the pale gray walls. It seemed the festival of shadows. Processions of shapes, obscure and indistinct, passed across the leaden-hued panels and vanished in the dusk corners. Every fresh blaze flung up by the wayward logs created new images. Now it was a funeral throng, with the bowed figures of mourners, the shrouded coffin, the plumes that waved like extinguished torches; now a knightly cavalcade with flags and lances, and weird horses, that rushed silently along until they met the angle of the room, when they pranced through the wall and vanished.

On a table close to where Herr Hippe sat was placed a large square box of some dark wood, while over it was spread a casing of steel, so elaborately wrought in an open arabesque pattern that it seemed like a shining blue lace which was lightly stretched over its surface.

Herr Hippe lay luxuriously in his armchair, looking meditatively into the fire. He was tall and thin, and his skin was of a dull saffron hue. Long, straight hair,—sharply cut, regular features,—a long, thin moustache, that curled like a dark asp around his mouth, the expression of which was so bitter and cruel that it seemed to distil the venom of the ideal serpent,— and a bony, muscular form, were the prominent characteristics of the Wondersmith.

The profound silence that reigned in the chamber was broken by a peculiar scratching at the panel of the door, like that which at the French court was formerly substituted for the ordinary knock, when it was necessary to demand admission to the royal apartments. Herr Hippe started, raised his head, which vibrated on his long neck like the head of a cobra when about to strike, and after a moment's silence uttered a strange guttural sound. The door unclosed, and a squat, broad-shouldered woman, with large, wild, Oriental eyes, entered softly.

"Ah! Filomel, you are come!" said the Wondersmith, sinking back in his chair. "Where are the rest of them?"

"They will be here presently," answered Madame Filomel, seating herself in an arm-chair much too narrow for a person of her proportions, and over the sides of which she bulged like a pudding.

"Have you brought the souls?" asked the Wondersmith.

"They are here," said the fortune-teller, drawing a large pot-bellied black bottle from under her cloak. "Ah! I have had such trouble with them!"

"Are they of the right brand,—wild, tearing, dark, devilish fellows? We want no essence of milk and honey, you know. None but souls bitter as hemlock or scorching as lightning will suit our purpose."

"You will see, you will see, Grand Duke of Egypt! They are ethereal demons, every one of them. They are the pick of a thousand births. Do you think that I, old midwife that I am, don't know the squall of the demon child from that of the angel child, the very moment they are delivered? Ask a musician, how he knows, even in the dark, a note struck by Thalberg from one struck by Listz!"

"I long to test them," cried the Wondersmith, rubbing his hands joyfully. "I long to see how the little devils will behave when I give them their shapes. Ah! it will be a proud day for us when we let them loose upon the cursed Christian children! Through the length and breadth of the land they will go; wherever our wandering people set foot, and wherever they are, the children of the Christians shall die. Then we, the despised Bohemians, the gypsies, as they call us, will be once more lords of the earth, as we were in the days when the accursed things called cities did not exist, and men lived in the free woods and hunted the game of the forest. Toys indeed! Ay, ay, we will give the little dears toys! toys that all day will sleep calmly in their boxes, seemingly stiff and wooden and without life,— but at night, when the souls enter them, will arise and surround the cots of the sleeping children, and pierce their hearts with their keen, envenomed blades! Toys indeed! oh, yes! I will sell them toys!"

And the Wondersmith laughed horribly, while the snaky moustache on his upper lip writhed as if it had truly a serpent's power and could sting.

"Have you got your first batch, Herr Hippe?" asked Madame Filomel. "Are they all ready?"

"Oh, ay! they are ready," answered the Wondersmith with gusto,— opening, as he spoke, the box covered with the blue steel lace-work; "they are here."

The box contained a quantity of exquisitely carved wooden manikins of both sexes, painted with great dexterity so as to present a miniature resemblance to Nature. They were, in fact, nothing more than admirable specimens of those toys which children delight in placing in various positions on the table,—in regiments, or sitting at meals, or grouped under the stiff green trees which always accompany them in the boxes in which they are sold at the toy-shops.

The peculiarity, however, about the manikins of Herr Hippe was not alone the artistic truth with which the limbs and the features were gifted; but on the countenance of each little puppet the carver's art had wrought an expression of wickedness that was appalling. Every tiny face had its special stamp of ferocity. The lips were thin and brimful of malice; the small black bead-like eyes glittered with the fire of a universal hate. There was not one of the manikins, male or female, that did not hold in his or her hand some miniature weapon. The little men, scowling like demons, clasped in their wooden fingers swords delicate as a housewife's needle. The women, whose countenances expressed treachery and cruelty, clutched infinitesimal daggers, with which they seemed about to take some terrible vengeance.

"Good!" said Madame Filomel, taking one of the manikins out of the box and examining it attentively; "you work well, Duke Balthazar! These little ones are of the right stamp; they look as if they had mischief in them. Ah! here come our brothers."

At this moment the same scratching that preceded the entrance of Madame Filomel was heard at the door, and Herr Hippe replied with a hoarse, guttural cry. The next moment two men entered. The first was a small man with very brilliant eyes. He was wrapt in a long shabby cloak, and wore a strange nondescript species of cap on his head, such a cap as one sees only in the low billiard-rooms in Paris. His companion was tall, long-limbed, and slender; and his dress, although of the ordinary cut, either from the disposition of colors, or from the careless, graceful attitudes of the wearer, assumed a certain air of picturesqueness. Both the men possessed the same marked Oriental type of countenance which distinguished the Wondersmith and Madame Filomel. True gypsies they seemed, who would not have been out of place telling fortunes, or stealing chickens in the green lanes of England, or wandering with their wild music and their sleight-of-hand tricks through Bohemian villages.

"Welcome, brothers!" said the Wondersmith; "you are in time. Sister Filomel has brought the souls, and we are about to test them. Monsieur Kerplonne, take off your cloak. Brother Oaksmith, take a chair. I promise you some amusement this evening; so make yourselves comfortable. Here is something to aid you."

And while the Frenchman Kerplonne, and his tall companion, Oaksmith, were obeying Hippe's invitation, he reached over to a little closet let into the wall, and took thence a squat bottle and some glasses, which he placed on the table.

"Drink, brothers!" he said; "it is not Christian blood, but good stout wine of Oporto. It goes right to the heart, and warms one like the sunshine of the South."

"It is good," said Kerplonne, smacking his lips with enthusiasm.

"Why don't you keep brandy? Hang wine!" cried Oaksmith, after having swallowed two bumpers in rapid succession.

"Bah! Brandy has been the ruin of our race. It has made us sots and thieves. It shall never cross my threshold," cried the Wondersmith, with a sombre indignation.

"A little of it is not bad, though, Duke," said the fortune-teller. "It consoles us for our misfortunes; it gives us the crowns we once wore; it restores to us the power we once wielded; it carries us back, as if by magic, to that land of the sun from which fate has driven us; it darkens the memory of all the evils that we have for centuries suffered."

"It is a devil; may it be cursed!" cried Herr Hippe, passionately. "It is a demon that stole from me my son, the finest youth in all Courland. Yes! my son, the son of the Waywode Balthazar, Grand Duke of Lower Egypt, died raving in a gutter, with an empty brandy-bottle in his hands. Were it not that the plant is a sacred one to our race, I would curse the grape and the vine that bore it."

This outburst was delivered with such energy that the three gypsies kept silence. Oaksmith helped himself to another glass of Port, and the fortune-teller rocked to and fro in her chair, too much overawed by the Wondersmith's vehemence of manner to reply. The little Frenchman, Kerplonne, took no part in the discussion, but seemed lost in admiration of the manikins, which he took from the box in which they lay, handling them with the greatest care. After the silence had lasted for about a minute, Herr Hippe broke it with the sudden question,—

"How does your eye get on, Kerplonne?"

"Excellently, Duke. It is finished. I have it here." And the little Frenchman put his hand into his breeches-pocket and pulled out a large artificial human eye. Its great size was the only thing in this eye that would lead any one to suspect its artificiality. It was at least twice the size of life; but there was a fearful speculative light in its iris, which seemed to expand and contract like the eye of a living being, that rendered it a horrible staring paradox. It looked like the naked eye of the Cyclops, torn from his forehead, and still burning with wrath and the desire for vengeance.

The little Frenchman laughed pleasantly as he held the eye in his hand, and gazed down on that huge dark pupil, that stared back at him, it seemed, with an air of defiance and mistrust.

"It is a devil of an eye," said the little man, wiping the enamelled surface with an old silk pocket-handkerchief; "it reads like a demon. My niece—the unhappy one—has a wretch of a lover, and I have a long time feared that she would run away with him. I could not read her correspondence, for she kept her writing-desk closely locked. But I asked her yesterday to keep this eye in some very safe place for me. She put it, as I knew she would, into her desk, and by its aid I read every one of her letters. She was to run away next Monday, the ungrateful! but she will find herself disappointed."

And the little man laughed heartily at the success of his stratagem, and polished and fondled the great eye until that optic seemed to grow sore with rubbing.

"And you have been at work, too, I see, Herr Hippe. Your manikins are excellent. But where are the souls?"

"In that bottle," answered the Wondersmith, pointing to the pot-bellied black bottle that Madame Filomel had brought with her. "Yes, Monsieur Kerplonne," he continued, "my manikins are well made. I invoked the aid of Abigor, the demon of soldiery, and he inspired me. The little fellows will be famous assassins when they are animated. We will try them to-night."

"Good!" cried Kerplonne, rubbing his hands joyously. "It is close upon New Year's Day. We will fabricate millions of the little murderers by New Year's Eve, and sell them in large quantities; and when the households are all asleep, and the Christian children are waiting for Santa Claus to come, the small ones will troop from their boxes and the Christian children will die. It is famous! Health to Abigor!"

"Let us try them at once," said Oaksmith. "Is your daughter, Zonéla, in bed, Herr Hippe? Are we secure from intrusion?"

"No one is stirring about the house," replied the Wondersmith, gloomily.

Filomel leaned over to Oaksmith, and said, in an undertone,—

"Why do you mention his daughter? You know he does not like to have her spoken about."

"I will take care that we are not disturbed," said Kerplonne, rising. "I will put my eye outside the door, to watch."

He went to the door and placed his great eye upon the floor with tender care. As he did so, a dark form, unseen by him or his second vision, glided along the passage noiselessly and was lost in the darkness.

"Now for it!" exclaimed Madame Filomel, taking up her fat black bottle. "Herr Hippe, prepare your manikins!"

The Wondersmith took the little dolls out, one by one, and set them upon the table. Such an array of villainous countenances was never seen. An army of Italian bravos, seen through the wrong end of a telescope, or a band of prisoners at the galleys in Liliput, will give some faint idea of the appearance they presented. While Madame Filomel uncorked the black bottle, Herr Hippe covered the dolls over with a species of linen tent, which he took also from the box. This done, the fortune-teller held the mouth of the bottle to the door of the tent, gathering the loose cloth closely round the glass neck. Immediately, tiny noises were heard inside the tent. Madame Filomel removed the bottle, and the Wondersmith lifted the covering in which he had enveloped his little people.

A wonderful transformation had taken place. Wooden and inflexible no longer, the crowd of manikins were now in full motion. The beadlike eyes turned, glittering, on all sides; the thin, wicked lips quivered with bad passions; the tiny hands sheathed and unsheathed the little swords and daggers. Episodes, common to life, were taking place in every direction. Here two martial manikins paid court to a pretty sly-faced female, who smiled on each alternately, but gave her hand to be kissed to a third manikin, an ugly little scoundrel, who crouched behind her back. There a pair of friendly dolls walked arm in arm, apparently on the best terms, while, all the time, one was watching his opportunity to stab the other in the back.

"I think they'll do," said the Wondersmith, chuckling, as he watched these various incidents. "Treacherous, cruel, bloodthirsty. All goes marvellously well. But stay! I will put the grand test to them."

So saying, he drew a gold dollar from his pocket, and let it fall on the table in the very midst of the throng of manikins. It had hardly touched the table, when there was a pause on all sides. Every head was turned towards the dollar. Then about twenty of the little creatures rushed towards the glittering coin. One, fleeter than the rest, leaped upon it, and drew his sword. The entire crowd of little people had now gathered round this new centre of attraction. Men and women struggled and shoved to get nearer to the piece of gold. Hardly had the first Liliputian mounted upon the treasure, when a hundred blades flashed back a defiant answer to his, and a dozen men, sword in hand, leaped upon the yellow platform and drove him off at the sword's point. Then commenced a general battle. The miniature faces were convulsed with rage and avarice. Each furious doll tried to plunge dagger or sword into his or her neighbor, and the women seemed possessed by a thousand devils.

"They will break themselves into atoms," cried Filomel, as she watched with eagerness this savage *mêlée*. "You had better gather them up, Herr Hippe. I will exhaust my bottle and suck all the souls back from them."

"Oh, they are perfect devils! they are magnificent little demons!" cried the Frenchman, with enthusiasm. "Hippe, you are a wonderful man. Brother Oaksmith, you have no such man as Hippe among your English gypsies."

"Not exactly," answered Oaksmith, rather sullenly, "not exactly. But we have men there who can make a twelve-year-old horse look like a four-year-old,—and who can take you and Herr Hippe up with one hand, and throw you over their shoulders."

"The good God forbid!" said the little Frenchman. "I do not love such play. It is incommodious."

While Oaksmith and Kerplonne were talking, the Wondersmith had placed the linen tent over the struggling dolls, and Madame Filomel, who had been performing some mysterious manipulations with her black bottle, put the mouth once more to the door of the tent. In an instant the confused murmur within ceased. Madame Filomel corked the bottle quickly. The Wondersmith withdrew the tent, and, lo! the furious dolls were once more wooden-jointed and inflexible; and the old sinister look was again frozen on their faces.

"They must have blood, though," said Herr Hippe, as he gathered them up and put them into their box. "Mr. Pippel, the bird-fancier, is asleep. I have a key that opens his door. We will let them loose among the birds; it will be rare fun."

"Magnificent!" cried Kerplonne. "Let us go on the instant. But first let me gather up my eye."

The Frenchman pocketed his eye, after having given it a polish with the silk handkerchief; Herr Hippe extinguished the lamp; Oaksmith took a last bumper of Port; and the four gypsies departed for Mr. Pippel's, carrying the box of manikins with them.

III. Solon

The shadow that glided along the dark corridor, at the moment that Monsieur Kerplonne deposited his sentinel eye outside the door of the Wondersmith's apartment, sped swiftly through the passage and ascended the stairs to the attic. Here the shadow stopped at the entrance to one of the chambers and knocked at the door. There was no reply.

"Zonéla, are you asleep?" said the shadow, softly.

"Oh, Solon, is it you?" replied a sweet low voice from within. "I thought it was Herr Hippe. Come in."

The shadow opened the door and entered. There were neither candles nor lamp in the room; but through the projecting window, which was open, there came the faint gleams of the starlight, by which one could distinguish a female figure seated on a low stool in the middle of the floor.

"Has he left you without light again, Zonéla?" asked the shadow, closing the door of the apartment. "I have brought my little lantern with me, though."

"Thank you, Solon," answered she called Zonéla; "you are a good fellow. He never gives me any light of an evening, but bids me go to bed. I like to sit sometimes and look at the moon and the stars,—the stars more than all; for they seem all the time to look right back into my face, very sadly, as if they would say, 'We see you, and pity you, and would help you, if we could.' But it is so mournful to be always looking at such myriads of melancholy eyes! and I long so to read those nice books that you lend me, Solon!"

By this time the shadow had lit the lantern and was a shadow no longer. A large head, covered with a profusion of long blonde hair, which was cut after that fashion known as *à l'enfants d'Edouard;* a beautiful pale face, lit with wide, blue, dreamy eyes; long arms and slender hands, attenuated legs, and—an enormous hump;—such was Solon, the shadow. As soon as the humpback had lit the lamp, Zonéla arose from the low stool on which she had been seated, and took Solon's hand affectionately in hers.

Zonéla was surely not of gypsy blood. That rich auburn hair, that looked almost black in the lamp-light, that pale, transparent skin, tinged with an under-glow of warm rich blood, the hazel eyes, large and soft as those of a fawn, were never begotten of a Zingaro. Zonéla was seemingly about sixteen; her figure, although somewhat thin and angular, was full of the unconscious grace of youth. She was dressed in an old cotton print, which had been once of an exceedingly boisterous pattern, but was now a mere suggestion of former splendor; while round her head was twisted, in fantastic fashion, a silk handkerchief of green ground spotted with bright crimson. This strange headdress gave her an elfish appearance.

"I have been out all day with the organ, and I am so tired, Solon!—not sleepy, but weary, I mean. Poor Furbelow was sleepy, though, and he's gone to bed."

"I'm weary, too, Zonéla;—not weary as you are, though, for I sit in my little book-stall all day long, and do not drag round an organ and a monkey and play old tunes for pennies,—but weary of myself, of life, of the load that I carry on my shoulders"; and, as he said this, the poor humpback glanced sideways, as if to call attention to his deformed person.

"Well, but you ought not to be melancholy amidst your books, Solon. Gracious! If I could only sit in the sun and read as you do, how happy I should be! But it's very tiresome to trudge round all day with that nasty organ, and look up at the houses, and know that you are annoying the people inside; and then the boys play such bad tricks on poor Furbelow, throwing him hot pennies to pick up, and burning his poor little hands; and oh! sometimes, Solon, the men in the street make me so afraid,—they speak to me and look at me so oddly!—I'd a great deal rather sit in your book-stall and read."

"I have nothing but odd volumes in my stall," answered the humpback. "Perhaps that's right, though; for, after all, I'm nothing but an odd volume myself."

"Come, don't be melancholy, Solon. Sit down and tell me a story. I'll bring Furbelow to listen."

So saying, she went to a dusk corner of the cheerless attic-room, and returned with a little Brazilian monkey in her arms,—a poor, mild, drowsy thing, that looked as if it had cried itself to sleep. She sat down on her little stool, with Furbelow in her lap, and nodded her head to Solon, as much as to say, "Go on; we are attentive."

"You want a story, do you?" said the humpback, with a mournful smile. "Well, I'll tell you one. Only what will your father say, if he catches me here?"

"Herr Hippe is not my father," cried Zonéla, indignantly. "He's a gypsy, and I know I'm stolen; and I'd run away from him, if I only knew where to run to. If I were his child, do you think that he would treat me as he does? make me trudge round the city, all day long, with a barrel-organ and a monkey,—though I love poor dear little Furbelow,—and keep me up in a garret, and give me ever so little to eat? I know I'm not his child, for he hates me."

"Listen to my story, Zonéla, and we'll talk of that afterwards. Let me sit at your feet";—and, having coiled himself up at the little maiden's feet, he commenced:—

"There once lived in a great city, just like this city of New York, a poor little hunchback. He kept a second-hand book-stall, where he made barely enough money to keep body and soul together. He was very sad at times, because he knew scarce any one, and those that he did know did not love him. He had passed a sickly, secluded youth. The children of his neighborhood would not play with him, for he was not made like them; and the people in the streets stared at him with pity, or scoffed at him when he went by. Ah! Zonéla, how his poor heart was wrung with bitterness when he beheld the procession of shapely men and fine women that every day passed him by in the thoroughfares of the great city! How he repined and cursed his fate as the torrent of fleet-footed firemen dashed past him to the toll of the bells, magnificent in their overflowing vitality and strength! But there was one consolation left him,—one drop of honey in the jar of gall, so sweet that it ameliorated all the bitterness of life. God had given him a deformed body, but his mind was straight and healthy. So the poor hunchback shut himself into the world of books, and was, if not happy, at least contented. He kept company with courteous paladins, and romantic heroes, and beautiful women; and this society was of such excellent breeding that it never so much as once noticed his poor crooked back or his lame walk. The love of books grew upon him with his years. He was remarked for his studious habits; and when, one day, the obscure people that he called father and mother—parents only in name—died, a compassionate book-vendor gave him enough stock in trade to set up a little stall of his own. Here, in his book-stall, he sat in the sun all day, waiting for the customers that seldom came, and reading the fine deeds of the people of the ancient time, or the beautiful thoughts of the poets that had warmed millions of hearts before that hour, and still glowed for him with undiminished fire. One day, when he was reading some book, that, small as it was, was big enough to shut the whole world out from him, he heard some music in the street. Looking up from his book, he saw a little girl, with large eyes, playing an organ, while a monkey begged for alms from a crowd of idlers who had nothing in their pockets but their hands. The girl was playing, but she was also weeping. The merry notes of the polka were ground out to a silent accompaniment of tears. She looked very sad, this organ-girl, and her monkey seemed to have caught the infection, for his large brown eyes were moist, as if he also wept. The poor hunchback was struck with pity, and called the little girl over to give her a penny,—not, dear Zonéla, because he wished to bestow alms, but because he wanted to speak with her. She came, and they talked together. She came the next day,—for it turned out that they were neighbors,—and the next, and, in short, every day. They became friends. They were both lonely and afflicted, with this difference, that she was beautiful, and he—was a hunchback."

"Why, Solon," cried Zonéla, "that's the very way you and I met!"

"It was then," continued Solon, with a faint smile, "that life seemed to have its music. A great harmony seemed to the poor cripple to fill the world. The carts that took the flour-barrels from the wharves to the storehouses seemed to emit joyous melodies from their wheels. The hum of the great business-streets sounded like grand symphonies of triumph. As one who has been travelling through a barren country without much heed feels with singular force the sterility of the lands he has passed through when he reaches the fertile plains that lie at the end of his journey, so the humpback, after his vision had been freshened with this blooming flower, remembered for the first time the misery of the life that he had led. But he did not allow himself to dwell upon the past. The present was so delightful that it occupied all his thoughts. Zonéla, he was in love with the organ-girl."

"Oh, that's so nice!" said Zonéla, innocently,—pinching poor Furbelow, as she spoke, in order to dispel a very evident snooze that was creeping over him. "It's going to be a love-story."

"Ah! but, Zonéla, he did not know whether she loved him in return. You forget that he was deformed."

"But," answered the girl, gravely, "he was good."

A light like the flash of an aurora illuminated Solon's face for an instant. He put out his hand suddenly, as if to take Zonéla's and press it to his heart; but an unaccountable timidity seemed to arrest the impulse, and he only stroked Furbelow's head,—upon which that individual opened one large brown eye to the extent of the eighth of an inch, and, seeing that it was only Solon, instantly closed it again, and resumed his dream of a city where there were no organs and all the copper coin of the realm was iced.

"He hoped and feared," continued Solon, in a low, mournful voice; "but at times he was very miserable, because he did not think it possible that so much happiness was reserved for him as the love of this beautiful, innocent girl. At night, when he was in bed, and all the world was dreaming, he lay awake looking up at the old books that hung against the walls, thinking how he could bring about the charming of her heart. One night, when he was thinking of this, with his eyes fixed upon the mouldy backs of the odd volumes that lay on their shelves, and looked back at him wistfully, as if they would say,—'We also are like you, and wait to be completed,'—it seemed as if he heard a rustle of leaves. Then, one by one, the books came down from their places to the floor, as if shifted by invisible hands, opened their worm-eaten covers, and from between the pages of each the hunchback saw issue forth a curious throng of little people that danced here and there through the apartment. Each one of these little creatures was shaped so as to bear resemblance to some one of the letters of the alphabet. One tall, long-legged fellow seemed like the letter A; a burly fellow, with a big head and a paunch, was the model of B; another leering little chap might have passed for a Q; and so on through the whole. These fairies—for fairies they were—climbed upon the hunchback's bed, and clustered thick as bees upon his pillow. 'Come!' they cried to him, 'we will lead you into fairy-land.' So saying, they seized his hand, and he suddenly found himself in a beautiful country, where the light did not come from sun or moon or stars, but floated round and over and in everything like the atmosphere. On all sides he heard mysterious melodies sung by strangely musical voices. None of the features of the landscape were definite; yet when he looked on the vague harmonies of color that melted one into another before his sight, he was filled with a sense of inexplicable beauty. On every side of him fluttered radiant bodies which darted to and fro through the illumined space. They were not birds, yet they flew like birds; and as each one crossed the path of his vision, he felt a strange delight flash through his brain, and straightway an interior voice seemed to sing beneath the vaulted dome of his temples a verse containing some beautiful thought. The little fairies were all this time dancing and fluttering around him, perching on his head, on his shoulders, or balancing themselves on his finger-tips. 'Where am I?' he asked, at last, of his friends, the fairies. 'Ah! Solon,' he heard them whisper, in tones that sounded like the distant tinkling of silver bells, 'this land is nameless; but those whom we lead hither, who tread its soil, and breathe its air, and gaze on its floating sparks of light, are poets forevermore!' Having said this, they vanished, and with them the beautiful indefinite land, and the flashing lights, and the illumined air; and the hunchback found himself again in bed, with the moonlight quivering on the floor, and the dusty books on their shelves, grim and mouldy as ever."

"You have betrayed yourself. You called yourself Solon," cried Zonéla. "Was it a dream?"

"I do not know," answered Solon; "but since that night I have been a poet."

"A poet?" screamed the little organ-girl,—"a real poet, who makes verses which every one reads and every one talks of?"

"The people call me a poet," answered Solon, with a sad smile. "They do not know me by the name of Solon, for I write under an assumed title; but they praise me, and repeat my songs. But Zonéla, I can't sing this load off of my back, can I?"

"Oh, bother the hump!" said Zonéla, jumping up suddenly. "You're a poet, and that's enough, isn't it? I'm so glad you're a poet, Solon! You must repeat all your best things to me, won't you?"

Solon nodded assent.

"You don't ask me," he said, "who was the little girl that the hunchback loved."

Zonéla's face flushed crimson. She turned suddenly away, and ran into a dark corner of the room. In a moment she returned with an old hand-organ in her arms.

"Play, Solon, play!" she cried. "I am so glad that I want to dance. Furbelow, come and dance in honor of Solon the Poet."

It was her confession. Solon's eyes flamed, as if his brain had suddenly ignited. He said nothing; but a triumphant smile broke over his countenance. Zonéla, the twilight of whose cheeks was still rosy with the setting blush, caught the lazy Furbelow by his little paws; Solon turned the crank of the organ, which wheezed out as merry a polka as its asthma would allow, and the girl and the monkey commenced their fantastic dance. They had taken but a few steps when the door suddenly opened, and the tall figure of the Wondersmith appeared on the threshold. His face was convulsed with rage, and the black snake that quivered on his upper lip seemed to rear itself as if about to spring upon the hunchback.

IV. THE MANIKINS AND THE MINOS

The four gypsies left Herr Hippe's house cautiously, and directed their steps towards Mr. Pippel's bird-shop. Golosh Street was asleep. Nothing was stirring in that tenebrous slum, save a dog that savagely gnawed a bone which lay on a dust-heap, tantalizing him with the flavor of food without its substance. As the gypsies moved stealthily along in the darkness, they had a sinister and murderous air that would not have failed to attract the attention of the policeman of the quarter, if that worthy had not at the moment been comfortably ensconced in the neighboring "Rainbow" bar-room, listening to the improvisations of that talented vocalist, Mr. Harrison, who was making impromptu verses on every possible subject, to the accompaniment of a citheru which was played by a sad little Italian in a large cloak, to whom the host of the "Rainbow" gave so many toddies and a dollar for his nightly performance.

Mr. Pippel's shop was but a short distance from the Wondersmith's house. A few moments, therefore, brought the gypsy party to the door, when, by aid of a key which Herr Hippe produced, they silently slipped into the entry. Here the Wondersmith took a dark-lantern from under his cloak, removed the cap that shrouded the light, and led the way into the shop, which was separated from the entry only by a glass door, that yielded, like the outer one, to a key which Hippe took from his pocket. The four gypsies now entered the shop and closed the door behind them.

It was a little world of birds. On every side, whether in large or small cages, one beheld balls of various-colored feathers standing on one leg and breathing peacefully. Love-birds, nestling shoulder to shoulder, with their heads tucked under their wings and all their feathers puffed out, so that they looked like globes of malachite; English bullfinches, with ashen-colored backs, in which their black heads were buried, and corselets of a rosy down; Java sparrows, fat and sleek and cleanly; troupials, so glossy and splendid in plumage that they looked as if they were dressed in the celebrated armor of the Black Prince, which was jet, richly damascened with gold; a cock of the rock, gleaming, a ball of tawny fire, like a setting sun; the Campanero of Brazil, white as snow, with his dilatable tolling-tube hanging from his head, placid and silent;—these, with a humbler crowd of linnets, canaries, robins, mocking-birds, and phoebes, slumbered calmly in their little cages, that were hung so thickly on the wall as not to leave an inch of it visible.

"Splendid little morsels, all of them!" exclaimed Monsieur Kerplonne. "Ah we are going to have a rare beating!"

"So Pippel does not sleep in his shop," said the English gypsy, Oaksmith.

"No. The fellow lives somewhere up one of the avenues," answered Madame Filomel. "He came, the other evening, to consult me about his fortune. I did not tell him," she added, with a laugh, "that he was going to have so distinguished a sporting party on his premises."

"Come," said the Wondersmith, producing the box of manikins, "get ready with souls, Madame Filomel. I am impatient to see my little men letting out lives for the first time."

Just at the moment that the Wondersmith uttered this sentence, the four gypsies were startled by a hoarse voice issuing from a corner of the room, and propounding in the most guttural tones the intemperate query of "What'll you take?" This sottish invitation had scarce been given, when a second extremely thick voice replied from an opposite corner, in accents so rough that they seemed to issue from a throat torn and furrowed by the liquid lava of many barrooms, "Brandy and water."

"Hollo! who's here?" muttered Herr Hippe, flashing the light of his lantern round the shop.

Oaksmith turned up his coat-cuffs, as if to be ready for a fight; Madame Filomel glided, or rather rolled, towards the door; while Kerplonne put his hand into his pocket, as if to assure himself that his supernumerary optic was all right.

"What'll you take?" croaked the voice in the corner, once more.

"Brandy and water," rapidly replied the second voice in the other corner. And then, as if by a concerted movement, a series of bibular invitations and acceptances were rolled backwards and forwards with a volubility of utterance that threw Patter *versus* Clatter into the shade.

"What the Devil can it be?" muttered the Wondersmith, flashing his lantern here and there. "Ah! it is those Minos."

So saying, he stopped under one of the wicker cages that hung high up on the wall, and raised the lantern above his head, so as to throw the light upon that particular cage. The hospitable individual who had been extending all these hoarse invitations to partake of intoxicating beverages was an inhabitant of the cage. It was a large Mino-bird, who now stood perched on his cross-bar, with his yellowish orange bill sloped slightly over his shoulder, and his white eye cocked knowingly upon the Wondersmith. The respondent voice in the other corner came from another Mino-bird, who sat in the dusk in a similar cage, also attentively watching the Wondersmith. These Mino-birds, I may remark, in passing, have a singular aptitude for acquiring phrases.

"What'll you take?" repeated the Mino, cocking his other eye upon Herr Hippe.

"*Mon Dieu!* what a bird!" exclaimed the little Frenchman. "He is, in truth, polite."

"I don't know what I'll take," said Hippe, as if replying to the Mino-bird; "but I know what you'll get, old fellow! Filomel, open the cage-doors, and give me the bottle."

Filomel opened, one after another, the doors of the numberless little cages, thereby arousing from slumber their feathered occupants, who opened their beaks, and stretched their claws, and stared with great surprise at the lantern and the midnight visitors.

By this time the Wondersmith had performed the mysterious manipulations with the bottle, and the manikins were once more in full motion, swarming out of their box, sword and dagger in hand, with their little black eyes glittering fiercely, and their white teeth shining. The little creatures seemed to scent their prey. The gypsies stood in the centre of the shop, watching the proceedings eagerly, while the Liliputians made in a body towards the wall and commenced climbing from cage to cage. Then was heard a tremendous fluttering of wings, and faint, despairing "quirks" echoed on all sides. In almost every cage there was a fierce manikin thrusting his sword or dagger vigorously into the body of some unhappy bird. It recalled the antique legend of the battles of the Pygmies and the Cranes. The poor lovebirds lay with their emerald feathers dabbled in their hearts' blood, shoulder to shoulder in death as in life. Canaries gasped at the bottom of their cages, while the water in their little glass fountains ran red. The bullfinches wore an unnatural crimson on their breasts. The mocking-bird lay on his back, kicking spasmodically, in the last agonies, with a tiny sword-thrust cleaving his melodious throat in twain, so that from the instrument which used to gush with wondrous music only scarlet drops of blood now trickled. The manikins were ruthless. Their faces were ten times wickeder than ever, as they roamed from cage to cage, slaughtering with a fury that seemed entirely unappeasable. Presently the feathery rustlings became fewer and fainter, and the little pipings of despair died away; and in every cage lay a poor murdered minstrel, with the song that abode within him forever quenched;—in every cage but two, and those two were high up on the wall; and in each glared a pair of wild, white eyes; and an orange beak, tough as steel, pointed threateningly down. With the needles which they grasped as swords all wet and warm with blood, and their beadlike eyes flashing in the light of the lantern, the Liliputian assassins swarmed up the cages in two separate bodies, until they reached the wickets of the habitations in which the Minos abode. Mino saw them coming,—had listened attentively to the many death-struggles of his comrades, and had, in fact, smelt a rat. Accordingly he was ready for the manikins. There he stood at the barbican of his castle, with formidable beak couched like a lance. The manikins made a gallant charge. "What'll you take?" was rattled out by the Mino, in a deep bass, as with one plunge of his sharp bill he scattered the ranks of the enemy, and sent three of them flying to the floor, where they lay with broken limbs. But the manikins were brave automats, and again they closed and charged the gallant Mino. Again the wicked white eyes of the bird gleamed, and again the orange bill dealt destruction. Everything seemed to be going on swimmingly for Mino, when he found himself attacked in the rear by two treacherous manikins, who had stolen upon him from behind, through the lattice-work of the cage. Quick as lightning the Mino turned to repel this assault, but all too late; two slender quivering threads of steel crossed in his poor body, and he staggered into a corner of the cage. His white eyes closed, then opened; a shiver passed over his body, beginning at his shoulder-tips and dying off in the extreme tips of the wings; he gasped as if for air, and then, with a convulsive shudder, which ruffled all his feathers, croaked out feebly his little speech, "What'll you take?" Instantly from the opposite corner came the old response, still feebler than the question,—a mere gurgle, as it were, of "Brandy and water." Then all was silent. The Mino-birds were dead.

"They spill blood like Christians," said the Wondersmith, gazing fondly on the manikins. "They will be famous assassins."

V. Tied Up

Herr Hippe stood in the doorway, scowling. His eyes seemed to scorch the poor hunchback, whose form, physically inferior, crouched before that baneful, blazing glance, while his head, mentally brave, reared itself, as if to redeem the cowardice of the frame to which it belonged. So the attitude of the serpent: the body pliant, yielding, supple; but the crest thrown aloft, erect, and threatening. As for Zonéla, she was frozen in the attitude of motion;—a dancing nymph in colored marble; agility stunned; elasticity petrified.

Furbelow, astonished at this sudden change, and catching, with all the mysterious rapidity of instinct peculiar to the lower animals, at the enigmatical character of the situation, turned his pleading, melancholy eyes from one to another of the motionless three, as if begging that his humble intellect (pardon me, naturalists, for the use of this word "intellect" in the matter of a monkey!) should be enlightened as speedily as possible. Not receiving the desired information, he, after the manner of trained animals, returned to his muttons; in other words, he conceived that this unusual entrance, and consequent dramatic *tableau,* meant "shop." He therefore dropped Zonéla's hand and pattered on his velvety little feet over towards the grim figure of the Wondersmith, holding out his poor little paw for the customary copper. He had but one idea drilled into him,—soulless creature that he was,—and that was, alms. But I have seen creatures that professed to have souls, and that would have been indignant, if you had denied them immortality, who took to the soliciting of alms as naturally as if beggary had been the original sin, and was regularly born with them, and never baptized out of them. I will give these Bandits of the Order of Charity this credit, however, that they knew the best highways and the richest founts of benevolence,—unlike to Furbelow, who, unreasoning and undiscriminating, begged from the first person that was near. Furbelow, owing to this intellectual inferiority to the before-mentioned Alsatians, frequently got more kicks than coppers, and the present supplication which he indulged in towards the Wondersmith was a terrible confirmation of the rule. The reply to the extended pleading paw was what might be called a double-barrelled kick,—a kick to be represented by the power of two when the foot touched the object, multiplied by four when the entire leg formed an angle of 45° with the spinal column. The long, nervous leg of the Wondersmith caught the little creature in the centre of the body, doubled up his brown, hairy form, till he looked like a fur driving-glove, and sent him whizzing across the room into a far corner, where he dropped senseless and flaccid.

This vengeance which Herr Hippe executed upon Furbelow seemed to have operated as a sort of escape-valve, and he found voice. He hissed out the question, "Who are you?" to the hunchback; and in listening to that essence of sibillation, it really seemed as if it proceeded from the serpent that curled upon his upper lip.

"Who are you? Deformed dog, who are you? What do you here?"

"My name is Solon," answered the fearless head of the hunchback, while the frail, cowardly body shivered and trembled inch by inch into a corner.

"So you come to visit my daughter in the night-time, when I am away?" continued the Wondersmith, with a sneering tone that dropped from his snake-wreathed mouth like poison. "You are a brave and gallant lover, are you not? Where did you win that Order of the Curse of God that decorates your shoulders? The women turn their heads and look after you in the street, when you pass, do they not? lost in admiration of that symmetrical figure, those graceful limbs, that neck pliant as the stem that moors the lotus! Elegant, conquering, Christian cripple, what do you here in my daughter's room?"

Can you imagine Jove, limitless in power and wrath, hurling from his vast grasp mountain after mountain upon the struggling Enceladus,—and picture the Titan sinking, sinking, deeper and deeper into the earth, crushed and dying, with nothing visible through the super-incumbent masses of Pelion and Ossa, but a gigantic head and two flaming eyes, that, despite the death which is creeping through each vein, still flash back defiance to the divine enemy? Well, Solon and Herr Hippe presented such a picture, seen through the wrong end of a telescope,—reduced in proportion, but alike in action. Solon's feeble body seemed to sink into utter annihilation beneath the horrible taunts that his enemy hurled at him, while the large, brave brow and unconquered eyes still sent forth a magnetic resistance.

Suddenly the poor hunchback felt his arm grasped. A thrill seemed to run through his entire body. A warm atmosphere, invigorating and full of delicious odor, surrounded him. It appeared as if invisible bandages were twisted all about his limbs, giving him a strange strength. His sinking legs straightened. His powerless arms were braced. Astonished, he glanced round for an instant, and beheld Zonéla, with a world of love burning in her large lambent eyes, wreathing her round white arms about his humped shoulders. Then the poet knew the great sustaining power of love. Solon reared himself boldly.

"Sneer at my poor form," he cried, in strong vibrating tones, flinging out one long arm and one thin finger at the Wondersmith, as if he would have impaled him like a beetle. "Humiliate me, if you can. I care not. You are a wretch, and I am honest and pure. This girl is not your daughter. You are like one of those demons in the fairy tales that held beauty and purity locked in infernal spells. I do not fear you, Herr Hippe. There are stories abroad about you in the neighborhood, and when you pass, people say that they feel evil and blight hovering over their thresholds. You persecute this girl. You are her tyrant. You hate her. I am a cripple. Providence has cast this lump upon my shoulders. But that is nothing. The camel, that is the salvation of the children of the desert, has been given his hump in order that he might bear his human burden better. This girl, who is homeless as the Arab, is my appointed load in life, and, please God, I will carry her on this back, hunched though it may be. I have come to see her, because I love her,—because she loves me. You have no claim on her: so I will take her from you."

Quick as lightning, the Wondersmith had stridden a few paces, and grasped the poor cripple, who was yet quivering with the departing thunder of his passion. He seized him in his bony, muscular grasp, as he would have seized a puppet, and held him at arm's length gasping and powerless; while Zonéla, pale, breathless, entreating, sank half-kneeling on the floor.

"Your skeleton will be interesting to science when you are dead, Mr. Solon," hissed the Wondersmith. "But before I have the pleasure of reducing you to an anatomy, which I will assuredly do, I wish to compliment you on your power of penetration, or sources of information; for I know not if you have derived your knowledge from your own mental research or the efforts of others. You are perfectly correct in your statement, that this charming young person, who day after day parades the streets with a barrel-organ and a monkey,—the last unhappily indisposed at present,— listening to the degrading jokes of ribald boys and depraved men,—you are quite correct, Sir, in stating that she is not my daughter. On the contrary, she is the daughter of an Hungarian nobleman who had the misfortune to incur my displeasure. I had a son, crooked spawn of a Christian!—a son, not like you, cankered, gnarled stump of life that you are,—but a youth tall and fair and noble in aspect, as became a child of one whose lineage makes Pharaoh modern,—a youth whose foot in the dance was as swift and beautiful to look at as the golden sandals of the sun when he dances upon the sea in summer. This youth was virtuous and good; and being of good race, and dwelling in a country where his rank, gypsy as he was, was recognized, he mixed with the proudest of the land. One day he fell in with this accursed Hungarian, a fierce drinker of that Devil's blood called brandy. My child until that hour had avoided this bane of our race. Generous wine he drank, because the soul of the sun our ancestor palpitated in its purple waves. But brandy, which is fallen and accursed wine, as devils are fallen and accursed angels, had never crossed his lips, until in an evil hour he was seduced by this Christian hog, and from that day forth his life was one fiery debauch, which set only in the black waves of death. I vowed vengeance on the destroyer of my child, and I kept my word. I have destroyed *his* child,—not compassed her death, but blighted her life, steeped her in misery and poverty, and now, thanks to the thousand devils, I have discovered a new torture for her heart. She thought to solace her life with a love-episode! Sweet little epicure that she was! She shall have her little crooked lover, shan't she? Oh, yes! She shall have him, cold and stark and livid, with that great, black, heavy hunch, which no back, however broad, can bear, Death, sitting between his shoulders!"

There was something so awful and demoniac in this entire speech and the manner in which it was delivered, that it petrified Zonéla into a mere inanimate figure, whose eyes seemed unalterably fixed on the fierce, cruel face of the Wondersmith. As for Solon, he was paralyzed in the grasp of his foe. He heard, but could not reply. His large eyes, dilated with horror to far beyond their ordinary size, expressed unutterable agony.

The last sentence had hardly been hissed out by the gypsy when he took from his pocket a long, thin coil of whipcord, which he entangled in a complicated mesh around the cripple's body. It was not the ordinary binding of a prisoner. The slender lash passed and repassed in a thousand intricate folds over the powerless limbs of the poor humpback. When the operation was completed, he looked as if he had been sewed from head to foot in some singularly ingenious species of network.

"Now, my pretty lop-sided little lover," laughed Herr Hippe, flinging Solon over his shoulder, as a fisherman might fling a net-full of fish, "we will proceed to put you into your little cage until your little coffin is quite ready. Meanwhile we will lock up your darling beggar-girl to mourn over your untimely end."

So saying, he stepped from the room with his captive, and securely locked the door behind him.

When he had disappeared, the frozen Zonéla thawed, and with a shriek of anguish flung herself on the inanimate body of Furbelow.

VI. THE POISONING OF THE SWORDS

It was New Year's Eve, and eleven o'clock at night. All over this great land, and in every great city in the land, curly heads were lying on white pillows, dreaming of the coming of the generous Santa Claus. Innumerable stockings hung by countless bedsides. Visions of beautiful toys, passing in splendid pageantry through myriads of dimly lit dormitories, made millions of little hearts palpitate in sleep. Ah! what heavenly toys those were that the children of this soil beheld, that mystic night, in their dreams! Painted cars with orchestral wheels, making music more delicious than the roll of planets. Agile men of cylindrical figure, who sprang unexpectedly out of meek-looking boxes, with a supernatural fierceness in their crimson cheeks and fur-whiskers. Herds of marvellous sheep, with fleeces as impossible as the one that Jason sailed after; animals entirely indifferent to grass and water and "rot" and "ticks." Horses spotted with an astounding regularity, and furnished with the most ingenious methods of locomotion. Slender foreigners, attired in painfully short tunics, whose existence passed in continually turning heels over head down a steep flight of steps, at the bottom of which they lay in an exhausted condition with dislocated limbs, until they were restored to their former elevation, when they went at it again as if nothing had happened. Stately swans, that seemed to have a touch of the ostrich in them; for they swam continually after a piece of iron which was held before them, as if consumed with a ferruginous hunger. Whole farm-yards of roosters, whose tails curled the wrong way,—a slight defect, that was, however, amply atoned for by the size and brilliancy of their scarlet combs, which, it would appear, Providence had intended for penwipers. Pears, that, when applied to youthful lips, gave forth sweet and inspiring sounds. Regiments of soldiers, that performed neat, but limited evolutions on cross-jointed contractile battle-fields. All these things, idealized, transfigured, and illuminated by the powers and atmosphere and colored lamps of Dreamland, did the millions of dear sleeping children behold, the night of the New Year's Eve of which I speak.

It was on this night, when Time was preparing to shed his skin and come out young and golden and glossy as ever,—when, in the vast chambers of the universe, silent and infallible preparations were making for the wonderful birth of the coming year,—when mystic dews were secreted for his baptism, and mystic instruments were tuned in space to welcome him, —it was at this holy and solemn hour that the Wondersmith and his three gypsy companions sat in close conclave in the little parlor before mentioned.

There was a fire roaring in the grate. On a table, nearly in the centre of the room, stood a huge decanter of Port wine, that glowed in the blaze which lit the chamber like a flask of crimson fire. On every side, piled in heaps, inanimate, but scowling with the same old wondrous scowl, lay myriads of the manikins, all clutching in their wooden hands their tiny weapons. The Wondersmith held in one hand a small silver bowl filled with a green, glutinous substance, which he was delicately applying, with the aid of a camel's-hair brush, to the tips of tiny swords and daggers. A horrible smile wandered over his sallow face,—a smile as unwholesome in appearance as the sickly light that plays above reeking graveyards.

"Let us drink great draughts, brothers," he cried, leaving off his strange anointment for a while, to lift a great glass, filled with sparkling liquor, to his lips. "Let us drink to our approaching triumph. Let us drink to the great poison, Macousha. Subtle seed of Death,—swift hurricane that sweeps away Life,—vast hammer that crushes brain and heart and artery with its resistless weight,—I drink to it."

"It is a noble decoction, Duke Balthazar," said the old fortune-teller and midwife, Madame Filomel, nodding in her chair as she swallowed her wine in great gulps. "Where did you obtain it?"

"It is made," said the Wondersmith, swallowing another great goblet-full of wine ere he replied, "in the wild woods of Guiana, in silence and in mystery. But one tribe of Indians, the Macoushi Indians, know the secret. It is simmered over fires built of strange woods, and the maker of it dies in the making. The place, for a mile around the spot where it is fabricated, is shunned as accursed. Devils hover over the pot in which it stews; and the birds of the air, scenting the smallest breath of its vapor from far away, drop to earth with paralyzed wings, cold and dead."

"It kills, then, fast?" asked Kerplonne, the artificial eyemaker,—his own eyes gleaming, under the influence of the wine, with a sinister lustre, as if they had been fresh from the factory, and were yet untarnished by use.

"Kills?" echoed the Wondersmith, derisively; "it is swifter than thunderbolts, stronger than lightning. But you shall see it proved before we let forth our army on the city accursed. You shall see a wretch die, as if smitten by a falling fragment of the sun."

"What? Do you mean Solon?" asked Oaksmith and the fortune-teller together.

"Ah! you mean the young man who makes the commerce with books?" echoed Kerplonne. "It is well. His agonies will instruct us."

"Yes! Solon," answered Hippe, with a savage accent. "I hate him, and he shall die this horrid death. Ah! how the little fellows will leap upon him, when I bring him in, bound and helpless, and give their beautiful wicked souls to them! How they will pierce him in ten thousand spots with their poisoned weapons, until his skin turns blue and violet and crimson, and his form swells with the venom,—until his hump is lost in shapeless flesh! He hears what I say, every word of it. He is in the closet next door, and is listening. How comfortable he feels! How the sweat of terror rolls on his brow! How he tries to loosen his bonds, and curses all earth and heaven when he finds that he cannot! Ho! ho! Handsome lover of Zonéla, will she kiss you when you are livid and swollen? Brothers, let us drink again,—drink always. Here, Oaksmith, take these brushes,—and you, Filomel,—and finish the anointing of these swords. This wine is grand. This poison is grand. It is fine to have good wine to drink, and good poison to kill with; is it not?" and, with flushed face and rolling eyes, the Wondersmith continued to drink and use his brush alternately.

The others hastened to follow his example. It was a horrible scene: those four wicked faces; those myriads of tiny faces, just as wicked; the certain unearthly air that pervaded the apartment; the red, unwholesome glare cast by the fire; the wild and reckless way in which the weird company drank the red-illumined wine.

The anointing of the swords went on rapidly, and the wine went as rapidly down the throats of the four poisoners. Their faces grew more and more inflamed each instant; their eyes shone like rolling fireballs; their hair was moist and dishevelled. The old fortune-teller rocked to and fro in her chair, like those legless plaster figures that sway upon convex loaded bottoms. All four began to mutter incoherent sentences, and babble unintelligible wickednesses. Still the anointing of the swords went on.

"I see the faces of millions of young corpses," babbled Herr Hippe, gazing, with swimming eyes, into the silver bowl that contained the Macousha poison,—"all young, all Christians,—and the little fellows dancing, dancing, and stabbing, stabbing. Filomel, Filomel, I say!"

"Well, Grand Duke," snored the old woman, giving a violent lurch.

"Where's the bottle of souls?"

"In my right-hand pocket, Herr Hippe"; and she felt, so as to assure herself that it was there. She half drew out the black bottle, before described in this narrative, and let it slide again into her pocket,—let it slide again, but it did not completely regain its former place. Caught by some accident, it hung half out, swaying over the edge of the pocket, as the fat midwife rolled backwards and forwards in her drunken efforts at equilibrium.

"All right," said Herr Hippe, "perfectly right! Let's drink."

He reached out his hand for his glass, and, with a dull sigh, dropped on the table, in the instantaneous slumber of intoxication. Oaksmith soon fell back in his chair, breathing heavily. Kerplonne followed. And the heavy, stertorous breathing of Filomel told that she slumbered also; but still her chair retained its rocking motion, and still the bottle of souls balanced itself on the edge of her pocket.

VII. Let Loose

Sure enough, Solon heard every word of the fiendish talk of the Wondersmith. For how many days he had been shut up, bound in the terrible net, in that dark closet, he did not know; but now he felt that his last hour was come. His little strength was completely worn out in efforts to disentangle himself. Once a day a door opened, and Herr Hippe placed a crust of bread and a cup of water within his reach. On this meagre fare he had subsisted. It was a hard life; but, bad as it was, it was better than the horrible death that menaced him. His brain reeled with terror at the prospect of it. Then, where was Zonéla? Why did she not come to his rescue? But she was, perhaps, dead. The darkness, too, appalled him. A faint light, when the moon was bright, came at night through a chink far up in the wall; and the only other hole in the chamber was an aperture through which, at some former time, a stove-pipe had been passed. Even if he were free, there would have been small hope of escape; but, laced as it were in a network of steel, what was to be done? He groaned and writhed upon the floor, and tore at the boards with his hands, which were free from the wrists down. All else was as solidly laced up as an Indian papoose. Nothing but pride kept him from shrieking aloud, when, on the night of New Year's Eve, he heard the fiendish Hippe recite the programme of his murder.

While he was thus wailing and gnashing his teeth in darkness and torture, he heard a faint noise above his head. Then something seemed to leap from the ceiling and alight softly on the floor. He shuddered with terror. Was it some new torture of the Wondersmith's invention? The next moment, he felt some small animal crawling over his body, and a soft, silky paw was pushed timidly across his face. His heart leaped with joy.

"It is Furbelow!" he cried. "Zonéla has sent him. He came through the stove-pipe hole."

It was Furbelow, indeed, restored to life by Zonéla's care, and who had come down a narrow tube, that no human being could have threaded, to console the poor captive. The monkey nestled closely into the hunchback's bosom, and as he did so, Solon felt something cold and hard hanging from his neck. He touched it. It was sharp. By the dim light that struggled through the aperture high up in the wall, he discovered a knife, suspended by a bit of cord. Ah! how the blood came rushing through the veins that crossed over and through his heart, when life and liberty came to him in this bit of rusty steel! With his manacled hands he loosened the heaven-sent weapon; a few cuts were rapidly made in the cunning network of cord that enveloped his limbs, and in a few seconds he was free!— cramped and faint with hunger, but free!—free to move, to use the limbs that God had given him for his preservation,—free to fight,—to die fighting, perhaps,—but still to die free. He ran to the door. The bolt was a weak one, for the Wondersmith had calculated more surely on his prison of cords than on any jail of stone,—and more; and with a few efforts the door opened. He went cautiously out into the darkness, with Furbelow perched on his shoulder, pressing his cold muzzle against his cheek. He had made but a few steps when a trembling hand was put into his, and in another moment Zonéla's palpitating heart was pressed against his own. One long kiss, an embrace, a few whispered words, and the hunchback and the girl stole softly towards the door of the chamber in which the four gypsies slept. All seemed still; nothing but the hard breathing of the sleepers, and the monotonous rocking of Madame Filomel's chair broke the silence. Solon stooped down and put his eye to the keyhole, through which a red bar of light streamed into the entry. As he did so, his foot crushed some brittle substance that lay just outside the door; at the same moment a howl of agony was heard to issue from the room within. Solon started; nor did he know that at that instant he had crushed into dust Monsieur Kerplonne's supernumerary eye, and the owner, though wrapt in a drunken sleep, felt the pang quiver through his brain.

While Solon peeped through the keyhole, all in the room was motionless. He had not gazed, however, for many seconds, when the chair of the fortune-teller gave a sudden lurch, and the black bottle, already hanging half out of her wide pocket, slipped entirely from its resting-place, and, falling heavily to the ground, shivered into fragments.

Then took place an astonishing spectacle. The myriads of armed dolls, that lay in piles about the room, became suddenly imbued with motion. They stood up straight, their tiny limbs moved, their black eyes flashed with wicked purposes, their thread-like swords gleamed as they waved them to and fro. The villainous souls imprisoned in the bottle began to work within them. Like the Liliputians, when they found the giant Gulliver asleep, they scaled in swarms the burly sides of the four sleeping gypsies. At every step they took, they drove their thin swords and quivering daggers into the flesh of the drunken authors of their being. To stab and kill was their mission, and they stabbed and killed with incredible fury. They clustered on the Wondersmith's sallow cheeks and sinewy throat, piercing every portion with their diminutive poisoned blades. Filomel's fat carcass was alive with them. They blackened the spare body of Monsieur Kerplonne. They covered Oaksmith's huge form like a cluster of insects.

Overcome completely with the fumes of wine, these tiny wounds did not for a few moments awaken the sleeping victims. But the swift and deadly poison Macousha, with which the weapons had been so fiendishly anointed, began to work. Herr Hippe, stung into sudden life, leaped to his feet, with a dwarf army clinging to his clothes and his hands,—always stabbing, stabbing, stabbing. For an instant, a look of stupid bewilderment clouded his face; then the horrible truth burst upon him. He gave a shriek like that which a horse utters when he finds himself fettered and surrounded by fire,—a shriek that curdled the air for miles and miles.

"Oaksmith! Kerplonne! Filomel! Awake! awake! We are lost! The souls have got loose! We are dead! poisoned! Oh, accursed ones! Oh, demons, ye are slaying me! Ah! fiends of Hell!"

Aroused by these frightful howls, the three gypsies sprang also to their feet, to find themselves stung to death by the manikins. They raved, they shrieked, they swore. They staggered round the chamber. Blinded in the eyes by the ever-stabbing weapons,—with the poison already burning in their veins like red-hot lead,—their forms swelling and discoloring visibly every moment,—their howls and attitudes and furious gestures made the scene look like a chamber in Hell.

Maddened beyond endurance, the Wondersmith, half-blind and choking with the venom that had congested all the blood-vessels of his body, seized dozens of the manikins and dashed them into the fire, trampling them down with his feet.

"Ye shall die too, if I die," he cried, with a roar like that of a tiger. "Ye shall burn, if I burn. I gave ye life,—I give ye death. Down!—down!—burn!—flame! Fiends that ye are, to slay us! Help me, brothers! Before we die, let us have our revenge!"

On this, the other gypsies, themselves maddened by approaching death, began hurling manikins, by handfuls, into the fire. The little creatures, being wooden of body, quickly caught the flames, and an awful struggle for life took place in miniature in the grate. Some of them escaped from between the bars and ran about the room, blazing, writhing in agony, and igniting the curtains and other draperies that hung around. Others fought and stabbed one another in the very core of the fire, like combating salamanders. Meantime, the motions of the gypsies grew more languid and slow, and their curses were uttered in choked guttural tones. The faces of all four were spotted with red and green and violet, like so many egg-plants. Their bodies were swollen to a frightful size, and at last they dropped on the floor, like overripe fruit shaken from the boughs by the winds of autumn.

The chamber was now a sheet of fire. The flames roared round and round, as if seeking for escape, licking every projecting cornice and sill with greedy tongues, as the serpent licks his prey before he swallows it. A hot, putrid breath came through the keyhole and smote Solon and Zonéla like a wind of death. They clasped each other's hands with a moan of terror, and fled from the house.

The next morning, when the young Year was just unclosing its eyes, and the happy children all over the great city were peeping from their beds into the myriads of stockings hanging near by, the blue skies of heaven shone through a black network of stone and charred rafters. These were all that remained of the habitation of Herr Hippe, the Wondersmith.

A Dead Secret

In what manner I became acquainted with that which follows, and from whom I had it, it serves not to relate here. It is enough that he *was* hanged, and that this is his story.

"And how came you," I asked, "to be—" I did not like to say hanged, for fear of wounding his delicacy, but I hinted my meaning by an expressive gesture.

"How came I to be hanged!" he echoed, in a tone of strident hoarseness. "You would like to know all about it—wouldn't you!"

He was sitting opposite to me at the end of the walnut-tree table in his shirt and trowsers, his bare feet on the bare polished oak floor. There was a dark bistre ring round each of his eyes; and they—being spherical rather than oval, with the pupils fixed and coldly shining in the centre of the orbits—were more like those of some wild animal than of a man. The hue of his forehead, too, was ghastly and dingy; blue, violet, and yellow, like a bruise that is five days old. There was a clammy sweat on his beard and under the lobes of his ears; and the sea-breeze coming gently through the open Venetians (for the night was very sultry), fanned his long locks of coarse dark hair until you might almost fancy you saw the serpents of the Furies writhing in them. The fingers of his lean hands were slightly crooked inward, owing to some involuntary muscular rigidity, and I noticed that his whole frame was pervaded by a nervous trembling, less spasmodic than regular, and resembling that which shakes a man afflicted with *delirium tremens.*

I had given him a cigar. After moistening the end of it in his mouth, he said, bending his eyes toward me, but still more on the wall behind my chair than on my face: "It's no use. You may torture me, scourge me, flay me alive. You may rasp me with rusty files, and seethe me in vinegar, and rub my eyes with gunpowder—but I can't tell you where the child is. I don't know—I never knew. How am I to make you believe that I don't know—that I never knew!"

"My good friend," I remarked, "you do not seem to be aware that, so far from wishing you to tell me where the child you allude to is, I am not actuated by the slightest curiosity to know any thing about any child whatever. Permit me to observe that I can not see the smallest connection between a child and your being hanged."

"No connection!" retorted my companion, with vehemence. "It *is* the connection—the cause. But for that child I should never have been hanged."

He went on muttering and panting about this child; and I pushed toward him a bottle of thin claret. (Being liable to be called up at all hours of the night, I find it lighter drinking than any other wine.) He filled a large tumbler—which he emptied into himself, rather than drank—and I observed that his lips were so dry and smooth with parchedness, that the liquid formed little globules of moisture on them, like drops of water on an oil-cloth. Then he began:

I had the misery to be born (he said) about seven-and-thirty years ago. I was the offspring of a double misery, for my mother was a newly-made widow when I was born, and she died in giving me birth. What my name was before I assumed the counterfeit that has blasted my life, I shall not tell you. But it was no patrician, high-sounding title, for my father was a petty tradesman, and my mother had been a domestic servant. Two kinsmen succored me in my orphanage. They were both uncles; one by my father's, one by my mother's side. The former was a retired sailor, rich, and a bachelor. The latter was a grocer, still in business. He was a widower, with one daughter, and not very well to do in the world. They hated each other with the sort of cold, fixed, and watchful aversion that a savage cat has for a dog too large for her to worry.

These two uncles played a miserable game of battledore and shuttlecock with me for nearly fourteen years. I was bandied about from one to the other, and equally maltreated by both. Now, it was my Uncle Collerer who discovered that I was starved by my Uncle Morbus, and took me under his protection. Now, my Uncle Morbus was indignant at my Uncle Collerer for beating me, and insisted that I should return to his roof. I was beaten and starved by one, and starved and beaten by the other. I endeavored—with that cunning which brutal treatment will teach the dullest child—to trim my sails to please both uncles. I could only succeed by ministering to the hatred they mutually had one for the other. I could only propitiate Collerer by abusing Morbus: the only road to Morbus's short-lived favor was by defaming Collerer. Nor do I think I did either of them much injustice; for they were both wicked-minded old men. I believe either of them would have allowed me to starve in the gutter; only each thought that, appearing to protect me, would naturally spite the other.

When I was about fifteen years old, it occurred to me, that I should make an election for good and all between my uncles; else, between these two knotty, crabbed stools I might fall to the ground. Naturally enough I chose the rich uncle—the retired sailor, Collerer; and although I dare say he knew I only clove to him for the sake of his money, he seemed perfectly satisfied with my hearty abuse of my Uncle Morbus, and my total abnegation of his society; for, for three years I never went near his house, and when he met me in the street I gave him the breadth of the pavement, and recked nothing for his shaking his fist at me, and calling me an ungrateful hound. My Uncle Collerer, although retired from the sea, had not left off making money. He lent it at usury on mortgages, and in numberless other crawling ways. I soon became his right hand, and assisted him in grinding the needy, in selling up poor tradesmen, and in buckling on the spurs of spendthrifts when they started for the race, the end of which was to be the jail. My uncle was pleased with me; and although he was miserably parsimonious in his housekeeping and in his allowance to me, I had hopes and lived on; but very much in the fashion of a rat in a hole.

I had known Mary Morbus, the grocer's daughter, years before. She was a sickly, delicate child, and I had often teased and struck and robbed her of her playthings, in my evil childhood. But she grew up a surpassingly beautiful creature, and I loved her. We met by stealth in the park outside her father's door while he was asleep in church on Sundays; and I fancied she began to love me. There was little in my mind or person, in my white face, elf-locks, and dull speech to captivate a girl; but her heart was full of love, and its brightness gilded my miserable clay. I felt my heart newly opened. I hoped for something more than my uncle's moneybags. We interchanged all the flighty vows of everlasting affection and constancy common to boys and girls; and although we knew the two fierce hatreds that stood betwixt us and happiness, we left the accomplishment of our wishes to time and fortune, and went on hoping and loving.

One evening, at supper-time—for which meal we had the heel of a Dutch cheese, a loaf of seconds bread, and a pint of small beer—I noticed that my Uncle Collerer looked more malignant and sullen than usual. He spoke little, and bit his food as if he had a spite against it. When supper was over, he went to an old worm-eaten bureau in which he was wont to keep documents of value; and, taking out a bundle of papers, untied and began to read them. I took little heed of that; for his favorite course of evening reading was bonds and mortgage deeds; and on every eve of bills of exchange falling due he would spend hours in poring over the acceptances and endorsements, and even in bed he would lie awake half the night moaning and crooning lest the bills should not be paid on the morrow. After carefully reading and sorting these papers, he tossed them over to me, and left the room without a word. Then I heard him going up stairs to the top of the house, where my room was.

I opened the packet with trembling hands and a beating heart. I found every single letter I had written to Mary Morbus. The room seemed to turn round. The white sheet I held and the black letters dancing on it were all I could see. All beyond—the room, the house, the world—was one black unutterable gulf of darkness. I tried to read a line—a line I had known by heart for months; but, to my scared senses, it might as well have been Chaldee. Then my uncle's heavy step was heard on the stairs.

He entered the room, dragging after him a small black portmanteau in which I kept all that I was able to call my own. "I happened to have a key that opens this," he said, "and I have read every one of the fine love-letters that silly girl has sent you. But I have been much more edified by the perusal of yours, which I only received from your good Uncle Morbus —strangle him!—last night. I'm a covetous hunks, am I? You live in hopes, do you? Hope told a flattering tale, my young friend. I've only two words to say to you," continued my uncle, after a few minutes' composed silence on his part, and of blank consternation on mine. "All your rags are in that trunk. Either give up Mary Morbus—now and forever, and write a letter to her here in my presence to that effect—or turn out into the street and never show your face here again. Make up your mind quickly, and for good." He then filled his pipe and lighted it.

While he sat composedly smoking his pipe, I was employed in making up my wretched mind. Love, fear, interest, avarice—cursed avarice—alternately gained ascendency within me. At length there came a craven inspiration that I might temporize; that by pretending to renounce Mary, and yet secretly assuring her of my constancy, I might play a double game, and yet live in hopes of succeeding to my uncle's wealth. To my shame and confusion, I caught at this coward expedient, and signified my willingness to do as my uncle desired.

"Write then," he resumed, flinging me a sheet of letter-paper and a pen. "I will dictate."

I took the pen; and following his dictation wrote, I scarcely can tell what now; but I suppose some abject words to Mary, saying that I resigned all claim to her hand.

"That'll do very nicely, nephew," said my uncle, when I had finished. "We needn't fold it, or seal it, or post it, because—he, he, he!—we can deliver it upon the spot." We were in the front parlor, which was separated from the back room by a pair of folding-doors. My uncle got up, opened one of these; and with a mock bow ushered in my Uncle Morbus and my Cousin Mary.

"A letter for you, my dear," grinned the old wretch; "a letter from your *true love*. Though I dare say you'll have no occasion to read it, for you must have heard it. I speak plain enough, though I am asthmatic, and can't last long—can't last long—eh, nephew!" This was a quotation from one of my own letters.

When Mary took the letter from my uncle, her hand shook as with the palsy. But, when I besought her to look at me, and passionately adjured her to believe that I was yet true to her, she turned on me a glance of scornful incredulity; and, crushing the miserable paper in her hand, cast it contemptuously from her.

"*You* marry my daughter," my Uncle Morbus piped forth—"you? Your father couldn't pay two-and-twopence in the pound. He owed me money, he owes me money to this day. Why ain't there laws to make sons pay their fathers' debts? You marry my daughter? Do you think I'd have your father's son—do you think I'd have your uncle's nephew for my son-in-law?" I could see that the temporary bond of union between my two uncles was already beginning to loosen; and a wretched hope sprang up within me.

"Get out of my house, you and your daughter, too!" cried my Uncle Collerer. "You've served my turn, and I've served yours. Now, go!"

I could hear the two old men fiercely, yet feebly, quarreling in the passage, and Mary weeping piteously without saying a word. Then the great street door was banged to, and my uncle came in, muttering and panting. "I hope you are satisfied now, uncle," I said.

"Satisfied!" he cried with a sort of shriek, catching up the great earthen jar, with the leaden top, in which he kept his tobacco, as though he meant to fling it at me. "Satisfied!—I'll satisfy you: go. Go! and never let me see your hang-dog face again!"

"You surely do not intend to turn me out of doors, uncle!" I faltered.

"March, bag and baggage. If you are here a minute longer, I'll call the police. Go!" And he pointed to the door.

"But where am I to go?" I asked.

"Go and beg," said my uncle; "go and cringe to your dear Uncle Morbus. Go and rot!"

So saying he opened the door, kicked my trunk into the hall, thrust me out of the room and into the street, and pushed my portmanteau after me, without my making the slightest resistance. He slammed the door in my face, and left me in the open street, at twelve o'clock at night.

I slept that night at a coffee-shop. I had a few shillings in my pocket;

and, next morning, I took a lodging at, I think, four shillings a week, in a court, somewhere up a back street between Gray's Inn and Leather Lane, Holborn. My room was at the top of the house. The court below swarmed with dirty, ragged children. My lodging was a back garret; and, when I opened the window, I could only see a narrow strip of sky, and a foul heap of sooty roofs, chimneypots and leads, with the great dingy brick tower of a church towering above all. Where the body of the church was I never knew.

I wrote letter after letter to my uncles and to Mary, but never received a line in answer. I wandered about the streets all day, feeding on saveloys and penny loaves. I went to my wretched bed by daylight, and groaned for darkness to come; then groaned that it might grow light again. I knew no one to whom I could apply for employment, and knew no means by which I could obtain it. The house I lived in and the neighborhood were full of foreign refugees and street mountebanks, whose jargon I could not understand. My little stock of money slowly dwindled away; and, in ten days, my mind was ripe for suicide. You must serve an apprenticeship to acquire that ripeness. Crowded streets, utter desolation and friendlessness in them, scanty food, and the knowledge that when you have spent all your money and sold your coat and waistcoat you must starve, are the best masters. They produce that frame of mind which coroners' juries call temporary insanity. I determined to die. I expended my last coin in purchasing laudanum at different chemists' shops—a pennyworth at each; which, I said, I wanted for the toothache; for I knew they would not supply a large quantity to a stranger. I took my dozen vials home, and poured their contents into a broken mug that stood on my wash-hand-stand. I locked the door, sat down on my fatal black portmanteau, and tried to pray; but I could not.

It was about nine in the evening, in the summer time, and the room was in that state of semi-obscurity you call "between the lights." While I sat on my black portmanteau, I heard through my garret window, which was wide open, a loud noise, a confusion of angry voices, in which I could not distinguish one word I could comprehend. The noise was followed by a pistol-shot. I hear it now, as distinctly as I heard it twenty years ago; and then another. As I looked out of the window I saw a pair of hands covered with blood, clutching the sill, and I heard a voice imploring help for God's sake! Scarcely knowing what I did, I drew up from the leads below and into the room the body of a man, whose face was one mass of blood—like a crimson mask. He stood upright on the floor when I had helped him in; his face glaring at me like the spot one sees after gazing too long at the sun. Then he began to stagger, and went reeling about the room, catching at the window curtain, the table, the wall, and leaving traces of his blood wherever he went—I following him in an agony—until he fell face-foremost on the bed.

I lit a candle as well as I could. He was quite dead. His features were so scorched and mangled, and drenched, that not one trait was to be distinguished. The pistol must have been discharged full in his face, for some of his long black hair was burnt off. He held, clasped in his left hand, a pistol which evidently had been recently discharged.

I sat by the side of this horrible object twenty minutes or more, waiting for the alarm which I thought must necessarily follow, and resolving what I should do. But all was as silent as the grave. No one in the house seemed to have heard the pistol-shot, and no one without seemed to have heeded it. I looked from the window, but the dingy mass of roofs and chimneys had grown black with night, and I could perceive nothing moving. Only, as I held my candle out of the window it mirrored itself dully in a pool of blood on the leads below.

I began to think I might be accused of the murder of this unknown man. I, who had so lately courted a violent death, began to fear it, and to shake like an aspen at the thought of the gallows. Then I tried to persuade myself that it was all a horrible dream; but there, on the bed, was the dreadful dead man in his blood, and all about the room were the marks of his gory fingers.

I began to examine the body more minutely. The dead man was almost exactly of my height and stoutness. Of his age I could not judge. His hair was long and black like mine. In one of his pockets I found a pocket-book, containing a mass of closely-written sheets of very thin paper, in a character utterly incomprehensible to me; moreover, there was a roll of English bank-notes to a very considerable amount. In his waistcoat pocket was a gold watch; and in a silken girdle round his waist, were two hundred English sovereigns and louis d'ors.

What fiend stood at my elbow while I made this examination I know not. The plan I fixed upon was not long revolved in my mind. It seemed to start up matured, like Minerva, from the head of Jupiter. I was resolved. The dead should be alive, and the live man dead. In less time than it takes to tell, I had stripped the body, dressed it in my own clothes, assumed the dead man's garments, and secured the pocket-book, the watch, and the money about my person. Then I overturned the lighted candle on to the bed, slouched my hat over my eyes, and stole down stairs. No one met me on the stairs, and I emerged into the court. No man pursued me, and I gained the open street. It was only, an hour after perhaps, as I crossed Holborn toward St. Andrew's Church, that I saw fire engines come rattling along; and, asking unconcernedly where the fire was, heard that it was "somewhere off Gray's Inn Lane."

I slept nowhere that night. I scarcely remember what I did; but I have an indistinct remembrance of flinging sovereigns about in blazing gas-lit taverns. It is a marvel to me now that I did not become senseless with liquor, unaccustomed as I was to dissipation. The next morning I read the following paragraph in a newspaper:

AWFUL SUICIDE AND FIRE
NEAR GRAY'S INN LANE.

Last night the inhabitants of Cragg's Court, Hustle-street, Gray's Inn Lane, were alarmed by volumes of smoke issuing from the windows of number five in that court, occupied as a lodging-house. On Mr. Plose, the landlord, entering a garret on the third floor, it was found that its tenant, Mr. ——, had committed suicide by blowing his brains out with a pistol, which was found tightly clenched in the wretched man's hand. Either from the ignition of the wadding, or from some other cause, the fire had communicated to the bed-clothes; all of which, with the bed and a portion of the furniture, were consumed. The engines of the North of England Fire Brigade were promptly on the spot; and the fire was with great difficulty at last successfully extinguished; little beyond the room occupied by the deceased being injured. The body and face of the miserable suicide were frightfully mutilated; but sufficient evidence was afforded from his clothes and papers to establish his identity. No cause is assigned for the rash act; and it is even stated that if he had prolonged his existence a few hours later, he would have come into possession of a fortune of thirty thousand pounds, his uncle, Gripple Collerer, Esq., of Raglan-street, Clerkenwell, having died only two days before, and having constituted him his sole heir and legatee. That active and intelligent parish officer, Mr. Pybus, immediately forwarded the necessary intimation to the Coroner, and the inquest will be held this evening at the Kiddy's Arms, Hustle-street.

I had lost all—name, existence, thirty thousand pounds, every thing—for about four hundred pounds in gold and notes.

"So I suppose," I said, as he who was hanged paused, "that you gave yourself up with a view of re-establishing your identity; and, failing to do that, you were hanged for murder or arson?"

I waited for a reply. He had lit another cigar, and sat smoking it. Seeing that he was calm, I judged it best not to excite or aggravate him by further questioning, but staid his pleasure. I had not to wait long.

"Not so," he resumed; "what I became that night I have remained ever since, and am now; that is, if I am any thing at all. The very day on which that paragraph appeared, I set off by the coach. My only wish was to get as far from London and from England as I possibly could; and, in due time, we came to Hull. Hearing that Hamburg was the nearest foreign port, to Hamburg I went. I lived there for six months in an hotel, frugally and in solitude, and endeavoring to learn German; for, on narrower examination of the papers in the pocket-book, I guessed some portions of them to be written in that language. I was a dull scholar; but at the end of six months, I had scraped together enough German to know that the dead man's name was Müller; that he had been in Russia, in France, and in America. I managed to translate portions of a diary he had kept while in this latter country; but they only related to his impressions of the towns he had visited. He often alluded, too, casually to his 'secret' and his 'charge;' but what that secret and that charge were, I could not discover. There were also hints about a 'shepherdess,' and 'antelope,' and a 'blue tiger'—fictitious names, I presumed, for some persons with whom he was connected. The great mass of the documents was in a cipher utterly inexplicable to my most strenuous ingenuity and research. I went by the name of Müller; but I found that there were hundreds more Müllers in Hamburg, and no man sought me out.

I was in the habit of going every evening to a lager-beer house outside the town, to smoke my pipe. There generally sat at the same table with me a little fat man in a gray great-coat, who smoked and drank beer incessantly. I was suspicious and shy of strangers; but, between this little man and me there gradually grew up a quiet kind of tavern acquaintance.

One evening, when we had had a rather liberal potation of pipes and beer, he asked me if I had ever tasted the famous Baierische or Bavarian beer, adding that it threw all other German beers into the shade, and liberally offering to pay for a flask of it. I was in rather merry humor, and assented. We had one bottle of Bavarian beer; then another, and another, till, what with the beer and the pipes and the wrangling of the domino-players, my head swam.

"I tell you what," said my companion, "we will just have one chopine of brandy. I always take it after Baierischer beer. We will not have it here, but at the *Grüne Gans*, hard by; which is an honest house, kept by Max Rombach, who is a widow's son."

I was in that state when a man having already had too much is sure to want more, and I followed the man in the gray coat. How many chopines of brandy I had at the *Grüne Gans* I know not; but I found myself in bed next morning with an intolerable thirst and a racking headache. My first action was to spring out of bed, and search in the pocket of my coat for my pocket-book. It was gone. The waiters and the landlord were summoned; but no one knew any thing about it. I had been brought home in a carriage, very inebriated, by a stout man in a gray great-coat, who said he was my friend, helped me up-stairs, and assisted me to undress. The investigation ended with a conviction that the man in the gray coat was the thief. He had, manifestly, been tempted to the robbery by no pecuniary motive; for the whole of my remaining stock of bank-notes, which I always kept in the pocket-book, I found in my waistcoat-pocket neatly rolled up.

That evening I walked down to the beer-house where I usually met my friend—not with the remotest idea of seeing him, but with the hope of eliciting some information as to who and what he was.

To my surprise he was sitting at his accustomed table, smoking and drinking as usual; and, to my stern salutation, replied with a good-humored hope that my head was not any worse for the *branntuein* overnight.

"I want a word with you," said I.

"With pleasure," he returned. Whereupon he put on his broad-brimmed hat and followed me into the garden behind the house, with an alacrity that was quite surprising.

"I was drunk last night," I commenced.

"Zo," he replied, with an unmoved countenance.

"And while drunk," I continued, "I was robbed of my pocket-book."

"Zo," he repeated with equal composure.

"And I venture to assert that you are the person who stole it."

"Zo. You are quite right, my son," he returned, with the most astonishing coolness. "I did take your pocket-book; I have it here. See."

He tapped the breast of his gray great-coat; and, I could clearly distinguish, through the cloth, the square form of my pocket-book, with its great clasp in the middle. I sprang at him immediately, with the intention of wrenching it from him; but he eluded my grasp nimbly, and, stepping aside, drew forth a small silver whistle, on which he blew a shrill note. In an instant a cloak or sheet was thrown over my head. I felt my hands muffled with soft but strong ligatures; and, before I had time to make one effort in self-defense, I was lifted off my feet and swiftly conveyed away, in total darkness. Presently we stopped, and I was lifted still higher; was placed on a seat; a door was slammed to; and the rumbling motion of wheels convinced me that I was in a carriage.

My journey must have lasted some hours. We stopped from time to time: to change horses, I suppose. At the commencement of the journey I made frantic efforts to disengage myself, and to cry out. But I was so well gagged, and bound, and muffled, that in sheer weariness and despair, I desisted. We halted at last for good. I was lifted out, and again carried swiftly along for upward of ten minutes. Then, from a difficulty of respiration, I concluded that I had entered a house, and was, perhaps, being borne along some underground passage. We ascended and descended staircases. I heard doors locked and unlocked. Finally, I was thrown violently down on a hard surface. The gag was removed from my mouth, and the mufflers from my hands; I heard a heavy door clang to, and I was at liberty to speak and to move.

My first care was to disengage myself from the mantle, whose folds still clung around me. I was in total darkness—darkness so black, that at first I concluded some infernal device had been made use of to blind me. But, after straining my eyes in every direction, I was able to discern high above me a small circular orifice, through which permeated a minute thread of light. Then I became sensible that I was not blind, but in some subterranean dungeon. The surface on which I was lying was hard and cold—a stone pavement. I crawled about, feeling with my hands, endeavoring to define the limits of my prison. Nothing was palpable to the touch, but the bare smooth pavement, and the bare smooth walls. I tried for hours to find the door, but could not. I shouted for help; but no man came near me.

I must have lain in this den two days and two nights—at least the pangs of hunger and thirst made me suppose that length of time to have elapsed. Then the terrible thought possessed me that I was imprisoned there to be starved to death. In the middle of the third day, as it seemed to me, however, I heard a rattling of keys; one grated in the lock; a door opened, a flood of light broke in upon me; and a well-remembered voice cried, "Come out!" as one might do to a beast in a cage.

The light was so dazzling that I could not at first distinguish any thing. But I crawled to the door; and then standing up, found I was in a small court-yard, and that opposite to me was my enemy, the man of the gray coat.

In a gray coat no longer, however. He was dressed in a scarlet jacket, richly laced with gold; which fitted him so tightly with the short tails sticking out behind, that, under any other circumstances, he would have seemed to me inconceivably ridiculous. He took no more notice of me than if he had never seen me before in his life; but, merely motioning to two servants in scarlet liveries to take hold of me under the arms, waddled on before.

We went in and out of half a dozen doors, and traversed as many small court-yards. The buildings surrounding them were all in a handsome style of architecture; and in one of them I could discern, through the open grated windows on the ground floor, several men in white caps and jackets.

A distant row of copper stewpans and a delicious odor, made me conjecture that we were close to the kitchen. We stopped some moments in this neighborhood; whether from previous orders, or from pure malignity toward me, I was unable then to tell. He glanced over his shoulder with an expression of such infinite malice, that, what with hunger and rage, I struggled violently but unsuccessfully to burst from my guards. At last we ascended a narrow but handsomely carpeted staircase; and, after traversing a splendid picture gallery, entered an apartment luxuriously furnished; half library and half drawing-room.

A cheerful wood fire crackled on the dogs in the fireplace; and, with his back toward it, stood a tall elderly man, his thin gray hair carefully brushed over his forehead. He was dressed in black, had a stiff white neckcloth, and a parti-colored ribbon at his button-hole. A few feet from him was a table, covered with books and papers; and sitting thereat in a large arm-chair, was an old man, immensely corpulent, swathed in a richly furred dressing-gown, with a sort of jockey cap on his head of black velvet, to which was attached a hideous green shade. The servants brought me to the foot of this table, still holding my arms.

"Monsieur Müller," said the man in black, politely, and in excellent English. "How do you feel?"

I replied, indignantly, that the state of my health was not the point in question. I demanded to know why I had been trepanned, robbed, and starved.

"Monsieur Müller," returned the man in black, with immovable politeness. "You must excuse the apparently discourteous manner in which you have been treated. The truth is, our house was built, not for a prison, but for a palace; and, for want of proper dungeon accommodation, we were compelled to utilize for the moment an apartment which I believe was formerly a wine-cellar. I hope you did not find it damp."

The man with the green shade shook his fat shoulders, as if in silent laughter.

"In the first instance, Monsieur," resumed the other, politely motioning me to be silent; for I was about to speak, "we deemed that the possession of the papers in your pocket-book" (he touched that fatal book as he spoke) "would have been sufficient for the accomplishment of the object we have in view. But, finding that a portion of the correspondence is in a cipher of which you alone have the key, we judged the pleasure of your company absolutely indispensable."

"I know no more about the cipher and its key than you do," I ejaculated, "and, before heaven, no secret that can concern you is in my keeping."

"You must be hungry, Monsieur Müller," pursued the man in black, taking no more notice of what I had said than if I had not spoken at all. "Carol, bring in lunch."

He, lately of the gray-coat, now addressed as Carol, bowed, retired, and presently returned with a tray covered with smoking viands and two flasks of wine. The servants half loosened their hold; my heart leaped within me, and I was about to rush toward the viands, when the man in black raised his hand.

"One moment, Monsieur Müller," he said, "before you recruit your strength. Will you oblige me by answering one question, Where is the child?"

"*Ja*, where is the child!" echoed the man in the green shade.

"I do not know," I replied, passionately; "on my honor I do not know. If you were to ask me for a hundred years, I could not tell you."

"Carol," said the man in black, with an unmoved countenance, "take away the tray. Monsieur Müller has no appetite. Unless," he added, turning to me, "you will be so good as to answer that little question."

"I can not," I repeated; "I don't know; I never knew."

"Carol," said my questioner, taking up a newspaper, and turning his back upon me, "take away the things. Monsieur Müller, good-morning."

In spite of my cries and struggles, I was dragged away. We traversed the picture gallery; but, instead of descending the staircase, entered another suite of apartments. We were crossing a long vestibule lighted with lamps, and one of my guards had stopped to unlock a door while the other lagged a few paces behind (they had loosened their hold of me, and Carol was not with us), when a panel in the wainscoat opened, and a lady in black—perhaps thirty years of age and beautiful—bent forward through the aperture. "I heard all," she said, in a rapid whisper. "You have acted nobly. Be proof against their temptations, and Heaven will reward your devotedness."

I had no time to reply, for the door was closed immediately. I was hurried forward through room after room; until at last we entered a small bed-chamber, simply but cleanly furnished. Here I was left, and the door was locked and barred on the outside. On the table were a small loaf of black bread, and a pitcher of water. Both of these I consumed ravenously.

I was left without further food for another entire day and night. From my window, which was heavily grated, I could see that my room overlooked the court-yard where the kitchen was, and the sight of the cooks, and the smell of the hot meat drove me almost mad.

On the second day I was again ushered into the presence of the man in black, and the man with the green shade. Again the infernal drama was played. Again I was tempted with rich food. Again, on my expressing my inability to answer the question, it was ordered to be removed.

"Stop!" I cried desperately, as Carol was about to remove the food, and thinking I might satisfy them with a falsehood; "I will confess. I will tell all."

"Speak," said the man in black, eagerly, "where is the child?"

"In Amsterdam," I replied at random.

"Amsterdam—nonsense!" said the man in the green shade impatiently, "what has Amsterdam to do with the Blue Tiger?"

"I need not remind you," said the man in black, sarcastically, "that the name of any town or country is no answer to the question. You know as well as I do that the key to the whereabouts of the child is *there,*" and he pointed to the pocket-book.

"Yes; *there,*" echoed the man in the green shade. And he struck it.

"But, sir—" I urged.

The answer was simply, "Good-morning, Monsieur Müller."

Again was I conducted back to my prison; again I met the lady in black, who administered to me the barren consolation that "Heaven would reward my devotedness." Again I found the black loaf and the pitcher of water, and again I was left a day and a night in semi-starvation, to be again brought forth, tantalized, questioned, and sent back again.

"Perhaps," remarked the man in black, at the fifth of these interviews, "it is gold that Monsieur Müller requires. See." As he spoke, he opened a bureau crammed with bags of money, and bade me help myself.

In vain I protested that all the gold in the world could not extort from me a secret which I did not possess. In vain I exclaimed that my name was not Müller; in vain I disclosed the ghastly deceit I had practiced. The man in black only shook his head, smiled incredulously, and told me—while complimenting me for my powers of invention—that my statement confirmed his conviction that I knew where the child was.

After the next interview, as I was returning to my starvation meal of bread and water, the lady in black again met me.

"Take courage," she whispered. "Your deliverance is at hand. You are to be removed to-night to a lunatic asylum."

How my translation to a madhouse could accomplish my deliverance, or better my prospects, did not appear very clear to me; but that very night I was gagged, my arms were confined in a strait waistcoat, and placed in a carriage, which immediately set off at a rapid pace. We traveled all night; and, in the early morning, arrived at a large stone building. Here I was stripped, examined, placed in a bath, and dressed in a suit of coarse gray cloth. I asked where I was? I was told in the Alienation-Refuge of the Grand Duchy of Sachs-Pfeiffiger.

"Can I see the head-keeper?" I asked.

The Herr Ober-Direktor was a little man with a shiny bald head and very white teeth. When I entered his cabinet he received me politely, and asked me what he could do for me? I told him my real name, my history, my wrongs; that I was a British subject, and demanded my liberty. He smiled, and simply called—"Where is Kraus?"

"Here, Herr," answered the keeper.

"What number is Monsieur?"

"Number ninety-two."

"Ninety-two," repeated the Herr Direktor, leisurely writing. "Cataplasms on the soles of the feet. Worsted blister behind the ears, a mustard plaster on the chest, and ice on the head. Let it be Baltic ice."

The abominable inflictions thus ordered were all applied. The villain Kraus tortured me in every imaginable way; and in the midst of his tortures, would repeat, "Tell me where the child is, Müller, and you shall have your liberty in half an hour."

I was in the madhouse for six months. If I complained to the doctor of Kraus's ill-treatment and temptations, he immediately began to order cataplasms and Baltic ice. The bruises I had to show were ascribed to injuries I had myself inflicted in fits of frenzy. The maniacs with whom I was caged declared, like all other maniacs, that I was outrageously mad.

One evening, as I lay groaning on my bed, Kraus entered my cell. "Get up," he said, "you are at liberty. I was bribed, by you know who, with ten thousand Prussian thalers to get your secret from you, if I could; but I have been bribed with twenty thousand Austrian florins (which is really a sum worth having) to set you free. I shall lose my place, and have to fly; but I will open an hotel at Frankfort for the Englanders, and make my fortune. Come!" He led me down-stairs, let me out of a private door in the garden; and, placing a bundle of clothes and a purse in my hand, bade me good-night.

I dressed myself, threw away the madman's livery, and kept walking along until morning, when I came to the custom-house barrier of another Grand Duchy. I had a passport ready provided for me in the pocket of my coat, which was found to be perfectly *en règle*, and I passed unquestioned. I went that morning to the coach-office of the town, and engaged a place in the *Eilwagen* to some German town, the name of which I forget; and, at the end of four days' weary traveling, I reached Brussels.

I was very thin and weak with confinement and privation; but I soon recovered my health and strength. I must say that I made up by good living for my former compulsory abstinence; and both in Brussels and in Paris, to which I next directed my steps, I lived on the best. One evening I entered one of the magnificent restaurants in the Palais Royal to dine. I had ordered my meal from the *carte*, when my attention was roused by a small piece of paper which had been slipped between its leaves. It ran thus:

Feign to eat, but eat no fish. Remain the usual time at your dinner, to disarm suspicion, but immediately afterwards make your way to England. Be sure, in passing through London, to call on Hildeburger.

I had ordered a *sole au gratin;* but when it arrived, managed to throw it piece by piece under the table. When I had discussed the rest of my dinner, I summoned the garçon, and asked for my bill.

"You will pay the head waiter, if you please, Monsieur," said he.

The head waiter came. If he had been a centaur or a sphinx I could not have stared at him with more horror and astonishment than I did; for there, in a waiter's dress, with a napkin over his arm, was Carol, the man of the gray coat.

"Müller," he said, coolly, bending over the table. "Your sole was poisoned. Tell me where the child is, and here is an antidote, and four hundred thousand francs."

For reply I seized the heavy water decanter, and dashed it with all the force I could command, full in the old ruffian's face. He fell like a stone, amid the screams of women, the oaths of men, and cries of *à la Garde! à la Garde!* I slipped out of the restaurant and into one of the passages or outlets which abound in the Palais Royal. Whether the man died or not, or whether I was pursued, I never knew. I gained my lodgings unmolested, packed up my luggage, and started the next morning by the diligence, for Boulogne.

I arrived in due time in London; but I did not call on "Hildeburger" because I did not know who or where Hildeburger was. I started the very evening of my arrival in London for Liverpool, being determined to go to America. I was fearful of remaining in England, not only on account of my persecutors, but because I was pursued every where by the spectre of the real Müller.

I took my passage to New York in a steamer which was to sail from the Docks in a week's time. It was to start on a Monday; and on the Friday preceding I was walking about the Exchange, congratulating myself that I should soon have the Atlantic between myself and my pursuers. All at once I heard the name of Müller pronounced in a loud tone close behind me. I turned, and met the gaze of a tall thin young man with a downy mustache, who was dressed in the extreme of fashion, and was sucking the end of an ebony stick.

"Monsieur Müller," he said, nodding to me easily.

"My name is not Müller," I answered, boldly.

"You have not yet called on Hildeburger," he added, slightly elevating his eyebrows at my denial.

I felt a cold shiver pass over me, and stammered, "N—n—no!"

"We had considerable difficulty in learning your whereabouts!" he went on with great composure. "The lady was obstinate. The screw and the water were tried in vain; but at length, by a judicious use of the cord and pulleys, we succeeded."

I shuddered again.

"Will you call on Hildeburger now!" he resumed quickly and sharply. "He is here—close by."

"Not now, not now." I faltered. "Some other time."

"The day after to-morrow!"

"Yes, yes," I answered eagerly, "the day after to-morrow."

"Well, Saturday be it. You will meet me here, at four in the afternoon! Good! Do not forget. *Au revoir*, Monsieur Müller."

He had no sooner uttered these words than he turned and disappeared among the crowd of merchants on 'Change.

I could not doubt, by his naming Saturday, as the day for our meeting, that he had some inkling of my intended departure. Although I had paid my passage to New York, I determined to forfeit it, and to change my course so as to evade my persecutors. I entered a shipping-office, and learned that a good steamer would leave George's Dock at ten that same night, for Glasgow. And to Glasgow for the present I made up my mind to go.

At a quarter before ten I was at the dock with my luggage. It was raining heavily, and there was a dense fog.

"This way for the Glasgow steamer—this way," cried a man in a Guernsey shirt, "this way, your honor. I'll carry your trunk!"

He took up my trunk as he spoke, and led the way down a ladder, across the decks of two or three steamers, and to the gangway of a fourth, where a man stood with dark bushy whiskers, dressed in a pea-coat, and holding a lighted lantern.

"Is this the Glasgow steamer?" I asked.

"All right!" answered the man with the lantern. "Look sharp, the bell's a-going to ring."

"Remember poor Jack, your honor," said the man in the Guernsey, who had carried my trunk. I gave him sixpence and stepped on board. A bell began to ring, and there was great confusion on board with hauling of ropes and stowing of luggage. The steamer seemed to me to be intolerably dirty and crowded with goods; and, to avoid the crush, I stepped aft to the wheel. In due time we had worked out of the dock and were steaming down the Mersey.

"How long will the run to Glasgow take, think you my man?" I asked of the man at the wheel. He stared at me as if he did not understand me, and muttered some unintelligible words. I repeated the question.

"He does not speak English," said a voice at my elbow, "nor can any soul on board this vessel, except you and I, Monsieur Müller."

I turned round, and saw to my horror the young man with the ebony cane and the downy mustache.

"I am kidnapped!" I cried. "Let me have a boat. Where is the captain?"

"Here is the captain," said the young man, as a fiercely bearded man came up the companion-ladder. "Captain Miloschvich of the Imperial Russian ship Pyroscaphe, bound to St. Petersburg, M. Müller. As Captain Miloschvich speaks no English you will permit me to act as interpreter."

Although I feared from his very presence that my case was already hopeless, I entreated him to explain to the captain that there was a mistake; that I was bound for Glasgow, and that I desired to be set on shore directly.

"Captain Miloschvich," said the young man, when he had translated my speech, and received the captain's answer, "begs you to understand that there is no mistake; that you are not bound for Glasgow, but for St. Petersburg; and that it is quite impossible for him to set you on shore here, seeing that he has positive instructions to set you on shore in Cronstadt. Furthermore, he feels it his duty to add that should you, by any words or actions, attempt to annoy or disturb the crew or passengers, he will be compelled to put you in irons, and place you in the bottom of the hold."

The captain frequently nodded during these remarks, as if he perfectly understood their purport, although unable to express them; and, to intimate his entire coincidence, he touched his wrists and ankles.

If I had not been a fool I should have resigned myself to my fate. But I was so maddened with misfortune, that I sprang on the young man, hoping to kill him, or to be killed myself, and to be thrown into the sea. But I was chained, beaten, and thrown into the hold. There, among tarred ropes, the stench of tallow-casks, and the most appalling sea-sickness, I lay for days, fed with mouldy biscuit and putrid water. At length we arrived at Cronstadt.

All I can tell you, or I know of Russia is, that somewhere in it there is a river, and on that river a fortress, and in that fortress a cell, and in that cell a knout. Seven years of my existence were passed in that cell, under the lashes of that knout, with the one horrible question dinning in my ears, "Where is the child?"

How I escaped to incur worse tortures, it is bootless to tell you. I have swept the streets of Palermo as a convict, in a hideous yellow dress. I have pined in the Inquisition at Rome. I have been caged in the madhouse at Constantinople, with the rabble to throw stones and mud at me through the bars. I have been branded in the back in the *bagnes* of Toulon and Rochefort; and every where I have been offered liberty and gold if I would answer the question, "Where is the child?" At last, having been accused of a crime I did not commit, I was condemned to death. Upon the scaffold they asked me, "Where is the child?" Of course there could be no answer, and I was—

Just then, Margery, my servant, who never will have the discrimination to deny me to importunate visitors, knocked at the door, and told me that I was wanted in the surgery. I went down stairs, and found Mrs. Walkingshaw, Johnny Walkingshaw's wife, who told me that her "master" was "took all over like," and quite "stroaken of a heap." Johnny Walkingshaw is a member of the ancient order of Sylvan Brothers; and, as I am club-doctor to the Sylvan Brothers, he has a right to my medical attendance for the sum of four shillings a year. Whenever he has taken an over-dose of rough cider he is apt to be "stroaken all of a heap," and to send for me. I was the more annoyed at being obliged to walk to Johnny Walkingshaw's cottage at two in the morning, because the wretched man had been cut short in his story just as he was about to explain the curious surgical problem of how he was resuscitated. When I returned he was gone, and I never saw him more. Whether he was mad and had hanged himself, or whether he was sane and had been hanged according to law, or whether he had ever been hanged, or never been hanged, are points I have never quite adjusted in my mind.

A Legend of Barlagh Cave

Some hundred years ago there lived upon the shores of this lake a young maiden named Aileen. She was beautiful, and of noble and generous disposition. Nigh to her father's home resided a youth called Connor, handsome as Apollo, and brave as Achilles. Aileen loved this youth, but was not loved in return; his affections were cast upon another maiden, worthy of love certainly, but not possessing one-half the charms of Aileen. The latter pined on in secret grief. Each day that she saw Connor go down to his boat and sail out to sea, a tide of blood would rush from her heart, and leave her almost fainting with excess of passion. She watched him when he sought the hills with his gun upon his shoulder, and her eyes traced him up the steep mountain paths with a sick yet loving gaze. But, oh! what untold agony that maiden suffered when, in the glorious summer evenings, as the sun was sinking in a golden sea, and the grey twilight was creeping like a fox from the hills, she behold Connor and his betrothed wandering along the fragrant beach, with twining arms and touching cheeks. Then the gorgeous clouds that floated in the western sky, those airy unsubstantial shapes of splendour, seemed to her distempered fancy to change into faces that stared at her with fierce mockery, while the azure heavens glowered upon her with myriads of sneering eyes. The low wind, as it wandered along the beach, sounded in her ear like derisive laughter. The very sea-birds that whirled above the calm surface of the lake, seemed to shriek wildly to her tales of anguish and despair. As time wore on, so much the deeper did her vain love eat into her soul and inflame her brain. Connor knew not this. He knew not that the hollow eyes and pale cheek which now never deserted Aileen, were all the fruits of love for him. When he met her, he was kind and gentle to the suffering girl—never dreaming that each soft word he uttered planted a fresh arrow in her torn bosom. Nay, once even he saved her from an imminent danger, and bore her in his arms to her father's cottage, when, if he had but known the despair that racked her heart, he would have left her to perish rather than restore her to a life which was nothing but one long calendar of anguish. At last, the passion that burned within her became too great to be concealed. She determined to make known to Connor her devouring secret. Before doing so, however, she thought she would consult the Spirit of the Hill, who dwelt in a vast breezy cave, on the summit of Cunna Conma, and endeavoured to discover from him some means of winning Connor to her side. One starry night, when the summer dews were falling like a gentle rain, and nought living was on foot save the fox and the wild cat, Aileen left her restless bed, and stealing softly from the house, took the wild and rugged path that led to the summit of the mountain. As she trod that broken and uncertain footway, strange fancies haunted her. The tall dark pines that fringed the narrow path seemed instinct with a sombre life, and nodded and whispered to each other gloomily. Indistinct and shadowy shapes rushed wildly through the thick brushwood, and chuckling laughter echoed through the trees. There was not an old grey stone that raised itself from out the coppice, which did not take the form and aspect of some terrible and unearthly thing. Aileen walked, surrounded by a mist of horrors. At length she reached the summit of the mountain, and wended her steps to the cave where dwelt the Spirit of the Hill. Large grey clouds continually veiled the entrance of this solemn place, and within, the plaintive winds chanted all night and day their mountain hymns. Aileen stood upon the rocky threshold, and with a bold and fearless voice, called upon the Spirit. A long, hollow moan, that sounded like the voice of some vanished year, replied to her summons.

"Spirit of the Hill!" she cried, "I summon thee to answer me. How shall I attain either happiness or death? Tell me, thou unseen being, how to win Connor or to die!"

A moment's pause, and then the answer came from the depths of the cave in tones like those of the tempest in a forest.

"Seek the cave of Barlagh tomorrow eve," said the hollow voice of the Spirit, "and there wilt thou find rest."

"Thanks, thanks!" cried Aileen, as the murmurs died away along the hill. "Tomorrow, then, I shall perhaps rest in Connor's arms."

She trod the downward path that night with a lighter step than she had known for months; and, happy in the belief that Heaven had at last taken pity on her hopeless love, she sought her bed, and sank lightly into slumber.

The evening sun was sinking into an amber sea, when Aileen, full of hope, sought this cave of Barlagh. As she urged her little boat through the rapids with a steady hand, her heart beat wildly in her bosom, and delightful visions full of bliss and love floated between her and the gorgeous sky. That destiny would lead Connor to the cave, and that there, through the intervention of the Spirit of the Hill, he would reward her attachment by a return of the passion, Aileen felt quite assured. No shadow of misfortune clouded her soul. No forbidding angel stood between her and the paradise of her imagination. The foaming waves of the rapids soon brought her little skiff abreast of the cavern's mouth, and sweeping round the rocky corner, she was about to enter, when a blue pigeon flew wildly out and almost skimmed her face. She started, and had scarcely time to utter an ejaculation of surprise, when a loud report rang through the echoing chambers of the cavern, and she fell back in the stern-sheets, with her life-blood welling from her bosom. Another second, and a boat shot out rapidly from the dusky cave, and Connor, who stood in the prow with his gun still smoking in his hand, beheld with horror the form of the bleeding girl. He jumped wildly into her boat, and lifting her in his arms, tried in vain to arrest the flight of her ebbing soul. Then there, with that solemn cave-temple rising grandly above her head, and none to look upon her agony save *Him* and the golden sun—there, in that hour of mortal trial, with the last energies of life quivering and flickering upon her lips, did Aileen pour into Connor's ear the history of her despairing love. She told him of her long days of misery and sorrow, of her sleepless nights, of her sick and wretched soul. She told him how deep, how ungovernable, was her love for him, and how she strove in vain to conquer it, but could not. She related how she had sought the Spirit of the Hill, and what reply he had given.

"He was right!" she said faintly, for her voice was growing weaker each moment, and the shades of death were creeping across her pale face. "The Spirit was right. I am dying in your arms, Connor; and is not that finding rest?"

Sadly and sorrowfully did Connor hang over the dying girl. Pained by her sad history, wrung with despair at having been the innocent cause of her death, nought but the remembrance that he had someone to live for prevented him from terminating his existence with his own hand. But he knew that there were longing eyes and anxious hearts which awaited his return, and he refrained. Aileen was now speechless, and the coldness of death was chilling her frame. Yet still her dying eyes sought his, and her white lips moved and told him, though he heard no sound, that her heart was uttering a fond farewell. This lasted but a few moments. When the last sunbeam had ceased to cast its golden shadow on the heavens and the ocean, her spirit fled.

Jubal, the Ringer

I

High in the brown belfry of the old Church of Saint Fantasmos sat Jubal the Ringer, looking over the huge town that lay spread below. A great black net-work of streets stretched far away on every side—the sombre web of intertwisted human passions and interests, in which, year after year, many thousand souls had been captured and destroyed.

Sleeping hills with clear-cut edges rose all about the dark town, which seemed to be lying at the bottom of a vast purple goblet, whose rim, touched with the whiteness of approaching day, looked as if they were brimming with the foam of some celestial wine. Deep in the distance rolled a long river, musical through the night, and shaking back the moon-beams from its bosom as if in play.

It was an old belfry, the belfry of Saint Fantasmos. It sprang from a vaulted arch with four groinings, which hung directly over the altar, so that one above in the bell-room could see, through the cracks in the stone ceiling, the silver lamps that lit the shrine, the altar-railings, the priest, the penitents below. Old flat mosses clung to the weather-beaten sides of the belfry, and the winds went in and out through it wheresoever they willed. From the very summit, which was pointed, there arose a tall iron rod, on which stood a golden cock, with head erect to catch the morning breeze, with feathers spread to bask in the morning sun. A golden cock, I said: alas! golden no longer. Wind and weather had used him badly, and he had moulted all his splendor. Battered, and gray, and rusty, with draggled tail and broken beak, he was no more the brave cock that he had been of yore. He had a malevolent and diabolical aspect. He looked as if he had made a compact with the demons of the night.

How blame him, if he had ceased to be an amiable cock? For years he had done his duty bravely to the town in all weathers, telling the points of the wind with unerring sagacity. The winds furious at having their secrets betrayed, would often steal softly down upon him in the disguise of a delicate breeze, and then burst upon him with the roar of a lion, in the hope of tumbling him from his sentinel's post. But they never caught him, for he was then young and agile, and he glided round at the slightest breath, so that the winds never could succeed in coming upon his broadside, but went off howling with anger to sea, where they wrecked ships, and buried them under the waves.

But the town neglected the poor cock, and he was never regilded or repaired, so that in time his pivots grew rusty, and he could no longer move with his former agility. Then the storms persecuted him, and the Equinox came down on him savagely twice a year, and buffeted him so that he thought his last hour was come; and those who passed by Saint Fantasmos on those tempestuous nights heard him shrieking with rage, through the wild aërial combats, till thinking it the voice of a demon high up in the clouds, they crossed themselves, and hurried home to bed.

So the cock, and the belfry, and Jubal the Ringer grew old together; but Jubal was the oldest of all, for the human heart ages more quickly than stone or copper, and the storms that assail it are fiercer and sharper than the winds or the rains.

II

Jubal sat in the window of the belfry, looking over the black town, and moaning to himself. The day had not yet risen, but was near at hand.

"This morn," he said, shaking his long hair, which was already sprinkled with gray, "this morn she will be wed. This morn she will stand in front of the altar below, the light from the silver lamps shining on her white forehead, that I love better than the moon; and her lover will put the gold ring upon her finger, and the priest will bless her with lifted hands, while I, through the cracks in the vaulted ceiling, will behold all this: I, who adore her: I who have loved her for years, and followed her with my eyes as she wandered through the fields in May, toying with the hawthorn hedges, herself more fragrant, whiter, purer than the blossoms which she gathered. I, who used to spend the early dawn traversing the woods, gathering the red wild strawberries while the silver dews still lay upon them, in order that I might place them secretly at her door! Ah! she never knew how in the cold winter nights I sat in the fork of the apple-tree outside her chamber-window, watching her light, and gazing on her shadow as it fell upon the blind. Sometimes the shadow would seem to lengthen, and come across the walk and climb the tree, and I would strive to fold it in my arms, as if it was my beloved in person; but it would suddenly recoil and elude me, and I could do nothing but kiss the branches where it had fallen, with my cold lips.

"One day, she went to gather white and yellow water-lilies, that swam on the surface of a pond. She held a long crook in her hand, with which she reached out and endeavored to bring them to shore. But they were cunning and slippery, and did not wish to be captured, by even so fair a maid as she; so when her crook touched them, they ducked their pearly and golden crests under the waters and escaped, coming up again all dripping and shining, and seeming to laugh at the eager girl. Being vexed at this, she stretched out her crook still farther, when the treacherous bank gave way, and my Agatha went down into the deep pond. I was near—I was always near her, though she knew it not—and I plunged in, and sought her amid the loathsome weeds. I brought her to shore, and chafed her fair forehead, and revived her. Then when she had recovered, I said to her: 'I am Jubal, the Ringer: I love you Agatha: will you make my lonely life happy forever?' With a look of wild horror she broke from me, and fled to her home.

"And I am despised, and she weds another. While the blessings are being given, and the church is white with orange-wreaths, and the poor wait in the porch for the nuptial bounty, I, who adore her, must sit aloft in this old belfry, and ring out jubilant chimes for the wedded pair.

"Aha! they know not Jubal, the Ringer. I can work the spells my mother worked, and I know the formulas that compel spirits. Agatha, thou false one, and thou, smooth-cheeked lover, who dreamst perhaps of her now, and thou, sacred priest, who givest away to another that which belongs to me, beware, for ye shall perish!"

Then Jubal laughed horribly, and spread his arms out as if he would embrace the night, and muttered certain strange sentences that were terrible to hear.

As he muttered, there came from the west a huge cloud of bats, that fastened themselves against the sides of the old belfry, and there was one for every stone, they were so numerous. And presently a ceaseless clicking resounded through the turret, as if myriads of tiny laborers were plying their pick-axes; a hail of falling fragments of mortar tinkled continually on the tin roofing of the Church of St. Fantasmos; and the bats seemed to eat into the crevices of the old belfry, as if they were about to sleep forever in its walls.

Presently the day rose. The sun-beams poured over the edges of the hills as the molten gold pours from the caldron of a worker in metals. The streets began to pulse with the first throbs of life, and Jubal, the Ringer, laughed aloud, for not a single bat was visible. The entire multitude had buried themselves in the walls of the belfry.

III

The street leading to the Church of St. Fantasmos was by nine o'clock as gay as the enamelled pages of a pope's missal. The road was strewn with flowers, and the people crushed the tender lily of the valley and the blue campanula and the spiced carnation under their feet. In and out between the throng of loiterers ran persons bearing boughs of the yellow laburnum in full blossom, until the way seemed arabesqued with gold. The windows on either side were filled with smiling faces, that pressed against the panes, like flowers pressing toward the light against conservatory casements. The linen of the maidens' caps was white as snow, and their cheeks were rose-red; and each jostled the other so as better to see the wedding procession of the fair Agatha and her gallant lover on its way to the altar of St. Fantasmos.

Presently the marriage cavalcade came by. It was like a page from a painted book. Agatha was so fair and modest; the bridegroom was so manly; the parents were so venerable with their white locks, and their faces lit with the beautiful sun-set of departing life.

As the procession passed beneath the windows, bunches of ribbons and flowers and bits of gay-colored paper, on which amorous devices were written, were flung to the bride and bridegroom by the bystanders; and a long murmur swelled along the street, of "GOD protect them, for they are beautiful and good!" And this lasted until they entered the gates of the church, where it was taken up by the poor people of the town who awaited them there. So, with benedictions falling upon them thick as the falling leaves of autumn, they passed into the Church of St. Fantasmos; but as they gained the threshold the bride looked up to the belfry, and there she fancied she beheld a man's head glaring at her with two fiery eyes, so that she shuddered and looked away. The next instant she looked up again, but the head was gone.

"The people who were not invited to the ceremony loitered in the yard without, intending to accompany the bride home when the sacred rite was concluded, and cheer her by the way with songs composed in her honor. While they waited, the chimes in the belfry began to peal.

"How now!" cried one. "It is too soon for the chimes to peal. The couple are not yet married."

"What can Jubal be dreaming of?" said a second.

"Listen," cried a third; "did you ever hear such discords. Those are not wedding chimes. It is the music of devils."

A terrible fear suddenly fell over the multitude as they listened. Louder and louder swelled the colossal discords of the bells. The clouds were torn with these awful dissonances; the skies were curdled with the groans, the shrieks, the unnatural thunders that issued from the belfry.

The people below crossed themselves, and muttered to one another that there was a devil in the turret.

There was a devil in the turret, for Jubal was no longer man. With his eyes fixed on the crack in the vaulted ceiling, through which he saw the marriage ceremony proceeding, and his sinewy arms working with super-human strength the machinery that moved the bells, he seemed the incarnation of a malevolent fiend. His hair stood erect; his eyes burned like fire-balls; and a white foam rose continually to his lips, and breaking into flakes, floated to the ground.

Still the terrible peals went on. The tortured bells swung now this way, now that, yelled forth a frightful diapason of sound that shook the very earth. Faster and faster Jubal tolled their iron tongues. Louder and louder grew the brazen clamor. The huge beams that supported the chimes cracked and groaned. The air, beaten with these violent sounds, swelled into waves that became billows, that in turn became mountains, and surged with irresistible force against the walls of the turret. The cock on the summit shivered and shrieked, as if the equinoxes of ten thousand years had been let loose on him at the same moment. The stones in the walls trembled, and from between their crevices vomited forth dust and mortar. The whole turret shook from base to apex.

Suddenly the people below beheld a vast cloud of bats issue from be-tween the stones of the belfry and fly toward the west.

Then it appeared as if the bells spent their last strength in one vast accumulated brazen howl, that seemed to split the skies. The turret rocked twice, then toppled. Down through the vaulted arch, crushing it in as if it had been glass; down through the incensed air that filled the aisle, on priest and bride and bridegroom and parents and friends, came a white blinding mass of stone and mortar, and the next instant there was nothing but a cloud of dust slowly rising, a splash of blood here and there, that the dry stones soaked in, and one battered human head with long hair, half-visible through the mass of ruin. It was Jubal dead, but also Jubal avenged.

When on the ensuing October the wild equinoxes came like a horde of Cossacks over the hills, to make their last assault upon the golden cock, they found neither bird nor belfry, and the mischief they did that night at sea, out of mere spite, was, the legend says, incredible.

Notes

"The Lost Room"

"The Lost Room" captures perfectly that dreadful feeling one has in dreams of failed efforts to flee peril, to achieve some inexplicably unobtainable goal, solve some evasive conundrum, or find one's way to a certain room. Anyone who has experienced this almost universal nightmare will relate all too closely to the terror of such events becoming tangible in the waking world. The narrator's early comfort, dissolving into the utter distress of a shifting reality, constitutes one of the most effectively morbid dramas in horror literature.

Yet the story could be interpreted as a fable about Fitz's own lost rooms when, in poverty, he was forced to give up his board and move in on friends. He wrote "The Lost Room" at the height of his powers, the same year he wrote the outstanding classic "The Diamond Lens," which it nearly equals in power, and a year before his equally famous "What Was It? A Mystery," which probably is not the equal of "The Lost Room."

Though relatively neglected in the shadow of "The Diamond Lens" and "What Was It? A Mystery," a half-dozen anthologists of the present century (among them R. C. Bull, James L. French, and Groff and Lucy Conklin) have regarded it highly, reprinting it from the William Winter-edited standard edition of O'Brien published in 1881 and reissued, sans poems, in 1885. The present text is from *Harper's New Monthly Magazine* for September 1858, where it first appeared.

Autobiographical references riddle Fitz's stories. The objects lovingly described in the opening third of this tale almost certainly belonged to him. The living situation—two rooms rented in a large mansion—were typical of his own generally impoverished circumstances. The discussion of Sir Florence O'Driscoll is taken directly from Fitz's family tree on the maternal side.

"The Lost Room" has been placed first in this modern edition so that it might at long last be given the focus it has always deserved.

"THE CHILD THAT LOVED A GRAVE"

"The Child That Loved a Grave" appeared in *Harper's New Monthly Magazine* for April 1861, from which the present text is taken. The story waited nearly a full century for its only revival, in Groff Conklin's 1958 paperback anthology *The Graveyard Reader* from Ballentine, itself a rare book today.

Penned at the height of his power, the tale is as moving as Dickens's "A Child's Dream of a Star," but lovelier and more poetic than the author Fitz was consciously emulating. The degree of sensitivity, without the least degree of mawkishness, is rare in Fitz's stories, although a less careful, overdone sentimentality is to be found in some of his nonsupernatural works.

In brevity and restraint and pure artistry, "The Child That Loved a Grave" ranks alongside the finest examples of the short-short story, weird or otherwise.

"THE DIAMOND LENS"

Of "The Diamond Lens" so much has been written that a catalog would be required to give every citation. At a glance, without making an enormous effort to identify every reprinting, I find it in twenty anthologies, and not only those with a supernatural orientation. The anthologists who've admired it include James L. French, Edward Everett Hale, Joseph Margolies, E. L. Pattee, Arthur Jessup, Greenberg and Waugh, Charles Dudley Warner, and many other notables. It has been continuously in print, usually in more than one book at a time, since 1865, the first of Fitz's stories to find its way into hardcover.

During his life he appeared exclusively in magazines and newspapers, but he was nonetheless well aware of the formidable success he had with "The Diamond Lens." It is difficult for us today to realize the impact a short story could have in the nineteenth century. It must be compared to the way a television program may occasionally become part of the American consciousness even if the program aired but once. Anyone who saw Rod Serling's "The Twilight Zone" in its first run can probably to this day synopsize a dozen episodes without ever having seen them again. Before mass media, the right story in the right magazine could easily become a cultural item for years to come. "The Diamond Lens" was such a story, and *The Atlantic Monthly* was the right place for it. For well over a century it has been recognized as one of the great works of world literature.

It was written at Thomas Bailey Aldrich's rooms at 105 Clinton Place while Fitz was otherwise homeless. On its appearance in the very first issue of *The Atlantic Monthly* for January 1858, Fitz became known as FitzLens O'Brien and other such sobriquets in Bohemian circles. In beauty, weirdness, and morbid sorrow, its praises cannot be too highly sung.

The present text is from the original *The Atlantic Monthly* appearance rather than from Winter's 1881 edition.

"The Pot of Tulips"

"The Pot of Tulips" is generally admitted to be one of Fitz's five or six best stories, alongside "The Diamond Lens," "The Lost Room," "What Was It? A Mystery," and "The Wondersmith." It's his only story that is squarely in that ghost story school that became so important for the rest of the Victorian era, and more than holds its own alongside the best-known ghost stories of the decades that followed.

Because of its somewhat scientific framework and the request that concludes the story, Harper Brothers received innumerable letters from people believing the story was a factual account. In *Harper's Weekly* there was soon printed the disclaimer, "that the whole was a pure effect of the imagination."

The story was sufficiently successful that Fitz felt safe in referring to it by title in his later story "What Was It? A Mystery" although the reference was deleted from the Winter-edited editions and all subsequent reprintings of that established classic. "The Pot of Tulips" has been in most editions of Fitz's stories, yet it has never been anthologized even among the considerable number of modern accumulations of Victorian ghost stories, a sad neglect. The next anthologist to consider "What Was It? A Mystery" for its umpteenth revival might properly reconsider and look at "The Pot of Tulips" for an excellent change of pace.

The text is from *Harper's New Monthly Magazine* for November 1855.

"The Bohemian"

Recognized in his day as a foremost example of the literary Bohemian and dandy—labels Fitz relished—"The Bohemian" takes on a degree of autobiographical importance. Surprisingly, he is critical of his social circle and the mannered decadence, greed, and ill-considered influence of his type.

A purely occult romance, it is not quite among Fitz's best work, but stands above works of other authors of his day, or even ours. Julian Hawthorne admired it sufficiently to place it in his *Lock and Key Library of the World's Best Mystery and Detective Stories* (1907) and it is relatively well known by right of its inclusion in the Winter standard edition. Slightly altered in the Winter editions, the present text is from the original in *Harper's New Monthly Magazine* for July 1855, the same year Fitz published his ghost story "The Pot of Tulips."

"SEEING THE WORLD"

As in several of Fitz's stories, "Seeing the World" is about a poet who might well be the author himself. In most of the more autobiographically inclined stories (in their emotional details at least and occasionally in the physical and historical details as well), the narrator appears pretty obviously to be Fitz himself. But in "Seeing the World" the narrator speaks *of* a figure akin to Fitz, rather than *as* the creative protagonist. In either point of view, however, the personalized content is poignant and revealing. "Seeing the World" addresses the artistic temperament that sees *too* clearly, that is driven mad by the extremeness of an ultimately useless talent, and shows the sadness and horror underlying the charming, dandified veneer of Fitz-James O'Brien. Anthologist and short story connoisseur Edward J. O'Brien (no relation) accutely judged the origin of Fitz's creativity as being "an interior life of great depth and terror."

In 1977 Michael Hayes edited for a London publisher *The Fantastic Tales of Fitz-James O'Brien*, consisting of six of the seven supernatural stories in Winter's edition, plus the only modern appearance of "Seeing the World" (in lieu of "The Bohemian"). The correct text is from *Harper's New Monthly Magazine* for September 1857, a bit different from what Hayes presented.

"WHAT WAS IT? A MYSTERY"

"What Was It? A Mystery" I found in over thirty anthologies between 1896 and 1984, without trying to find them all. It has been a standard in both general fiction compilations and in collections of supernatural tales. It appealed to such noted editors as Charles Dudley Warner, Dorothy Scarborough, J. W. McSpadden, James L. French, Arthur Jessup, Herbert

Dale, Isaac Asimov . . . some anthologists using it in more than one of their volumes.

Written in snatches at the abode of Thomas Bailey Aldrich, this is likely the most influencial single story aside from those of Poe in the development of modern supernatural horror. Ambrose Bierce's "The Damned Thing" and "Staley Fleming's Hallucination" borrow from it, as does Guy de Maupassant's equally classic "The Horla." H. G. Wells owes a debt to Fitz's story for inspiring *The Invisible Man,* if indirectly, while F. Marion Crawford with "The Upper Birth" and James Brendan Connolly with "The Illimitable Senses" assuredly read "What Was It? A Mystery" before penning their own versions.

William Winter altered the story in his edition, which has been the source of most reprintings. Some editors shortened it even further. This is the first reprinting of the complete text from *Harper's New Monthly Magazine* for March 1859, although I make no claim that Winter's version should generally be usurped from here on out. His editing was judicious and well considered for maximum impact of the horrific intent; but the complete text, Fitz's own, has a more personal tone, in keeping with his tendency to write fantastic tales as though they were autobiographical.

"The Wondersmith"

"The Wondersmith" is a first-rate homage to Hoffmann, a tale of pure evil and automatons in "an atmosphere surcharged with magic," to quote Joseph J. Reilly from *Catholic World,* March 1920, in an essay aptly titled "A Celtic Poe." The theme of creations destroying their creators shows the influence of Mary Shelley's *Frankenstein* (1818). Edward J. O'Brien singled this story for special praise in his 1925 edition of Fitz's *Collected Stories* (a selection drawn from Winter's editions).

This was Fitz's next story for *The Atlantic Monthly* after the success of "The Diamond Lens." It has been revived only a few times in our century, beginning with *Classic Tales by Famous Authors,* Volume V (1902), and in modern fantasy anthologies from the hands of Sam Moskowitz, Hugh Lamb, and the team of Sean Manley and Gogo Lewis. The present text is taken directly from *The Atlantic Monthly* for October 1859.

"A Dead Secret"

"A Dead Secret" was Fitz's earliest success at the purely macabre tale. In it is every evidence of the classic horror he would later write. The text is from *Harper's New Monthly Magazine* for November 1853, from which it has never before been reprinted.

"A Legend of Barlagh Cave"

"A Legend of Barlagh Cave" was integrated into the novella "The Phantom Light" as a fireside tale told by one of the characters. The novella was serialized in R. Kemp Philp's short-lived *The Home Companion* published weekly in London; the legend occurs in the fifth installment published January 31, 1852. By the time it appeared, Fitz had already left England and arrived in New York with almost no money in his pockets.

The larger text of "The Phantom Light" merits passing discussion, although the supernatural element was deemed too insignificant to justify inclusion of it here. In the first half of the story there are various references to Irish folklore, but the only occurrence within the story *per se* is the sighting of a will o' the wisp as an evil omen. The phantom light is thereafter dispensed with, rendering the choice of title somewhat suspect.

The story develops as a sentimental love story such as Fitz was to write now and then with some success. The real sparks of life enter during scenes with Uncle Tot, an eccentric old inventor who sets off various malfunctioning devices. These moments of highly effective comedy are all the story has to recommend it, besides, of course, the legend encountered midway in the narrative.

Only "An Arabian Nightmare" is known to predate "The Phantom Light," and is short by comparison. So the novella must be counted Fitz's first substantial story, already revealing his fascination for the supernatural. It's also one of his few tales to make use of his Irish homeland as a setting. In the story's preface, he says of the southwestern coast of Ireland, "There were entrancing stories . . . and many a night in boyhood I listened eagerly to the tale," and, "There was not a moss-covered stone throughout that land but had its tradition; and some there were that had whole centuries of legends heaped upon them." None of these prefacing observations have a tiddle to do with the story he tells, but in themselves reveal the cultural origins of his love for an uncanny tale.

"Jubal, the Ringer"

The best of Fitz's uncollected stories is "Jubal, the Ringer," a Romanticist piece reminiscent Poe hybridized with Victor Hugo. The mood is flawless, a superior horror yarn throughout. Its only revival was in a limited edition anthology from The Strange Company, Wisconsin, *In the Dark and Other Rare Ghost Stories* published in 1988.

This was among the stories Fitz listed as his own favorites. Yet it was overlooked by Winter. The text is from *The Knickerbocker* for August 1858.

FITZ-JAMES O'BRIEN was an Irish-born American writer. From his arrival in New York in 1852 until he died of an infected wound in the Civil War, O'Brien contributed numerous poems and minor stories to the magazines. His importance rests on a handful of brilliantly original science fiction tales, which were influential not only on subsequent science fiction but also on the development of the short-story genre.

JESSICA AMANDA SALMONSON has published five novels, of which *Ou Lu Khen and the Beautiful Madwoman* is the most recent. She is also a poet *(Innocent of Evil)* and World Fantasy Award-winning anthologist *(Amazons!)*. Her most recent books include a collection *A Silver Thread of Madness;* an anthology, *Heroic Visions II;* and a contemporary horror novel, *Anthony Shriek.*